WAITING
★ FOR ★
CALLBACK

WAITING ★FOR★ CALLBACK

Perdita & Honor Cargill

SIMON & SCHUSTER

First published in Great Britain in 2016 by Simon and Schuster UK Ltd
A CBS COMPANY

1 3 5 7 9 10 8 6 4 2

Simon & Schuster UK Ltd
1st Floor
222 Gray's Inn Road
London WC1X 8HB

www.simonandschuster.co.uk

Simon & Schuster Australia, Sydney
Simon & Schuster India, New Delhi

A CIP catalogue record for this book
is available from the British Library.

PB ISBN 978-1-4711-4483-7
eBook ISBN 978-1-4711-4484-4

Typeset in the UK by M Rules
Printed and bound by CPI Group (UK) Ltd, Croydon, CR0 4YY

MIX
Paper from
responsible sources
FSC® C020471

Simon & Schuster UK Ltd are committed to sourcing paper
that is made from wood grown in sustainable forests and supports the Forest
Stewardship Council, the leading international forest certification organisation.
Our books displaying the FSC logo are printed on FSC certified paper.

Dead-ication

Scraps 2001–2015

OK, you never mastered 'fetch', but you were an all-round excellent dog and the best writing companion ever. We miss you (and if we earn you'll get your urn).

I'm dressed as a spider, waiting to go onstage to impersonate a carrot.

It could be worse: I could be dressed as a carrot, waiting to go onstage to impersonate a carrot. That would be even more humiliating, but even in a black leotard I'm feeling pretty exposed. This carrot monologue was absolutely not my choice. I'd have chosen just about anything else (maybe something with death or trauma or at least an abusive mother in it), definitely not something that involved an arachnid pretending to be a vegetable. It isn't exactly a meaty role.

This is entertainment.

Or what passes as entertainment on gala night at ACT.

I'm sweating right down into my black tights and I very much want to go to the loo.

Again.

The dance number that's on before me is winding up and I'm running out of escape options. My mind is a complete blank. I can't remember a single word. I think I might be sick. Not just a little bit sick in my mouth, but projectile-vomit sick.

'You're on, Elektra,' says someone from the wings.

And somehow I am on and I open my mouth and the words are there ...

'It's dark and it's cold.
And under the ground nobody
can hear you scream ...'

And then I don't want to escape. I don't want to get off the stage. I remember how much I love this feeling. I'll just stay here with my face turned up to the lights and soak up all the energy until I'm the sort of spider who can take on the world and win (well, it's been known).

I'm high on drama.

★
CHAPTER 1

*'I mean nothing really happens in your life until
you're fourteen or fifteen.'*

Chloë Moretz

'Funny to think she wants Elektra.'

'Thanks for the vote of confidence, Dad.' There
were times in this house when not enough respect
was given to my fragile teenage psyche.

'What worries me is where it will all *end*,' said
my mum. (I take it back: please continue to ignore
my fragile teenage psyche.) 'I just don't know how
healthy it is. Look at Lindsay Lohan.'

'You told Mrs Haden it was "all very exciting",' I
said.

'Well, it is exciting.' Mum looked a bit shamefaced.
'I just *worry*.' (She still worried if at fifteen I took the
bus on my own.) 'And Mrs Haden didn't say she

definitely wanted you. She just invited us in for a chat. She did sound keen though.'

'You *have* to say yes.'

Tactical error.

'We don't *have* to do anything,' they said together.

'Please. It would be my *dream*.'

'Would it really?' Dad sounded sceptical.

'I want to be an actor.'

'What, more than being the editor of *Vogue* or discovering the cure for cancer?'

'Actually, yes.' (Well, obviously, I would quite like to 'discover' the cure for cancer, but unless I literally stumble upon it I don't think that's going to happen.)

'We should at least listen to Elektra,' said Mum. She pulled up a chair for me at the big white kitchen table and we all sat around it like it was some weird, domestic board meeting. Our kitchen was *very* white and plain with just one large black-and-white photo of a tomato on the wall. All the photos in our house were black and white; colour photos would have offended my architect dad's aesthetic sensibilities. Even our dog (Digby – my parents' son substitute and favourite) was a Dalmatian; a red setter would have been out of the question. He (Dad not Digby) has a very low tolerance for colour and mess; to him they're the same thing. It's a sort of chromatic traumatic thing. It is genuinely painful for him to enter my bedroom.

I tried to look rational and adult, although I

4

wasn't feeling either (or looking the part – I was wearing an old nightie which only just covered my bum and dated from my Snoopy era).

'Are you sure this isn't just another phase? What if you go off acting like you went off climbing and . . . ballet?' Mum whispered the last word.

Dad let out a snort. 'Ha, I'd forgotten the climbing lessons. Bit of a low point.'

'To be fair,' said Mum, 'acting's the one thing that Elektra hasn't gone off. She's been going to ACT every Thursday for years.'

ACT (or Act-up Children's Theatre) was just a local, after-school theatre group, not the sort of Academy for the Performing Arts where they fitted maths and physics round the students' bursts of spontaneous and yet perfectly choreographed song and dance routines. And I loved it all the more for that.

'Remember when she played Tinkerbell?' Mum added.

'That was the time she fell off the stage, wasn't it?' said Dad.

They both laughed a little bit too much. 'I am still here,' I said. My Tinkerbell had been inspired. I'd just relied too much on my wings when I was caught up in the moment.

'Sorry, darling,' said Mum. 'You were brilliant last night.'

'Well, this Haden woman obviously thought

Elektra was a credible carrot.' Dad's tone suggested he didn't necessarily share her opinion.

'She should know; apparently, she's been an acting agent for ages. She's got her own company – she gave me her card.' Mum dropped it on to the table and we all looked at the little white rectangle nervously as if the woman herself might materialize. 'Lens knows her.'

Lens was our teacher at ACT. I loved Lens (not just because he looked like Will Smith, although that helped). He was the only person who could have persuaded me that the carrot monologue was the way to go. He was probably also the only person who could have persuaded an acting agent to come and see a show featuring performing vegetables.

'It all seems legitimate,' said Mum.

God, I hadn't imagined the agent might be illegitimate. What did that even mean?

'Maybe she's just got a space on her books for a performing vegetable,' Dad suggested.

I ignored him. 'You think we should say yes, don't you, Mum?' It was always important in our family triangle to try and get on the right side of the 2:1.

'I don't know, darling. We don't want anything to interfere with school. It's not long until your GCSEs ...'

'It's *ages* till I have to worry about my exams.' Thank God, because I was still some way off mastering circle theorems. 'And look at Emma Watson; she's meant to be, like, really brainy.'

'Don't say "like",' they both said together (as they so often did).

I ignored the interruption (as I so often did). 'She got loads of As and A stars *and* she went to university all over the place *and* now she's, like, literally running the UN or something.' Also I kept seeing photos of her in magazines with preppy hot guys on both sides of the Atlantic (admirable, but not a point that was likely to help me right now).

'Don't misuse "literally",' said Dad, who cares about the strangest things. 'And I thought it was Hermione who was really brainy?' He used to read me the *Harry Potter* books at bedtime until the plots got a bit heavy and Mum stopped keeping my room tidy.

'Well, yes, but—' I began.

'Schoolwork matters anyway – exams or no exams,' my mother interrupted.

'Natalie Portman went to Harvard and speaks six languages,' I countered. 'And Dakota Fanning went to NYU.'

'I have no idea who you're talking about,' said Dad.

I struggled to think of clever *well-behaved* actors that they might have heard of (I wasn't going to risk bringing up clever badly behaved actors like Lindsay Lohan or any number of others). I knew *everything* about these people (including things I very much wished I could unknow), something that had at least as much to do with my embarrassing addiction to gossip sites and trashy mags as it did with my acting obsession. It probably wasn't entirely healthy.

'And you wouldn't mind if it was time off for violin or something,' I went on.

My father snorted – probably because no one could forget my short- lived but nonetheless painful violin phase.

'I'm right though, aren't I? You wouldn't be worried if this agent lady wanted to represent me for a youth orchestra or something. You should hear the things that go on at Pro Corda courses.' Rumour had it those classical musicians spent more time sticking their tongues down one another's throats than they did mastering Mozart (or any other dead musical genius) and nobody ever assumed they'd all end up in rehab.

My phone barked. (I wasn't too cool for novelty ringtones and it was a homage to Digby, who I sincerely loved, despite his favoured child status.)

'Don't even think about answering that,' Mum said, giving me a look.

'I wasn't going to,' I lied.

'Who is it?'

I considered saying, 'None of your business,' but thought better of it. 'Moss.'

'Moss can wait.'

I considered saying, 'You always tell me it's important not to neglect my friends,' but I thought better of that too: there were bigger things at stake right now. 'Look, I probably won't get any parts anyway.'

'Then *why* do you want to do it?' asked Dad in his annoyingly logical way.

'Because I *might*,' I mumbled through an unwieldy mouthful of toast. Digby padded in, sat by my feet and looked adoringly at me (well, more likely at the toast; he was a slave to carbs).

'But if you don't you might get terribly upset. How will you deal with so much *rejection?*' said Mum.

Like fifteen-year-old girls weren't used to rejection.

'It would be me that would have to deal with it. You're always telling me I have to take risks in life and now the first chance of a big one comes along and you're both all weird about it.'

My phone gave a single bark. **PICKKKKK UPPPPPP!**

Can't. Parents.

Have they said yes?

Not yet ☹

My mother swooped in like some sort of vulture (well, a vulture in cashmere and pressed jeans) and confiscated my phone. It was like social services ripping a newborn baby from its teenage mother.

'This is an important conversation and you are not going to sit here paying more attention to your phone than to us.'

Obviously, I was not OK with the whole taking-the-phone thing – there are boundaries – but there are also times when just being in the right is not enough.

'Come on, Julia, we need to make a decision on this.' Dad was keen to get the conversation back on track. Probably because he wanted it over so he could check *his* phone. 'Pros and cons: let's list them.'

Dad's a committed list-maker. This was something we had in common, although his lists were never random like mine, which were almost *always* random (and usually embarrassing). Also Dad's lists didn't look anything like mine because he was the sort of person who could draw perfectly straight lines freehand and he was severely limited in his choice of stationery and ink.

After some – occasionally heated – discussion, here's what we came up with:

Pros	Cons
Teach resilience	Undermine morale
Professionalism	Loss of childhood
Creative outlet	Distraction from study
Fun	Too much fun
~~Money~~	

I didn't really get why we argued about money. To me, it was an obvious 'pro'. At first sight, to Dad (sole breadwinner), it was a 'pro', but to my mother (primary spender) it was surprisingly a 'con'. To listen to her, you'd have thought that possession of a bank account by anybody under the age of twenty-one was a passport to depravity.

'What do you think I'm going to do if I earn any money? Buy hard drugs?'

She shuddered. 'It's not unknown.'

'But it's *me*. I don't even like taking *Calpol*. I'm not going to morph into some Hollywood substance abuser because someone pays me a couple of hundred pounds to do some acting for them.'

'Some hope,' said Dad, which (assuming he was talking about the money) was harsh but probably true.

We weren't getting anywhere. One minute my parents were worried I was going to face a life of rejection and low self-esteem (and would probably get anorexia) and the next that I wouldn't be able to deal with a three-film deal (and would probably get anorexia). We broke, exhausted, for more toast (me – an eating disorder was a *spectacularly* remote risk) and more coffee (them).

It was time to bring out my trump card.

'It would look amazing on my personal statement for uni.'

Within five minutes, they were talking about calling Mrs Haden ('just to discuss it'). I fled the kitchen (reclaiming my stolen property en route). I needed to talk to Moss about important things like what we'd wear to the Oscars.

'Elektra, get off the phone and go and get dressed!' my mum yelled from the kitchen after a few minutes.

'Just talking to Moss!' I yelled back.

'Don't shout!' yelled my dad.

'Sorry!' I yelled back.

'I mean it, Elektra. Get off the mobile or you'll get a brain tumour!' My mother was apparently allowed to shout (although her whisper would have bored through most walls too).

'Did your mum just say you'd get a brain tumour?' Moss was listening in. Hard not to.

'Yep.'

'From talking on the phone?'

'Yep, high-risk thing to do.'

'Seriously? God, it must be tiring being your mum.'

I think it probably was.

From: Stella at the Haden Agency
Date: 4 November 16:21
To: Julia James
Cc: Charlotte at the Haden Agency
Subject: Meeting to discuss possible representation (Elektra James)
Attachments: Directions.doc

Dear Julia,

We are so pleased that you and Elektra are going to come in and talk to us about *possible* representation. I was just telling Charlie (my assistant) about what a wonderfully *vibrant* carrot Elektra was!

I perfectly understand that an after-school appointment would suit best and I could offer you next Monday 10 November at 5 p.m.? Let me know if that works. I've attached a map with directions; we're directly above the Mayfield Dental Practice – once you see the metre-high model of a molar, you'll know you've found the right place!

We're looking forward to meeting you both.

Best wishes,

Stella Haden

CHAPTER 2

'Stuff happens [at school] that stays behind closed doors. I wouldn't be here now if it didn't, because I've put that into what I do.'

Alex Pettyfer

'So, are you getting off school early to meet her?' asked Moss as we sat on the bus to school the following Monday.

'Who?' I asked distractedly, searching through my bag for my French homework.

'Your agent,' said Moss, 'and how unreal is it that I just asked that?'

'Well, it's not real. She's not my agent.' Neither of us could say the word 'agent' in a normal voice; it still sounded like it should be in italics or capitals or quotes or something.

'She's not your agent *yet*,' said Moss with an

optimism that owed everything to our friendship. 'Today's the day.'

'I can't even let myself think about it I want it to happen so much.' Also it made me a bit sweaty. 'And no, I'm not missing any lessons; my mum "kindly" arranged the meeting for after school.' I rifled through my bag for the hundredth time. 'Aaaargh, it's definitely not here.'

'What have you lost this time?' Moss was used to this morning routine.

'My French homework. I've forgotten it ... again.'

'Who cares? You're going to be a Hollywood star.'

That was true of course (sure), but right now it was Monday morning and there was a lot to be got through before five o'clock – including French unfortunately.

'I'll help you look.' Moss dumped the entire contents of my bag on to the seat between us: a tampon that had exploded half out of its wrapper like a small escaping mouse (but, to the boys on the bus, scarier); two mini Oreo packets, sadly empty; a copy of *Grazia* (cover story: *Alex Pettyfer on dating his co-stars* – hopefully, useful at some point, but right now less useful than my French homework); random exercise books and textbooks for every subject except French.

'Madame Verte will give me detention. That'll

15

make her happy – she's such a cow.' (Her real name is Mrs Green and she comes from Essex.)

'I'll keep you company. I got a detention from Mrs Lawal on Friday.'

'What for?'

'I was late for physics ... again.'

Figured. Moss and I spend a lot of bonding time in detention together.

'Have you told Archie about the meeting?' she asked.

'Take a wild guess.'

'That would be no then.'

'No.'

'Is that because you still haven't talked to him?'

I shook my head and she looked at me in despair. I'd been in the same class at ACT as Archie Mortimer for nearly a term, but it wasn't that simple.

Archie was fit. The sort of fit that is universally acknowledged – tall, good body (and yes, I'd Facebook stalked for evidence), face full of bones (I know that all faces are full of bones, but his are perfectly arranged). This isn't subjective and I'm not exaggerating. I'm not saying this like it's a good thing. It would be much better for me if I were the *only one* irresistibly drawn to his understated, outsider, in-the-eye-of-the-beholder charms. That would maybe work quite well all round. But no, nobody's calling Archie Mortimer's charms understated.

Of course I hadn't talked to him.

In my head, we had entire conversations and I was witty and adorable with just the right number of quirks. Basically, I was every leading lady in every romcom and he was smitten and always followed the script.

Imaginary dating: it's the way forward.

But in Real Life there was a Status Gap between me and Archie, and you should *always* respect the Status Gap. He had been in an episode of some BBC series about murders and scones or something (serious status points), he was at least one year older than me (more points – school years are like castes) and also there's the universally fit thing, see above (*many* more points). I couldn't risk talking to him in case I went red and/or blotchy.

He did try to talk to me sometimes. Not talk as in 'have a conversation', just talk as in 'say unavoidable words every now and again'. Stuff like, 'Hey, Elektra, what's up?' (me – mumble, mumble)/'Hey, Elektra, how's school?' (me – mumble, mumble)/'Hey, Elektra, Lens wants us to [insert random teacher instruction that I'd missed because of Archie's proximity] (me – mumble, mumble, blush). No matter how much I wanted to, I couldn't categorize it as conversation, far less banter, far less flirty banter.

'I can't wait to get to school,' Moss said, stirring me from my Archie thoughts.

That was a first. 'I'm guessing not because you're excited about assembly.'

'No. It's because I'll get to see Flissy's face when you tell *her* about your agent.'

'There's no way I'm telling Flissy!'

'Why not? She'll be so jealous, her face will be hilarious.'

Moss was right. Being approached by an actual agent had the potential to impress Flissy (only about half as much as if I'd been spotted by a modelling agent, but still a lot). Nothing I had ever done to date had impressed Flissy. It was tempting.

'And Talia too. Go on, *pleeeease*. I will literally pay you.'

Flissy and Talia were inseparable, a sort of power couple of meanness (Flissy) and hotness (Talia). They didn't like us and we didn't like them. We all knew where we stood.

'Really?'

'Well, not literally, no.'

'Not worth it. They'll just persecute me for a whole term.'

'If it was me, I couldn't resist,' said Moss, but then she was always braver (stupider?) than me.

'I'm not going to tell *anyone*.'

'You have to tell Jenny and Maia,' said Moss. She looked guilty.

'So, what you mean is you've already told Jenny

18

and Maia?' No answer. It was maybe OK; we hung out with them quite a lot. Jenny was sweet and chill; Maia was really funny and our number-one source of gossip. I don't know how Maia did it, but she knew everything about everyone. That was a life skill.

'Tell them not to tell anyone else,' I said sternly, 'especially Maia. Seriously. It'll just be humiliating if nothing happens.'

Even though I had the meeting set up, I wasn't counting my chickens. I couldn't even see any chickens yet.

I always spend a lot of my day at school watching time pass. This is partly because every single classroom has a huge clock on the wall the better to terrorize us in exams and partly because there are very few lessons that wouldn't be improved by being at least ten minutes shorter. But today I was even more time-obsessed and time was not helping by running way more slowly than it usually did (even on a Monday). Double history felt like we were experiencing the Franco-Prussian War in real time; chemistry went a bit faster only because I managed to google 'teen actor red carpet fails' on my phone under the desk; French was livened up by the handing down of the predicted detention at 11.52 a.m.; I'm not even going to talk about sports or double maths. I knew that geography, the last lesson of the day, was going to be a long forty minutes.

'So, five more problems that might be faced by residents of shanty towns. Come on, who's going to volunteer?' asked Mrs Gryll. 'Nobody? I'm thrilled to see you've all prepared so comprehensively for this lesson. Right, who's going to give me just *one*? Elektra?'

The pressure. OK, admittedly it wasn't that hard a question, but I was finding it increasingly difficult to concentrate as we got closer to the bell. Also I was involved in a particularly distracting bit of list-making (potential Romeos to my Juliet).

'Elektra? Do I have to wait until global warming has melted the ice caps before I get this answer?'

I think that was geography banter. 'Er ... fires?' I offered, putting Archie out of my head and scribbling down 'RPatz'. No prizes for originality. I folded the paper and passed it under the table to Jenny.

'Excellent. Fires are indeed a serious risk and problem in overpopulated areas. Jenny? Jenny, are you even here with us? What is wrong with you all?'

Jenny looked up guiltily. 'Sorry. Erm, what was the question again?'

'You'd know if you weren't so busy with whatever

else is going on in this classroom today. Why don't you share what you're writing with all of us?'

Classic. It's like there's one big teacher script.

'It's just a list ... for English?' Poor attempt at a save by Jenny.

'I do enjoy English,' said Mrs Gryll, wandering out from behind her desk and stretching out her hand for the note.

'"Hot guys to play MY Romeo. Suggestions, please",' she read. 'Whose Romeo would this be? Yours, Jenny?'

'Mine,' I said in a very small voice.

'You're playing Juliet?' Mrs Gryll asked me.

'Yes ... In my head.'

'Freak,' muttered Flissy, not quite quietly enough.

'And this is for English? Strange. I could have sworn your set play was *Waiting for Godot*.'

How did teachers know so much?

'"Douglas Booth ... RPatz."' She began to read out the names on the list.

'Sweet to see you're still making lists of imaginary boyfriends, Elektra,' said Flissy. 'It's like a throwback to Year Seven.'

Brutal. I ignored her.

'Aaaw, Flissy, it's like that time when you wrote all those poems in your maths book to that guy Hen—'

'Oh my God, shut up, Talia,' hissed Flissy.

21

'And then you wanted him to notice you so you—'

Flissy hurled her exercise book at Talia to make her stop. It was a harsh blow, not least because the exercise book probably weighed about the same as Talia.

'Yeah, well, at least some of us have moved beyond crushes,' said Flissy, reasserting her position in the class hierarchy. She'd have batted her eyelashes had the weight of mascara not made that a physical impossibility. 'You'll understand when you have a boyfriend. Sorry, *if* you ever have a boyfriend.'

Moss and I looked at each other. Flissy talking about her boyfriend (which was something she did multiple times a day) was enough to make anyone want to die alone with cats.

Mrs Gryll had been ignoring this little exchange in favour of a close study of my Romeo candidates. 'Well, girls, if you want my opinion, this is a predictable and slightly insipid list.'

Seriously? Did she even know who these people were? Insipid?

'Who'd be on your list, Mrs Gryll?' asked Maia.

'Gregory Peck,' said Mrs Gryll and smiled in a way that was troubling in a teacher.

'What's he in?' I asked because we seemed to have forgotten about shanty towns and that could only be a good thing.

'He's dead,' she replied.

'I'm so sorry,' I said because a) it was obviously a recent loss and still painful for her and b) I was potentially still in a bit of trouble.

'Gregory would have been my perfect Romeo,' said Mrs Gryll (you could practically see the little heart emojis).

'Show us a picture, *pleeease*.' Maia was teacher's pet so perfectly placed to keep us off topic.

'We should get on ...' But Mrs Gryll was weakening. 'OK, just one then we're straight back to inadequate infrastructure.' She searched on her laptop and then there he was in all his black-and-white glory on the smart board.

That is not sarcasm. Gregory Peck is so going on my Romeo list. Anyone that looks like that (even if they're dead) deserves a wider fan base than middle-aged geography teachers.

★
CHAPTER 3

*'As an actor, you get to try all sorts of different
hats on and share hats and own hats and rent
hats and give them back. And have them taken
from you. And I think that's wonderful.'*
Shailene Woodley

Just like Stella's email had said, the agency offices
were above a dentist's surgery. There was just a
small sign by the side doorway that we'd have
missed if we hadn't been looking for it:

Second Floor
The Haden Agency
Leading Children's Theatrical Agency Since 1990

Maybe they'd camouflaged it on purpose to avoid
hundreds of hopeful candidates with newly washed

hair and a copy of the *Wicked* lyrics dropping by on the 'off chance'. The whole by-invitation-of-Mrs-Haden thing should have made me less nervous, but it didn't.

This meeting still felt like a test.

But then quite a lot of things I have to do feel like a test.

1. **Actual tests** (obviously) – and at my school there are loads. A bad experience with a physics test (hydraulics – I got my pascals mixed up with my newtons) was fresh in my mind.

2. **Appearance tests** (subcategories virtual and actual, virtual being the way more important category). I've got a bad feeling that weight had it's own category too – but not on my list.

3. **Daily fashion tests** – I was resigned to failing this Monday to Friday because nobody could persuade me that it was worth making any effort to style and accessorize our gross school uniform.

4. **Social tests** – 'You didn't get invited to Talia's house party? Seriously?' 'Your profile pic only got thirty likes? Seriously?' Ability to pass social tests was brutally correlated to results in 2 and 3 above.

5. *Endless* 'good child' tests – 'No, I didn't say you *had* to be back before ten o'clock, but if you were half as responsible as [insert the name of any of my friends] you would have been' (Mum) or 'If you spent more time on geometry, you'd find it infinitely more rewarding' (Dad – and no, actually, I wouldn't).

This list could be a lot longer, but it's too depressing.

No question this meeting was a test. And the whole fear factor wasn't helped by the dentist smell in the stairwell. (What was that? Formaldehyde? Antiseptic? Weird mixture of bone and mint?) The agency office was just a small room with two tables facing each other, both laden with bulky, old-fashioned computers with wires pooling everywhere. It wasn't how I'd imagined it; not exactly Hollywood glamour.

'Mrs James, Elektra, thank you for taking the time to come in and meet with us.' Mrs Haden motioned for us to sit opposite her. She was seriously tall and the sort of skinny that would get me on the lunchtime watch list at school. She looked pretty serious; yep, definitely a test (I'd found a new hardcore category – 'professional tests').

'Thank *you* for seeing us, Mrs Haden,' Mum said, putting on her too-polite voice.

'Please, you must both call me Stella.'

I was too intimidated to call her anything.

'And this is Charlie,' Stella said, gesturing to the woman at the second desk who was practically hidden behind her computer. Charlie, who was a lot younger than Stella and a whole lot shorter, just waved vaguely at us and went back to whatever she was doing.

One entire wall of the office was covered in headshots of kids of different ages. Under each was a name and some had code-like dates and initials scrawled under them too. Stella saw me looking. 'They're our clients. You must know Daisy Arnold? She's at ACT with you, isn't she?'

I nodded. Daisy was gorgeous and tiny like a doll – all blonde ringlets and big round blue eyes. She had a sort of retro-perfect thing going on and never had smudged mascara or a fist-sized hole in her tights like the rest of us. Daisy was also so lovely that it was impossible to hate her for any of that.

'Your photo could be going up there too, Elektra.'

If that involved looking like most of the kids on that wall, then maybe not. Daisy fitted right in.

'So tell me, Elektra, how did you get into acting?'

The first question in any test is usually the easy one, but I was already struggling. I mean, how much backstory did she want? I could tell her all about my early Barbie voice-over years, the intense doctors and nurses phase with Freddy from next door (he's moved away now, probably to be nearer to his therapist), but that might be oversharing. I just really liked acting, I always had – and no question I was better at it than at lots of other things (netball, maths, ballet obviously). I hadn't given it up which was more than could be said for any other after-school thing I'd started. But what 'got me into it'? I should have said something/anything a) because silence is scary when you're the one meant to be filling it and b) because I handed my mum the opportunity to jump right in and answer (loudly) for me. Basic error.

'Well ... Elektra has just always loved the opportunity to explore being other characters ...'

At that precise moment, I did want to explore being another character – like someone else's daughter.

I quickly cut over Mum and started waffling on about my classes at ACT. I was selective. For example, I didn't tell Stella that it had been kind of grim at first because most of the other kids thought I was weird and posh. I didn't tell her that I wasn't that keen on warming up to retro Britney Spears compilation tapes or that I struggled with some drama 'games' (usually the ones that involve pretending to be any non-human form). I was pretty sure Stella didn't need to know any of that, so I just told her that I liked making words come alive and I especially liked it when they were so real that I was suddenly someone or something completely different. And that was true.

'And what made you choose the monologue I heard last week?' Stella asked.

'Um ... well ... my teacher, Lens, chose it.' Which I know wasn't the 'right' answer. I should have said something about being touched by the raw energy of the spider/carrot's spiritual journey. Because I was ninety-nine per cent sure the monologue was an extremely meaningful metaphor. I just wasn't sure what it was a metaphor for.

'Well, it was very good.' Stella must have seen the look on my face because she added, 'But obviously we try to find our clients non-vegetable parts too.'

'Thank you.' I probably blushed; I blush easily. I definitely blushed when my phone started barking.

'Sorry, sorry, sorry.' I began a frantic search in my messy bag.

'It's *fine*,' said Stella, raising her voice over the woofs.

Mum's glare would have melted girders. She fished out my phone in seconds and switched it to silent. It felt like every perfect child on The Wall was looking at me. This was all making me a bit sweaty.

'But you had fun doing it?' Charlie put me out of my misery. She pulled her chair over and came to join us.

'Doing what?' It's possible I was not at my most impressive. Also I found Charlie quite distracting.

She was working a sort of gothy headteacher look: jet-black hair; very tight black skirt; unchipped black nail polish; three tiny crosses in her right ear and a skull tattoo that stretched all over the back of one hand.

'Performing? Being onstage?'

I tried to explain what it had felt like which was so much more than 'fun', and Stella and Charlie were both smiling and nodding and I relaxed a little. I think I'd finally said something they wanted to hear.

'So, Elektra, do you really think you want to be an actor?' asked Stella.

It was a simple enough question and I knew or thought I knew what the right answer was. Of course I wanted to be an actor – but now she was actually asking the question I hesitated . . .

I knew that I wanted someone to ask me to act in their television drama or their film right now. I knew that I wanted to be onstage in front of an audience (or even without an audience). I knew I wanted my photo on The Wall. I knew I wanted an agent. I knew I wanted to be Juliet to both Douglas Booth's and Gregory Peck's Romeo. I knew lots of things in my head and in my imagination. But Stella was asking: 'Do you want to do this *for real*,' and that was a massively big question.

Stella, my mother and Charlie were all leaning forward in their chairs, waiting for my answer.

God, the pressure. 'I just ... I know I want to do it *now*, but I think it's maybe a better job when you're fifteen than when you're thirty.'

Stella stared at me. My mum fidgeted. Even Charlie looked embarrassed. The perfect children on The Wall judged me. I blushed (again).

There was silence for a long moment and then Stella smiled and said, 'Quite right, Elektra; I think you'll handle this just fine.' She paused and exchanged a look with Charlie. 'Look, I know you'll need to go away and think about this ...' I wouldn't. 'But from our side I might as well just say straight away that we'd love to represent you.'

I'd passed a test. I was *stupefied*.

Stella started talking to my mum all about how contracts and fees worked and when I'd recovered a bit I snuck a look at my phone under the desk. There was a whole scroll of text messages from Moss.

Good luck

GOOD LUCK

GOOOODDDDD LUCKKKKKKK

I just called you

But you didn't pick up

Which is annoying

Because I wanted to be nice

And wish you LUCCCCKKKKK.

It was typical of Moss both that she'd remembered to phone me to wish me luck and that she'd been about an hour too late. She was pretty much always an hour late for everything. In fairness, it was typical of me that I'd forgotten to switch off my phone. I pretty much always forgot stuff.

'We need to get your Spotlight form filled in.' Stella pulled me back into the conversation. 'It's a sort of CV.'

Personal details were easy: height, eye colour (brown – which sounds better than 'muddy' which is what they actually are), hair (brown – more mediocrity right there), etc. My 'native' accent is, apparently, Received Pronunciation (aka RP – just a tiny bit on the posh side of normal). Then things started to go downhill.

'Do you have any other accents?'

I looked at Stella questioningly.

'You know, can you do an American accent or an Irish accent or a Scottish accent?'

I shook my head.

'You must watch American TV shows? *Friends*?'

I shook my head (I mean, I'd seen it, but I wasn't an expert).

'*Pretty Little Liars*?'

I nodded. I may have watched several hundred episodes.

'Great. Then you probably can do an American

standard accent. That's always the most useful one. Have a go.'

I had one of these blank moments when I couldn't think of anything to say. There was a yellow Post-it stuck on Stella's desk: 'Remember call Jamie's mum _after_ 5 p.m. re *Potato Boy* CBBC casting.' I tried not to get distracted by imagining what sort of show CBBC were planning that could possibly be titled *Potato Boy* and read it out in what I hoped was the right sort of American accent.

Apparently, it wasn't *any* sort of American accent – I watched as Stella wrote NONE.

'Do you speak any other languages?'

'A little bit of French,' put in my mother from the sidelines. I could tell she was still nervous by the way she was holding her handbag on her knee like a large and expensive body shield.

'Could you cope with a script in French?' asked Stella.

My mother and I looked at each other and shook our heads. Stella wrote NONE in the 'Other Languages' category.

'Never mind,' she said kindly. 'OK, let's move on to skills.'

Now we were talking. This was where my optimistic if scattered attendance at after-school activities was going to pay off.

'Instruments?' Stella asked, pen poised.

'Piano and er ... violin,' I offered.

'Both at grade five or above?'

'Er ... no.'

'Neither?'

'No.'

'Singing?'

'I sing.' Everybody sang, right?

'Trained? Musical theatre? Classical? School choirs?'

'No.' Maybe not.

'Dance? Jazz? Tap? Ballet? Circus skills?'

I shook my head. Mum had slumped into a mortified heap beside me. All those hours of ferrying me to after-school clubs and I was a total failure.

'Not to worry,' Stella said briskly. 'I'm sure there's something we can put down. How about swimming, skating, fencing, horse riding ... ?'

I sensed my mother twitch into excited life, but I put out a hand to restrain her.

'Would I have to be good enough to do them on-screen?' I asked.

'Or onstage, yes.'

'Well ... better just leave that blank too,' I suggested, keen to have this over. I'd never realized actors were so talented. I'd just thought they were good at pretending and either hot enough to look good on a red carpet and/or twenty feet tall in high definition (surely achievement enough right there) or weird enough to play 'character' parts without too much time in hair and make-up. But no; they can all speak in tongues and walk a tightrope while singing a show tune.

Stella didn't seem that bothered by my hopelessness. She shoved my mostly blank Spotlight form into the out tray on her desk and gave my mother (who must have been wishing she had lots of other better-skilled children) a list of photographers who could take my headshots.

'Turn up in a black or white top with a simple neckline; that photographs best,' Stella advised. 'Choose a photo that looks like you, no make-up and no touching up; it never does to disappoint them when you walk through the door.'

Which I was pretty sure was good Life Advice in general.

Stella's Words of Wisdom

1.

There are far more parts for boys than girls and far more girls than boys looking for parts. My gender would certainly be a disadvantage.

2.

Most parts for child actors are playing younger versions of adult actors. The adult actors are cast first. Most actresses are skinny, blonde and beautiful. In other words, my hair 'etc.' was a disadvantage.

3.

Unlike Real Life, most roles require an accent that's either cut-glass Queen's English or Cockney — my accent being somewhere in the middle was a disadvantage.

4.

My teeth had better stay perfectly straight. Braces or, worse, wonky teeth would certainly prove to be a disadvantage.

5.

There are more parts for teeny little cute girls than for girls at an 'awkward' age. My age would be a disadvantage (although if I hung in there till sixteen there were 'coming-of-age' roles -bring it on).

6.
Puberty generally was a disadvantage (they had no idea). If I got fatter or spottier or too much taller or too busty (I wished), I'd be dropped like a Christmas jumper in January.

7.
If I got lucky and was picked for a great role, I'd probably be typecast and never work again, i.e. any early success would be a disadvantage.

8.
Obviously, failure at any stage would also be a disadvantage.

9.
All child actors would probably soon be replaced by CGI which would be creepy and a disadvantage.

From: Stella at the Haden Agency
Date: 14 November 16:51
To: Julia James
Cc: Charlotte at the Haden Agency
Subject: RE: Elektra James – contract

Dear Julia,

Thank you for sending over the signed contract today. Charlie and I are both so pleased that Elektra wants to join our stable of talent!

We think we've become pretty good at telling which children will enjoy this mad(!) world, but we are very conscious that the reality of what can be quite a tough business is sometimes a shock. If Elektra is unhappy or struggling or even if you feel that she is just losing her wonderful enthusiasm for acting, we really would urge you to let us know straight away. We're here to help support her.

We look forward to hearing from you.

Kind regards,

Stella

P.S. Do tell Elektra that Charlie was so impressed by her ringtone that she too has downloaded her very own animal alert (a cow)! I confess to mixed feelings about this!

☆
CHAPTER 4

'I'm just normal. Acting is a hobby between my A levels.'

Nicholas Hoult

'It's official. Mum sent back the *signed* contract today. I'm in business. I am "Under New Management".' Which I know made me sound a bit like a restaurant, but I just liked the idea of being under any kind of (non-parental) 'management'.

Eulalie made a strange Frenchy (to be fair she was French), yelpy sort of sound that I took to mean that she was almost as excited as I was. 'We must make some shopping.'

I loved Eulalie (and not just because she loved shopping). Years ago – before I was even born – she'd rescued Mum's lovely (now dead) father from

39

the clutches of her awful (and still living) mother, Granny Gwen. She was my favourite 'grandmother' (and, genetics aside, definitely the one I had the most in common with).

'*Chérie*, you need beautiful clothes for going to see all the famous directors. Nothing from that horrible Large Shop.' She helped herself to most of the salad (which I appreciated because there was less left for me).

'You mean Top Shop ... I don't think it will be quite like that. I mean, I'm not sure I'll be meeting famous directors.'

'But of course, *bien sûr*. How else are you going to act for them?'

It was a fair point, but still sort of unimaginable.

'We'll go to Harrods.' (Just assume that every 'h' is silent and every 'r' is rolled – the longer Eulalie lived in London, the stronger her French accent seemed to get.)

'You spoil Elektra.' Mum brought over extra salad just for me which was pretty passive-aggressive parenting.

'I enjoy spoiling her,' said Eulalie without the slightest shame. Her spoiling me is something we both get a lot out of.

'Eulalie doesn't believe that gifts, guilt and Oxfam goats have to go together *every time* like Granny Gwen does,' said Dad who adored Eulalie.

Everyone adored Eulalie, even Mum who really should have been a bit more conflicted.

'Boats?' asked Eulalie, looking bewildered. 'Yachts?'

'Goats,' repeated Dad.

'Gots?'

'What's the French for goats, Elektra? Chevrons? Or is that cheese?'

'Don't ask me. Mum, what's the French for goats?'

My mother's shrug at least was pretty Gallic.

Apparently, languages wouldn't be on my parents' 'Skills' sections either. Also 'goat' is surprisingly difficult to mime. Eulalie decided that she might as well talk about yachts (I'm pretty sure she knew a lot more about them anyway). Not just yachts but partying on yachts with actors. Typically, it was a bit inappropriate. In her world, excessive amounts of champagne and non-stop parties and affairs were just a bit of harmless fun.

'Honestly, Eulalie, I can't quite believe that *******
[I won't use the name of the actress because I'd be sued] would have done *that* with ****** [high-profile actor, same problem].'

My mother did that *tssk* thing (it's actually quite hard to do, but she's good at it).

'I promise you, Julia, it's true,' said Eulalie. She paused for impact. 'I was there.'

No question that if Eulalie had actually been

41

there when ******* did what she said she'd done to ****** then it was an even more scandalous story. I knew (we all knew) that Eulalie was a little bit truth challenged, but it wasn't completely impossible.

'Everybody is knowing that he is the father of at least two of her children,' Eulalie went on.

'Well, I know that's not true.' Mum sounded very sure.

'Were you there too?' I asked her. She didn't answer, just punished me with more vegetables.

'She was having the new bosoms after the third baby and the new face after the third husband.'

'That I do believe,' said Mum.

'I need to see it,' said Eulalie and it took us a moment to realize she was talking about the contract and not about the actress's 'improvements'.

I carried the document over to the table like a high priest bearing precious offerings to an altar.

'"Talent Representation Agreement …"' read Eulalie. 'You're the *talent* – no?'

'Indeed I am,' I said, ignoring my parents rolling their eyes at each other. Eulalie nodded as though that was how she described me every day.

'"… I hereby authorize the Haden Agency to negotiate contracts for the delivery of my professional services as an artist or otherwise in the fields of film, television, stage, radio broadcasting, modelling—"' Eulalie broke off. 'Modelling?' Even she looked a bit surprised.

'It's a catch-all,' I explained. I wasn't quite sure what that meant, but it was pretty clear that I wasn't going to be sent out for any modelling jobs any time soon.

'You pay them *twenty per cent* of all the monies you are making?'

'Well, it's eighty per cent of something or a hundred per cent of nothing,' I said. I was new to this but not stupid.

'It could be eighty per cent of nothing,' said Mum. 'Stella made it quite clear that Elektra might not get any parts or at least not for a long time.'

Eulalie shrugged like that could *never* happen. 'You need to think positive thoughts, then it will happen for sure. Close your eyes, Elektra, and imagine yourself in your dream role.'

I felt like a bit of an idiot, but because it was Eulalie I did exactly what she said (also that way I couldn't see my parents' expressions).

'So, describe to us what are you seeing,' Eulalie said like some sort of spirit guide.

What I was actually seeing was either a) nothing if I closed my eyes really tightly or b) my dad smirking if I didn't. Also it was hard to concentrate because Digby was licking my leg under the table. 'Er, Joan of Arc?' I don't know where that one came from, but it would be a great role (except for the traumatic haircut). This was quite hard. A mean, gorgeous girl in St Trinian's (or a nice but 'plain' girl who gets a makeover and turns out to be seriously fit)? Any part in Doctor Who? (Except for a dalek because I'd get claustrophobic.) None of these would mean anything to Eulalie.

'Juliet,' I said because I'd practised fantasizing about that one. I opened my eyes. 'Have any of you ever heard of an actor called Gregory Peck?'

It was like I'd said, 'Have any of you ever heard of the Pope or Napoleon or Queen Elizabeth?' There was outrage at my ignorance.

'So, first we watch Roman Holiday and second we go to Harrods,' said Eulalie when she'd recovered the power of speech.

Dad's phone started ringing in the other room. 'It'll be work,' he explained. 'I'll leave it.'

'What are you building now, Bertie?' asked Eulalie.

We'd all given up explaining to her that Dad didn't actually build anything. And yes, he was called Bertie. It was just a cross he had to bear.

'Not enough actually. It's quiet at the moment. Too quiet. There's a limit to how excited I can get about kitchen extensions.'

Dad usually got excited about things like rectilinear elevations or bespoke brushed metal cladding (nope, I've no idea either).

'Well, you can always come over and help me renovate my *boiseries*.'

I don't know what Eulalie was talking about, but there was no question she was flirting. She flirts with everyone: man, woman, child, dog.

'I'm not sure what *boiseries* are, Eulalie, but no doubt it would be a pleasure.'

Sacré bleu, he was flirting back.

Sometimes I struggled being in this family.

Moss turned up just when Eulalie was leaving – which in one way was bad because they adore each other, but in another way was good because they'd have spent ages talking about fashion and their shoe fetishes and I'd have felt left out. Moss and I grabbed Digby and a packet of custard creams and headed up to my room to 'revise'.

My messy room's nice but it's very cold. That's how I like it (the cold bit – I'm neutral about mess as it's just there) but Moss gets shivery so we piled (Digby included) under the duvet.

'So, what happens next?' she asked.

I looked at Moss a bit blankly. 'I'm not sure. I suppose I wait.'

'What did they say would happen?'

'I think they'll just phone me if there's something they think I could try for.'

'You'd better not lose your phone then.'

I started to object to that slur on my character, but to be fair I had form on losing my phone. 'Well, they'll probably phone my mum. Until I'm sixteen, I need to get permission from her even to audition.'

'I'll need permission from my mum to do anything until I'm at least twenty-one.'

'Anything?'

'Anything.'

'Well, that's going to be embarrassing.'

Moss groaned and crammed a whole biscuit into her mouth.

'Do you want to see my headshot?' I asked.

'Yes!'

I pulled it up on my phone. 'What do you think?'

She gave it the sort of close, critical examination it deserved. 'Wow ... It's like you but not like you. It's like a better you. Sort of a glossy version of you.'

'Thank you, I think.'

'You should totally make it your new Facebook profile pic.'

'No way. It's too ... perfect.' I meant the photograph, not me obviously.

'Flissy has her profile pic taken professionally.'

Of course she did. Flissy had her hair blow-dried and wore a smoky eye to school. 'I'm not going to start competing with Flissy.' There was only so much narcissism that someone outside her crew would get away with.

'What was the photographer like?'

'Old, quiet, quite sweet. It was still scary though. I felt really self-conscious.' And weirdly aware of my teeth. In the end, I'd had to act being a super-confident actor (with no teeth hang-ups) getting her headshots done.

'Well, it was only one photo. It can't have been that scary.'

'You have no idea – it took forever to get that shot.' Literally hours – respect to models; at least I could eat biscuits while he was fiddling with the lighting. 'I'm like an expert now.' I took back my phone. 'Come on, I'm going to take your headshot now. Give me your best pose … Chin down … Neck back and up, sweetie …'

'He called you "sweetie"?'

'Yes, but in a nice not weird way. Concentrate. Eyes to me … Time for a few with your hair up … No, not like that … Leave it down …'

'It's my ears, right? They always look weird in photos.'

She did have very big ears. 'They're only ears; nobody's ears are a huge selling point. Stop pouting.'

'I wasn't pouting.'

'You so were. That was a Flissy-level pout. Come on, I want to get the perfect shot, face slightly to the left … NOT YOU, DIGBY.' He was photobombing. 'Now to the right, Moss … *Relax* your face.'

'What does that even mean?'

'I don't know, but the photographer said it to me *a lot*. Try blowing out through your mouth like a pony – that was another of his top tips.' It was a direction too far. Moss lost it. I wasn't going to get the *perfect* shot. I had some quite funny ones though.

'Are you scared about auditions and – I don't know – *doing* stuff in front of people?' Moss asked when we'd got ourselves together.

I thought about it. 'Nah. I mean, I probably will be, but it's not real yet so not much point getting worried about it.'

'I couldn't do it.'

Moss had had a seriously traumatic experience as a gryphon in our Year Seven production of *Alice in Wonderland* and I doubted if she'd ever get on a stage again.

'There must be some stuff you wouldn't want to do.'

'Like what?'

'Don't know. Getting naked? Advertising tampons?'

I hadn't really thought about things like that. 'Aaaargh, I'm not sure. Maybe not being naked.'

'Imagine being stark naked on a ten-metre-high screen. In high definition. With people you know in the audience. Are you chill with that?'

'Not exactly "chill".' Not even a little bit chill.

'What about horror movies?'

'I think I'd be OK with horror.'

'Seriously, Elektra? You can't even watch *Doctor Who* without holding on to me or Digby.'

That was true. Now I came to think about it there was quite a lot of stuff I wouldn't want to do. This was making me anxious, and when I was anxious I made lists. My room might be messy, but I liked my mind to be tidy. I scrabbled for something to write on (back of a letter from school about signing up for sports teams that I'd 'forgotten' to hand in) and a pen (actually an eyeliner, but I was rubbish at using eyeliner so it was a reasonable redeployment). 'I need something to lean on.'

'Use Digby,' suggested Moss, hefting him from her side of the bed to mine.

'No, he won't stay still while there are crumbs in the bed to be hoovered up. I'll use a pillow.'

Out of the Question

1. Any role that involves total or partial nudity. (This rule had more to do with Moss's comments about high definition than morality. Also I might review it if I get boobs.)
2. Any role that involves anything more than kissing. (This rule had nothing to do with morality either and I was going to keep it under regular review.)

3. Any role where the love interest is a man who is old enough to be my father. (It is a poor reflection on the people that make films that I might have to review that one at some (*much* later) point too.)

4. Any role in a commercial advertising a 'female sanitary' product (especially if it has a sporty theme); incontinence products; head-lice treatments; wart treatments; zit cream; or anything medical to do with bottoms.

5. Any role in a horror movie.

6. Any role that involves real spiders, large or small, household or Amazonian, venomous or herbivorous.

7. Any role that involves bugs. (Including beetles – except ladybirds – any grubs or larvae and maggots and basically anything that wriggles.)

8. Any role that involves snakes, garden or venomous, etc. (Snakes are basically evil. On my hierarchy of bad things, they are close to the top. I'm not hot on amphibians either, but the list was getting long and I was aiming to be professional.)

9. Any role that involves heights, by which I obviously mean any height in excess of my own.

10 Any role that involves singing or dancing.

(More of a can't than a won't – which might also be true of Rule 2).

'Digby!' Dad was shouting from the foot of the stairs.

Digby pricked up his ears, but proximity to the biscuits won out and he stayed where he was.

'Come on, boy. Come down and watch the match with me.' Dad sounded a bit needy.

Digby looked unenthusiastic. I prodded him with my foot. 'Go on, Diggers, you don't want to miss kick-off.' One of Digby's duties as the favoured sibling was to watch every Chelsea match with my dad (from the sofa obviously). Dad insisted that it was meaningful bonding for them both. Which was an unusual way to look at watching football with an elderly dog.

Moss (who'd spent enough time in our house to be unsurprised by any of this) got out of bed and bribed Digby from the room. 'You'll need a list of off-screen things you wouldn't ever do as well,' she said, climbing back in and making a serious duvet grab.

'Like what?'

'Well, like pretty much anything Lindsay Lohan does. Also don't store any photos in the Cloud.'

'I don't think anyone's going to be interested in my photos.'

'Not now maybe but one day.'

'What, one day someone's going to hack my account and share what? That photo of us in Christmas jumpers in front of Starbucks?'

Actually, that would be quite humiliating.

From: Stella at the Haden Agency
Date: 19 November 15:24
To: Julia James
Cc: Charlotte at the Haden Agency
Subject: RE: Elektra
Attachments: Spotlight entry info.doc

Dear Julia,

Thank you for sending Elektra's 8 x 10 headshots. They're perfect.
And yes, it's absolutely fine to have photoshopped out the spot!!
We're putting Elektra's entry up on Spotlight now – her PIN is
attached if she wants to look herself up!

I'm sorry that I missed your call. We will start putting Elektra up
for jobs straight away, but I should warn you both that things slow
down in the run up to Christmas (don't forget to keep us informed
of all and any holiday plans!) and it may be a while until you hear
from us. I know that it's difficult after all the excitement of signing,
but the best advice for Elektra (and you) is *just to get on with life
as normal* in the meantime.

Once again, we'd just like to say we're delighted to have Elektra
on board!

Kind regards,

Stella

CHAPTER 5

'There has to be certain chemistry between the two characters and we had that straight away, I think.'

Hailee Steinfeld (on screen-testing with Douglas Booth)

Chocolate Buttons?

I didn't recognize the number so I scanned the room to see who was enjoying retro chocolate instead of concentrating on miming 'going to the supermarket in the style of an animal you relate to on a spiritual level' (one of the more dignified of the ACT exercises).

Archie Mortimer. Hell, yes.

Obviously, an offer of chocolate is good from just about anyone, but coming from Archie it was especially welcome. Maybe there was something there I could work with (also I was hungry for chocolate).

Yeeeesssss. This was intended to convey enthusiasm and not desperation.

Catch . . .

I was up for that except that I wasn't the sort of girl who could catch Buttons in her mouth and look good doing it. Correction, I wasn't the sort of girl who could catch full stop. I was also struggling to think of a witty answer that conveyed this problem without making me look lame.

Can't

Maybe he'd think the single word answer was enigmatic.

You'll need to come over here then

Promising.

Can't

Witty banter was still escaping me.

I'll pass them along

I looked at Archie, ready to flash my sexy and enigmatic half-smile (I'd been practising in the mirror for just such a moment), but he wasn't looking at me; he wasn't even looking at his phone. Actually, he looked pretty absorbed by Jay's attempt to convey the agonies of the self-checkout as experienced by a rhino.

I scanned the room.

Daisy was also eating Buttons.

There were two possibilities: a) Archie had also supplied Daisy with Buttons or b) the Buttons were Daisy's and I'd just been engaging in flirty banter (or trying to) with Daisy.

As Daisy was checking her phone and I'd remembered that Archie didn't have my number, b) was looking the most likely, but even option a) was not ideal. It could be chocolate evidence that Archie fancied Daisy and/or that Daisy fancied Archie.

It figured. Archie was Archie and I'm guessing all the girls and at least two of the guys fancied him and we all had some sort of crush on Daisy. So sharing chocolate with Daisy was OK; it was just a case of disappointed expectations.

Now I was pretty sure where the Chocolate Buttons were coming from I could trace their progress along the line: Lizzy (dull, good at accents), Issam (nice, funny), Maria (no idea, never talked), Christian (mouthy, shouty show-off with serious acne) and 'Big' Brian.

I really did not like 'Big' Brian. I disliked him even more than I disliked Christian (which was a lot). Brian was sixteen, but looked eight because he was so short. He was seriously aggressive, annoyingly talented and up himself, and was destined for success playing (very short) thugs and the sort of boy who tears the wings off butterflies with his teeth. Being short wouldn't stop Brian: he'd just slot right in to a long-standing Hollywood tradition – Tom Cruise who says he's 5'7" (sure), Mark Wahlberg claims 5'8" (really?), Daniel Radcliffe 5'5" (tops). Good news for short actresses, good news for Daisy, bad news for me.

'Oi.' Brian prodded me. 'Got something for you, yeah?' He held up the little purple bag. 'Jump for it.' He waggled the bag above my head, which would have been impossible except for the fact that he was standing on a bench. It was quite humiliating, but a girl has to make an effort for chocolate.

'Oops, missed again. And again.'

He was tormenting me in much the same way I used to torment Digby with treats – before I grew out of teasing dumb animals.

'Too slow. Sorry.' Brian emptied the bag into his mouth. I wasn't surprised: yet more disappointed expectations.

'Elektra, Brian – I don't know what's going on, but I'd prefer it if whatever it was went on after class.' Now we'd annoyed Lens and it was really hard to do that.

Archie raised his eyebrows and smirked at me. Great, now he thought I was voluntarily communicating with Big Brian. Status points lost right there.

'Elektra, you're up next,' said Lens. 'What animal do you feel a spiritual connection with?'

I should have been giving this some thought. But then I'd been distracted. 'Er ... a bushbaby.' Well, I liked bushbabies. Also I suspected that I was looking a little startled.

'Awesome. Let's see your bushbaby in the supermarket then.'

I regretted my choice before I was even on my feet. I didn't really know what bushbabies looked like apart from the fact that they had big eyes. I didn't know what their bodies were like, how they moved. I didn't know what mannerisms they had. I should have gone for meerkat. I was an expert on meerkats (well, at least the ones that are in the insurance business). Everyone was looking at me. The pressure.

'Motivation,' prompted Lens.

I projected my hunger for chocolate on to my formless, wordless bushbaby.

'Have you started?' asked Lens a couple of minutes later.

I had, but obviously not in a way that was going to bring Spielberg to his knees. I wasn't feeling it. What had my bushbaby experienced? She could be a deeply traumatized bushbaby. For all I knew, her parents and two small sisters could have died in a tragic road accident. Or not. How was I supposed to *become* the bushbaby without this vital information?

'Elektra, come on. Think movement, think instinct, think curiosity, think fear, think not looking like you're thinking.' Lens was on his feet. I think that what I was looking at was *his* 'bushbaby in a supermarket', but it was hard to be sure.

Lens got paid for this.

I could never admit to anyone how much fun it was.

Daisy caught up with me as I was collecting my coat and looking for my phone at the end of class and gave me a big hug. 'We're agency sisters! Stella told me. I'm so pleased for you.'

'Aaaaw, thanks.' I looked round to check no one was within earshot. Archie and Issam were near, but they were laughing so hard about something that they couldn't have been listening.

'Are you not telling anyone?' asked Daisy.

'Well, I told Lens and I'm really glad you know, but no, I don't want a big announcement. I probably won't get anything.' It had been a couple of weeks since we'd sent back the contract and since then nothing. Radio silence. 'Or if I do ever get anything everyone will work it out.'

She nodded like she understood. 'But you will get stuff. Stella's great. She's really nice too.'

'A bit scary.'

'Yep, but she's nice. Charlie too. Look, anything

you want to know just ask me. I've got to run, my gran's picking me up.'

I thanked her (also for the Buttons which had in fact been celebratory Buttons – which was another reason they should not have ended up being snaffled by Brian). Where was my phone? Practically everyone had left. Lens was doing that thing with the keys that made it really obvious that although he loved us all dearly he wanted to go home.

'See you later, Elektra,' said Archie on his way out of the door and I gave an awkward little wave because … well, because that's how smooth I am.

I could hear familiar barking coming from under a pile of props. A pile of props I hadn't been anywhere near.

My phone defied the laws of physics.

✩ CHAPTER 6

*'I was bullied by my teachers . . . Can you believe
that? This math teacher gave me an F because she
said I smiled too much. And I'm great at math! I
think they just found it weird that I wanted to act,
you know?'*

Chloë Moretz

'And when he said "see you later" he might have
meant that he *wanted* to see you later.' Moss and I
were hanging by the school gates after a particularly
trying Wednesday and she was analysing my recent
dazzling 'exchange' with Archie. 'He *might* have
meant that it would be nice if you guys were to meet
up . . . later.'

I just looked at her with the sort of despair that
that suggestion deserved.

'Well, why would you be in his cover pic if he wasn't into you?'

Maybe I'd been a bit overexcited about that. 'We're all in his cover pic, the whole class.'

I got my phone out to show her. I was just a tiny pixel at the back of a wide group shot. Daisy was much more in focus than I was. Even Brian was.

'... Your legs look nice?' It was the best Moss could offer. It was so cold that everything we said came out of our mouths with its own little puff of steam.

'You can only see one of them.'

'No, two ...' She looked closer. 'Oh, sorry, I don't think that other one is yours.'

'No, it's Issam's.' It wasn't a flattering mistake, but in fairness I was really hard to make out and there were a lot of limbs in that photo.

'You're going to kill me.'

'What have you done, Moss?' But I had a sinking feeling I knew exactly what she'd done because she still had my phone. 'Oh, God, you liked it, didn't you?'

'To be precise, you liked it. It was an accident.'

It was not an accident. 'He'll think I'm a weird stalker.' I was freaking out.

'Well, you are.'

Brutal.

'He won't even notice.'

'He will notice. Everyone will notice.'

'Just unlike it then,' she said.

'I have, but it's probably too late.' And now I felt paranoid that not only would he think I'd 'liked' his photo, he would also think I'd 'unliked' it. So I would look weird, desperate *and* indecisive.

'But you need to let him know you're interested. He's not going to just realize, it's not like you give out "come and talk to me" vibes.'

'I do!'

'I love you, Elektra, but you are seriously a long way along the sarcastic spectrum which doesn't always make you the most approachable person.'

She sounded like my mum. And my dad. And quite a few other people now I came to think about it.

'Archie did hold me in his manly arms last week.'

'*Whaaaaaat!*'

'It was only because we were partners in the Trust Game.'

'What's the Trust Game? And can I play it with Archie too?'

'We all stand in pairs and you have to close your eyes and fall back and trust the other person to catch you. And no you can't.' It's been known to go horribly wrong. But it hadn't that time and the Trust Game was now my absolutely favourite drama game.

'Was there any ... tension?'

'Not enough. But I sometimes think he's watching me in class.'

'That's definitely a good sign. He's probably a little bit obsessed with you.'

'Or maybe I'm just a little bit obsessed with him and super aware of his every glance.'

Moss grimaced; that was possible.

Actually, that was true.

'Maybe you should take up smoking and then you can go outside and smoke together on your break and get close.' Moss waggled her eyebrows in a frankly disturbing way. 'That's how Aba got with Rob on their cello course.'

'Yep, I can totally see how that would work ... except I don't think he smokes ... Also we don't get breaks ... Also I'm not taking up smoking for a guy; even the smell makes me sick so I'd probably throw up which would not be smooth ... Also my mum would kill me.'

'All good points. So maybe not my best idea?'

'Maybe not. Anyway, he's probably got a girlfriend,' I said, examining my hair for split ends.

'He probably doesn't. Most guys don't. Not if they can get a girl without committing.' Moss read a lot of advice columns, but not much of it translated to our lives. 'Maybe he'll be at the social. Can you wait that long?'

The social was the annual party run by the PTA for our year and up and boys from St John's (the closest boys' school) were invited (i.e. made to come). It wasn't until after the Christmas holidays and the fact that we were already talking about it was a tragic reflection on our social lives. But it was the only exception to our school's strict 'No Boys' policy (well, except for a smuggling incident involving a girl in the sixth form, her boyfriend and the changing rooms, but nobody would give us any details and that was Never Going to Happen Again).

'How is that possible? Archie doesn't even go to St John's.'

Moss shrugged. 'It's probably for the best.'

It probably was. The classy venue for the social was the sports hall.

Nothing good has ever happened to me in a sports hall.

'Elektra!' I spun round to see my mother striding towards the gates, waving a hairbrush in a manic fashion to get my attention. Like I/anyone could have missed her; I'm pretty sure they heard her in the staffroom.

'Aaaaw, look, everyone, Elektra's mummy's come to pick her up in her little car. That's *so* sweet,' Flissy said, calling a black cab on her iPhone, applying lipgloss and embarrassing me all at the same time. Which was impressive multitasking. But as soon as my mum got within hearing distance the charm offensive was turned on. 'Hello, Mrs Jones,' she said.

'James,' I corrected, but they both ignored me.

Moss was miming being sick behind Flissy's back. I loved Moss.

'I adore your bag.' Flissy was literally talking down to her. My (short) mum looked pathetically pleased by the attention. She hadn't noticed that Flissy was carrying the newer, shinier version of the same bag.

'I do hope Elektra isn't too upset.' *What the?* Flissy had a weird expression on her face. I think it was meant to be concern, but that was obviously an unfamiliar emotion for her.

'Upset? Elektra, what happened?'

'Nothing,' I said, trying to steer Mum towards the car (which was a perfectly ordinary size).

'About the biology test? Oh, she didn't tell you her mark? Eeek, sorry, Elektra!' Sure, she was really sorry. 'I probably wouldn't have told my mum either – wouldn't have wanted her to *worry*.' Flissy smiled 'sweetly'. 'Must go, my taxi's here. So nice to talk to you, Mrs Jones.'

On the one hand, Flissy had just admired my mother's handbag and told the truth. On the other hand, she was toxic.

I hugged Moss and hurried my mother away from the gates and into the car before anyone else could say anything to her and before she could say anything about anything in front of anybody. Luckily, she was distracted.

'Darling! Your agent called!'

Thank God she hadn't said that in front of Flissy.

'And?' I tried to sound casual, but I'm not sure I managed it.

'You've got an audition! Seat belt, seat belt.'

'What for? What? Really? When?' I was buckling and babbling.

'Well, in about ...' she looked at her watch while reversing very dangerously out of the car park, 'fifty minutes.'

It wasn't meant to happen like this. Somehow I was meant to feel prepared and ready to be cast. I didn't. I was going in there metaphorically naked. I needed time to prepare – dramatically (I'd planned on begging Lens to give me lots of one-to-one tuition before every audition), physically (I had a spot lurking in my left eyebrow) and emotionally (I was so not calm).

'Have I got any lines to learn?' I asked Mum, looking at my watch, but hardly able to read the time I was so stressy.

'No,' said my mother, narrowly missing running over my maths teacher (wasted opportunity), 'but don't worry. Stella's filled me in on everything you need to know. They're looking for a dead girl – well, to be accurate, a good actress who can convincingly portray a dead girl.' She was obviously parroting Stella.

'A dead girl? How hard can that be?' I was

crushed. At first sight, it didn't sound like the role had a lot of potential.

'Well, Stella said they were looking for a strong actress.'

'She was just trying to be nice. What if this is my first audition because she thinks that's all I can do – be dead.'

My mother looked at me carefully.

'Keep your eyes on the road, Mum, or I *will* be a dead child.'

She didn't say anything, just handed me a tube of spot concealer.

Now I came to think about it (and now that I only had about twenty-five minutes to go) maybe convincingly portraying a dead girl *did* require talent. I mean, what exactly did dead girls look like?

What do dead girls look like? It was an emergency so I texted Moss.

???????????

Audition!!!!!!!!

Oh. My. God. And then, **How dead?**

'How dead am I?' I asked my mum.

'What do you mean?'

'Well, like, have I just drawn my last breath or am I practically decomposing? Do I have a tinge of blue about the lips or am I at the maggots stage?'

My mother shuddered. 'I don't know, Elektra. Stella just said dead.'

'You didn't *ask*?' I wailed.

'She sounded busy.'

I don't know how dead I am, I texted Moss, wishing there were an emoticon for despair (there probably was, but not on my ancient phone).

I meant how did you die? Disease? Knife? Poison? Gunshot wound to the head? Or sleep? She was right on it.

'Mum, did you ask how I died?' I asked, wondering how you could die of sleep.

She shook her head. It didn't seem to have occurred to her to find out anything useful at all.

Mosssss, nightmare. I don't know how I died.

I think it will make a difference. Not sure what Google images to look at.

Yep, presumably, dead girls who'd just gone through something very violent – or worse – would look different to girls who'd just quietly stopped breathing. Maybe it was a period drama and I had been carried away by consumption or whatever it was that carried teenage girls away in period dramas – although I wasn't sure I was thin enough to carry off death by consumption. Maybe it was a ghost thing – then the character *would* have potential. Cool but unlikely.

Google pics of dead girls are gross and prob not very helpful. Suggest you go with the flow. You will be a beautiful corpse.

I won't be a beautiful corpse. I am wearing school uniform ☹

Even Moss couldn't think of an upbeat reply to that one.

'Mum, have I got time to go home and get changed? I can't go like this.'

'We've hardly got time to get there full stop. Don't worry. Stella said your school uniform would be perfect.'

'But it's *purple*. I can't die in *purple*.' I was prepared to do my very best, even in these difficult circumstances, but how good could I be wearing purple polyester?

'The colour brings out your eyes,' Mum said (lied), but nothing was going to reconcile me to looking like an aubergine. Also my skirt (bought 'to last') was at least three sizes too big. I was a tragic, droopy, nervous aubergine with mud-brown eyes. Maybe I was going to die of shame.

I tried calling Lens, but he didn't pick up. Then I tried Daisy ... Nope, she wasn't picking up either. What if she was my competition? Daisy would be a beautiful corpse. Eulalie didn't answer either. I needed her to tell me how *super/sensationnelle/craquante* I was.

What I didn't need to do was sit in the car with my stressy mum.

★ CHAPTER 7

'Go into every audition knowing that you're an equal and expect to be treated as such.'

Romola Garai

The audition was somewhere in Soho and usually I'd have been fascinated by all the gay bars and sex shops (*what* or *who* was behind those weird beaded curtain things? Did I even want to know? Yes.) But I was too busy getting really freaked out about being late for the audition and not knowing how to be dead so we could have been anywhere. We ended up parking on a single yellow line and Mum started trying to clean me up like I was a toddler, still rubbing away at some ink marks on my arms with a saliva-damp tissue as we ran to the address that Stella had given her.

I'd expected some flashy media offices with

multiple screens in reception and those arty bottles of Coca-Cola lined up like a gallery display; instead, it was just some rented rooms in a run-down old building.

There was a typed notice sellotaped to the door:

AUDITIONS FOR GREENLIGHT PROJECT 2
SECOND FLOOR

Even without that, we'd have known that we were in the right place by the two girls in school uniform, pretty much the same age as me, coming out as we were going in. They looked at me and I looked at them: everyone sizing up the competition (predictably they had more flattering uniforms).

Even my mum was quiet on the way upstairs. There was a narrow landing and at the end of it, standing guard in front of a closed door, a pale young man wearing a lilac pashmina.

'Name?' he asked so listlessly that he could have been near death himself.

'Elek—' Mum began.

'Elektra James,' I cut across her because I knew my own name.

Mr Pashmina ticked me off without even looking up and gestured up at a tatty half-landing. 'First door to the right and take a seat. They'll see you in a mo.'

Six other 'dead schoolgirl' hopefuls were sitting on narrow hard-backed chairs in a tiny waiting room. None of them were Daisy (thankfully). I was on my own, Stella's only hope. The room was stuffy. It was like a dentist's waiting room, but without the weird smell (good) or the trashy magazines (bad). Five of the girls were accompanied by anxious-looking women (I'm guessing their mums); one girl was with an even more stressed-out-looking man (definitely her dad: they looked practically identical). There was an extra mother pacing by the barred window.

All the girls were wearing school uniform. One of them was working a real St Trinian's look; if they were looking for a slutty dead schoolgirl, she would definitely get the part. You could tell the girls who'd done this before: they'd brought something to read. One particularly cool girl, who was rocking a simple black-and-white uniform as if it were indie Chanel, was knitting.

My mother started saying hello to everyone, but one of the mothers gestured to a large sign on the wall that said **Perfect Quiet, Please, Taping** in thick red marker and Mum (who always obeyed signs) lapsed into embarrassed silence.

I was grateful.

The 'mo' Mr Pashmina promised stretched into what seemed like hours. Every ten minutes or so, a subdued or excited-looking girl would come in, collect a random parent and depart, followed five minutes later by Mr Pashmina with his clipboard. He would stage-whisper the next name and a girl would get up and follow him.

I tried to look like I was silently wishing them good luck, but deep down I wasn't. Who would?

I was the last girl to be called. I had reread a discarded *Evening Standard* three times by then (the top news story, *Psychic sheep predicts election victory*, still made no sense), my phone battery had died and I was a weird mixture of really nervous and really, really bored. I'd got to the stage of wishing I'd brought my physics homework with me (Ohm's law which is less relaxing than it sounds).

I followed Mr Pashmina, ignoring my mother who was pointlessly fumbling in her handbag for the hairbrush. I was shaking a little and I needed to go to the loo, even though I'd already been for about a hundred nervy micro wees.

The audition room was really small. There were two women sitting behind a desk, one of them watching replays on a camcorder. They looked a bit tired and the room smelled of ham sandwiches. I'm not sure what I'd expected at an audition, but it wasn't this.

The older woman smiled warmly at me. 'Hello, come on in. You're Elektra James?'

I nodded and she made a tick against my name on a depressingly long list.

'I'm Lily and this is Anna. Did your agent ...' She looked down at her list. 'Oh, yes, Stella Haden – did Stella have a chance to explain the role to you?'

'Sort of; I know it's a dead schoolgirl. I don't know what sort of dead. I mean I don't know how she died.'

'Oh, don't worry about that at this stage. It's early days.' It didn't seem to occur to Lily that I might worry less if I had some idea what I was meant to be doing.

'I haven't learned any lines or anything.'

'No, that's because the role is a non-speaking one.'

Ah. They laughed and I blushed and because they were nice they tried to pretend they'd just been coughing.

'OK, let's get your ident done first,' said Lily.

I looked at her blankly.

She handed me a big rectangle of wipe-clean card. It was mostly empty space, but across the bottom was written *Dead Drop* (which I guessed was the name of whatever this was) and Greenlight (which I'd worked out was the name of the production company) and 3rd December.

'Here.' She passed me a black marker pen. 'Just write your name on the card, hold it up in front of you and we'll take a photo. Stand over by the white wall. No, don't hold it in front of your face. The whole point is that we can see who you are. Yes, that'll do. Now turn to each side . . . Perfect.'

The other woman, Anna, captured me on her camera looking like a criminal.

As soon as she took the picture, I had a nasty feeling that I might have spelled my name wrong. I was feeling a bit brain foggy.

That was pretty much the most active thing I had to do. After that, they just photographed me from every angle and measured my height. Why? I was going to be dead, presumably lying down – surely I could just curl up a bit into the desired length? Maybe not. What did I know?

Less than five minutes later, I found myself back out in the corridor and went to reclaim my mother.

She started up before we'd left the room, far less the building.

'How *was* it, darling?'

Cringe.

I made 'don't talk now' faces at her, but she was practised at ignoring those. We passed Mr Pashmina on the way out.

'Thank you *so* much for seeing Elektra,' she gushed (loudly). '*Such* an exciting experience for her. So, we just wait to hear now, do we?'

Cringe.

Mr Pashmina just looked blank. He'd obviously forgotten who we were. Just as well.

I dragged Mum down the narrow stairs and out into the now dark street. The cold air smelled of coffee and cake from the cafe next door. It was a really good smell, cinnamon and chocolate *and* vanilla in the mix. I was hungry, but I could see a couple of the 'dead schoolgirls' and their mothers inside and I didn't trust Mum to keep her voice down or, even worse, not to start talking to them, so I steered her back to the car. We had a parking ticket; of course we did.

'So, tell me what happened in there?' Mum said, shoving the ticket into her bag. I was impressed that she wasn't freaking out about the ticket or saying it was my fault (which it sort of was).

I shrugged. 'Not much really.'

'What did they ask you to do?'

'Really nothing.' Which was disappointing for both of us.

'*Something* must have happened. What did they say to you?' She hates it when I don't tell her stuff; it's a problem – she needs to work on her attachment (to me) issues.

Obviously, the first thing I did when I got in the car was plug my phone into the charger and check my messages.

Just stay calm, smile at them and do what they say. (Daisy, the pro.)

Just enjoy yourself, it's all good experience. (Lens, the teacher.)

You will be FABULEUSE. (This was followed by a long line of not entirely appropriate emoticons about half of which wouldn't display on my screen – Eulalie had a new iPhone and was getting in touch with her inner teenager by downloading multiple weird apps) **How can they not love you? You are YOU.** (getting pretty French and existential there.)

Don't panic. There are lots of images of dead girls in school uniform. Even purple school uniform. Moss would probably have nightmares for years and I wouldn't even get the part.

I scrolled down; fifteen texts between them, all pretty much saying the same thing – it would be *great*, I would be *great* (except for a typically random one from my dad that was just a really poor joke about cows). But I wasn't feeling great. There's something depressing about reading advice after you've already done something and when you're pretty sure you didn't take any of it.

'Elektra, would you get off that phone for five minutes and talk to me?' My mum was still trying to get my attention.

'I'm not *not* telling you,' and for once I wasn't, 'but honestly nothing much happened. They just sort of looked at me and measured me and took photos.'

'That was it? Really? They didn't say what would happen next?'

'Nope, that was it.'

And neither of us could draw much encouragement from that.

'So, about that biology test.'

Great. The car ride home was going to be a long one.

From: Stella at the Haden Agency
Date: 11 December 11:25
To: Julia James
Cc: Charlotte at the Haden Agency
Subject: *Straker* (working title) project
Attachments: Casting brief.doc; character scenes.doc

Dear Julia,

Would Elektra be free for a meeting at 5 p.m. on Wednesday 17 December at the Spotlight Offices, 7 Leicester Place, WC2 with Janey (director, Suited Casting)?

The meeting is to put some scenes (attached) on tape for a great role in an upcoming feature, working title *STRAKER*. I should warn you that the casting team are looking at a lot of girls, but whatever happens this is fantastic audition experience for Elektra! I've attached the casting brief they sent over as well as the scenes so that you have as much information as possible – but please can I stress that this project is **<u>Top Secret</u>**. Let me know if Elektra's available as soon as possible, please. And can I remind you both that the number-one rule for auditions is to be on time? (Early is even better!)

Kind regards,

Stella

P.S. Well done to Elektra for getting her first audition under her belt for the Greenlight *Dead Drop* project last Wednesday. I'll let you know if we hear anything. ☺

Attachment: Casting Brief

STRAKER (working title) is a fast action drama set in post-apocalyptic Europe. Straker and her family, psychologically damaged by the harrowing events that have shaken their world, must fight against the Warri tribes who are the only other survivors.

Production Details

Production Dates:	To be confirmed
Company:	Panda Productions/Universal
Director:	Sergei Havelski
Casting:	Suited Casting Ltd
Location:	TBC but to include London, Northern Ireland & Hungary
Pay category:	Paid

Character Breakdown

Straker, female, playing age about fifteen years, white, accent RP/ neutral.
Pretty, slim with long hair and an innocent expression that belies her *tough inner and physical resilience* (no make-up at audition, please).

This character has several key scenes with dialogue and we are looking for an able young actress to carry this role.

The details of this project are currently confidential and it is important that the character breakdown and summary and scenes attached are not discussed with, or especially shown to, any third party.

⭐ CHAPTER 8

*'I could eat out in the woods, I would eat bugs ... I
can take care of myself.'*

Tom Cruise

'Dad and I are going out,' said Mum in the sort of
voice I'd have used to announce a Nobel Prize win
(or getting the jeans I really wanted in the sale).
'Eulalie is coming over to chill out with you.'

'Did you just say "chill out"? No, don't answer that;
let's just move on. I don't really need a babysitter.'

'I know, but I thought that you'd have fun.'

'Are you sure it wasn't because you were worried
that the minute you left me alone a) a burglar
would break down the front door and attack me,
b) the kitchen would spontaneously combust and
c) I'd invite over a hundred friends and have an
impromptu house party during which everything

that hadn't already been burgled or burnt would be trashed?'

'The first two, yes.'

'That's actually quite insulting.'

'Sorry, darling. Now what should I wear?'

'Where are you going?' I asked.

'Just a restaurant but a nice one.'

'Your blue dress definitely and wear heels.'

'I can't walk in them.'

'Wear them anyway,' I said firmly.

Her phone rang. 'Oh, hello, Stella.' She listened and I held my breath. 'Oh, I don't think so, no.'

'*What?*' I mouthed at her.

'She's right here. I can ask her.' She turned to me. 'Stella wants to know if you have any mime skills. You don't, do you?'

I definitely did not have any mime skills. 'What are we talking? Basic? Advanced?'

'Did you hear that, Stella? Hang on, I'll put you on speaker.'

'Pretty advanced.' Stella's voice sounded tinny. 'It's for a European co-production; they seem to be taking their mime pretty seriously.'

'I could learn?'

'No, it's for something that's shooting next week. The girl that they cast has broken her arm.'

I could see how that would get in the way of the miming.

'Could I wing it?' I asked.

Stella laughed. 'No, Elektra, you definitely could not wing it. But I appreciate the enthusiasm. Don't worry, there'll be other non-mimey roles. I'll be in touch.' And she rang off.

'Oh, well,' said Mum, 'I've never been a big fan of mime.'

Me neither but that really was missing the point.

'Come on, I'll run the *Straker* lines with you before I get changed.'

'Seriously, Eulalie, you have to help me,' I pleaded, opening the door to her (Mum, perfectly styled, had already gone to meet Dad).

'Of course I am helping you,' said Eulalie, putting down two large shiny Selfridges bags and kissing me on both cheeks (twice). 'What is the emergency?'

'I need to run my lines for the *Straker* audition. Mum's been driving me mad because she keeps doing it with a weird accent and with *actions*.' For someone that didn't like mime, she used a lot of gestures.

'I too will be doing it with a weird accent, but no actions I am promising.'

'Yes, but it will be your own weird accent and not some strange actor-y thing. Do you want me to make you coffee?'

'Can you do a tiny little espresso, please?'

'I don't think I can,' I said, looking at the kettle and the ground coffee.

She glanced at her watch. 'A tiny glass of wine?'

That I could do. I poured her a large glass and we went to get comfy in the sitting room.

'What is he being about, this *Straker*?'

'I don't know very much, but it's crazy exciting. Basically, the world has all but ended and Straker – who's my character ... well, the character I'm up for – is all, like, super traumatized and complex. She has a romance with Jan, who's the son of the chief of the Warri tribe, and they're basically responsible for the survival of the human race or something like that.'

Eulalie looked confused which was fair enough.

'Look, it's not in the gritty realism genre.' I handed her the scene I had to prepare. 'Have a read.'

Scene 8: Interior. Damp is coursing down the rough walls of the mud shelter.
Straker and Winona [Straker's mother] are sitting cross-legged on the floor. There is a shallow pot in front of them. Straker is shaking, clearly afraid. The atmosphere is strained.

STRAKER

(*trembling*) I can't do it.

WINONA

Yes you can. You have no choice. I know
you're hungry.

STRAKER

I'm so, so hungry.(*Puts her hand out to the
bowl, but draws back again, disgusted.*)

WINONA

(*fiercely*) EAT them.

STRAKER

I can't. They're ... wriggling!

WINONA

(*picking up a fat white maggot and eating
it whole*) EAT the bugs, Straker. Just EAT
the bugs!

STRAKER

It's horrible.

WINONA

Not as horrible as death.

'So, you are wanting me to play this fierce Winona?'

'Yes, please.'

We ran through it a couple of times. I was word perfect, but that wasn't very impressive because I only had fourteen words and I'd been practising non-stop since Stella had sent them through four days ago.

'Do you think I've got the disgust down well?' I asked. I should have. I was borderline phobic about maggots and in denial about acting with them (if you can act 'with' a maggot).

'Yes, you are very revolting,' said Eulalie. 'I am not understanding this.'

'What bit?' I asked her.

'The bugs,' she said.

'It's because there's been a big eco-disaster and they're, like, practically the only survivors and there's no food – well, no Sainsbury's or anything – so they have to eat bugs to survive.'

'I am understanding *that*,' she said. 'But bugs are *délicieuse*!'

'No, I don't think they are,' I said with some certainty.

'Have you ever eaten them?'

'No.' Obviously not.

'Ah, you are missing something, *chérie*. The maggoty ones like these are sort of mushroomy and nutty; crickets, they are more crunchy, like little prawns in their shells.'

'How do you even know this?' Anyway, I didn't like mushrooms or nuts.

'One of the most romantic nights of my life was sitting under the stars in a beach bar in Mexico, eating bugs. I was with Sebastian. He was very, very handsome.'

I'm sure he was; they always were. 'I wouldn't eat bugs for any guy,' I said. Not even Archie (but I didn't say that out loud).

'Not *for* a man, *chérie*, *with* a man. It is not AT ALL the same thing.'

'Still no,' I said firmly.

'We can do a googly on bug recipes?' she suggested hopefully, getting out her iPad.

'Better not.' I didn't want to look at hundreds of Google images of bugs, cooked or not. 'I can't start imagining that Winona is serving me a delicacy or I'm going to totally muck this scene up. This is a dystopian, miserable, messed-up meal scene, not a Mexican seduction. Can we do it one more time?'

'Perfect,' Eulalie said when we'd finished. 'So, what are the costumes being like? This can be a problem with these end-of-the-world movies; sometimes the costumes are not so good.'

'I think if you're eating maggots there probably

isn't a functioning department store' I said. 'Will you do my French homework for me?'

'*Bien sûr*, but fill up my glass because French grammar is so very, very stressful.'

I went out to the kitchen to get the bottle of wine for her; it seemed like a fair bargain. As I walked back into the room, I saw her shaking her head over my exercise book, '*Non, non, non!* This is terrible!'

'What?' Had she stumbled over my 37 per cent test result on the imperfect subjunctive?

'This is a very bad comprehension,' she said. 'Marianne is in the *supermarché* doing the shopping for her *maman* and it is saying here that Marianne is buying *quatre pommes*. This is not possible. She has *trois frères et deux sœurs*: plainly, she is needing many more than *quatre pommes*.'

'They never make any sense,' I said. 'Last week there was a whole page on "having fun babysitting"; nobody ever has fun babysitting.'

My phone barked. It was Moss.

BuzzFeed has spoken

And what has BuzzFeed said?

I'll be in a 'meaningful relationship' within three months

Yeah, right

BuzzFeed is never wrong

She attached a pic. Yep, her quiz results were pretty conclusive.

BuzzFeed is sometimes wrong. It said I was a Ravenclaw and I'm obvs a Hufflepuff.

True, but I'm cautiously optimistic. What are you up to?

Doing French homework with Eulalie

You mean Eulalie is doing your French homework?

Yes

Would she do mine? The long exercise on comparative and superlative adverbs, p.79 of text-book. It starts (appropriately) with 'I have the worst teacher in the school'.

We were in different sets for French because Moss was less hopeless than me. 'Eulalie, will you do Moss's French homework too?'

'Of course, *chérie*. Just pour me a little tiny extra glass of wine.'

From: Charlotte at the Haden Agency
Date: 19 December 14:38
To: Julia James
Cc: Stella at the Haden Agency
Subject: RE: Holidays and update

Dear Julia,

Thank you for letting us have Elektra's holiday dates. That's great. And thank you for your messages about *Straker* (working title). No, we still haven't heard anything from the casting team about rearranging the auditions. We'll let you know if and when we do. I'm afraid this is just how it goes.

We did hear back from the casting team on *Dead Drop*, but unfortunately they're not taking it any further with Elektra this time. All good experience though!

We're not aware of anything coming up in the immediate future that would be a good fit for Elektra so do have a relaxing Christmas holiday. Fingers crossed for an exciting New Year!!

Best,

Charlotte

WAITING

- Only a little bit distracted by Christmas and New Year.
- No good parties (not even any bad parties).
- Number of auditions: 0.

From: Jonathan Tibble, Deputy Head, Berkeley Academy
Date: 6 January 16:01
To: Parents of Year 10; Parents of Year 11; Parents of Year 12;
Parents of Year 13
Subject: Social with St John's School, 9 January

Dear Parents,

I hope that everyone enjoyed the festive season and that the girls are rested and ready for a productive term.

The PTA has emailed details for this year's social (this Friday, 9 January). I would encourage all the girls to attend, as mixed, friendly events are an important chance to develop social skills and our association with St John's School is longstanding.

That said, I would like to take this chance to remind you (and ask you to remind your daughters) that *our expectations are that the girls will behave as well at the social event as at any other school event*. In particular, I would like to stress the strict Berkeley Academy rules regarding alcohol, cigarettes, etc. (I refer you to the School Handbook).

Whilst I am optimistic that all will go well, poor behaviour will incur sanctions.

Best wishes,

Mr Tibble

Berkeley Academy: Believing and Achieving since 1964

★
CHAPTER 9

'I think everyone goes to more parties than me ...'
Daniel Radcliffe

Moss was leaning off the edge of the bed, trying to mouth-hoover up dropped Maltesers that were just a bit too far away.

'You look like a stingray.'

'What? Why? Do stingrays wear neon leg warmers? Is it the blue eyeshadow? It is the blue eyeshadow, isn't it?' Moss had come over to mine to get ready for the social. It was eighties-themed which explained the neon leg warmers and the eyeshadow. In so far as they could ever be explained.

'No, it's because they, like, swim along, hoovering stuff up from the sea floor.'

'Wow, so much general knowledge.'

'What can I say? My *Children's First Encyclopedia* serves me well. There are tons more Maltesers in the box or are you enjoying the chase?'

'I only like Maltesers when they play hard to get. They may roll away, but that's just tactics. Mmm …' Moss finally caught one. It was obviously the start of a beautiful relationship.

'Are you practising for this evening? The chase part, not the stingray part obviously.'

'I live in hope. Also I'm a bit bored. I mean, I don't have a Hollywood action film to keep me occupied.'

'Yeah, right. I wish. I'm so not getting that *Straker* part. The clue is in the word "action" which isn't exactly me.' I was pretty sure that none of my sports teachers would have endorsed me for a role requiring 'tough inner and physical resilience'. 'Anyway, Stella phoned to say the audition's been postponed again so it'll probably never happen.'

'It *has* to happen. It's got everything: post-apocalyptic harrowing events, romance, *psychological damage*.'

Of course I'd told Moss about my 'confidential film project'. More than half our conversations were about 'secret' things (and about half of them actually were secret). And, not only had I told her, I'd shown her the scenes and practised them with her too. I would not have been a true friend if I hadn't given her the opportunity to try and say the line 'EAT the bugs, Straker. Just EAT the bugs!', with a straight face (she failed).

'Well, if it does happen, it won't be with me. It's a big part so it'll go to someone who actually knows what they're doing. And literally *nothing* else is happening on the acting front.'

'Does it get to you?'

'What?'

'Waiting.'

I shrugged. I knew it was part of the process, so I wanted to be all cool about it. But I was no good at being patient. At all. Ever.

'If you want a lift, you need to come now,' called my dad from the bottom of the stairs.

We stampeded down and there was a bit of pause when Dad saw us. I like to think it was awe. Well, it was something anyway.

Mum came out of the kitchen to check us over. 'I think I may have had that very skirt,' she said. As 'that very skirt' was a ball of lime-green taffeta that made me look like I was half girl-half Granny Smith apple, I hoped she was joking.

The hall was all decked out with random garlands. I think the ugliest ones had been put there to add to the eighties vibe, but the highest-up ones were just left over from various sporting events. It was dark which was a sound design decision. Most of the girls had gone all out with so much neon netting and Lycra it was a full-on fire hazard, but the boys had ducked the theme. (Except for one boy wearing tight orange leggings. Brave but misguided. He was like a walking biology diagram.)

Moss and I made a beeline for the food, partly to give us time to acclimatize to the shock of being in the same room as the opposite sex, but mostly because, well, it was food.

'Ohmigod, they have Party Rings.' I hadn't seen those things since Year Two birthday parties and it was irrationally exciting.

'Shall we just take the bowl and go and eat them at home?' asked Moss hopefully.

Tempting but no. Socials were a rite of passage. We needed to experience at least one – if only so we could be as rude about them as all the girls in the upper years.

'This is like some messed-up, twenty-first-century version of the Meryton Assembly in *Pride and Prejudice*,' I said, surveying the room. (Surveying the room is very much what people do in Jane Austen novels and *Pride and Prejudice* was our set text for English.)

'That is a freakishly geekish thing to say,' said Moss. 'And *how* is it like that?'

'*One*, all us girls have been looking forward to it for weeks because we never get to see boys. *Two*, more girls have turned up than guys and that fact is really annoying the girls and they're becoming competitive with one another to get the most attention. *Three*, there are lots of single-sex groups and occasionally two girls "take a turn about the room" to increase their chances of getting pulled. *Four*, the boys will all complain about how lame it was and the girls will talk about it for months. *Five*, none of the fathers will have any interest in what happened and all the mothers will ask too many questions.'

'You're right. We are totally at the start of a Georgian romcom,' said Moss. 'With the sad exception of costumes.' She tugged down her purple puffball, which was riding up, but unfortunately only on one side. I passed her a purple Party Ring as an edible accessory.

'I'd forgotten how good these were. I didn't appreciate them properly when I was seven. They're so— *Eurgh!*' Moss recoiled in horror.

'That was a quick change of opinion.'

'No,' Moss whispered, 'look at *that*.'

I followed her gaze to a gymnastics bench in a corner, not nearly far enough away from the table, where Flissy was sucking some poor guy's face. It really put me off my Party Ring (they may be ruined forever by the association). We both stared. It was oddly compelling: as much as you wanted to, you couldn't look away.

'That's repulsive,' said Moss way, way too loudly.

'Oh, hey, guys.' Flissy sat up proudly. She was wearing little more than an electric-blue leotard and very shiny footless tights – she'd probably matched her costume to her make-out location. She rarely addressed us, but she had a point to make. 'This is my *boyfriend* James.'

'It would be a bit weird if it was some other guy.'

'What? Why?' James asked. He seemed deeply confused by the sophistication of the conversation.

'Because you've been sucking each other's faces for the last five minutes.'

'Oh, it's been much longer than that.' Flissy smirked.

The token PTA father in charge of refreshments looked deeply uncomfortable.

'Let's leave them to it,' said Moss because a) they were already back on it and b) it was depressing.

The music was being provided by one of the many 'DJs' the boys' school had to offer – guys who'd selflessly volunteered to take charge of the music in return for a raised platform on which to show off gravity-defying gelled hair and get a bird's-eye view of the dance floor for more time-efficient perving. The whole 'I'm a DJ thing' was clearly working for this one because Talia and three other girls had already joined him.

The music was really dance-y and Moss and I

got properly into it. We got some attention, but I can't be sure that it was the right sort; my dancing style is not universally appreciated. I was halfway through an original rendition of the *Grease* finale (well, that's what I'd say if challenged) when Moss grabbed my arm.

'Elektra, I know that boy.'

'What? Where?' Her enthusiasm suggested that it wasn't anyone I knew. This was a bit of a breakthrough.

'He just moved in practically next door to us.' She pointed at a guy with shaggy white-blond hair who was leaning against a pillar and watching the party like it was some sort of nature documentary. He was fit if you liked the skinny, arty-boy vibe. Which Moss plainly did. But she was not alone; a small huddle of girls on the other side of the room were watching him too and swaying awkwardly. Moss looked at them bitterly. 'Look at Kasha and Melly perving on him. Bit desperate – they don't even know him.'

'You didn't tell me about winning the boy-next-door lottery.' What were the odds? A sixty-five-year-old single accountant lived next door to me. On the other side there was a woman with seven cats.

'Torr!' Moss called, waving her arm only slightly manically.

Blond boy looked around, confused.

'Torr!' Moss tried again, going bright red, as well she might.

He caught sight of her and grinned.

'Oh. My. God. He's got a *sexy-lopsided-grin*,' I whispered. This was something we'd read about, but never (despite intensive research) encountered in the flesh. It was fortunate that skinny, arty boys were not my type: Moss and I had a strict non-compete policy.

'It's Moss, right? How are you?' He came towards us.

'I'm good. What are you doing here?' Moss giggled, more (I hope) for the benefit of the staring girls than for Torr.

'I've just started at St John's ... Strangely enough, I didn't choose to crash this thing.'

'Yeah, I know, so *lame*, right?' said Moss.

'I'm coming round to the neon fishnet look actually,' I said.

Moss dug her nails into my arm. 'Ha, funny.' I hadn't been joking. 'Torr, this is Elektra.'

'Good to meet you, Elektra.' Torr cracked out his arty-boy speciality grin.

'We came ironically, but this is killing me,' said Moss. She was clearly trying to reassemble (assemble?) the aloof and mysterious arty persona that had been destroyed by the Party Rings and cheesy dancing.

'Yeah, I feel you. This is not really my kind of scene.' (He was doing the whole Darcy 'above the company' thing.)

'What is your scene?'

'I'm more into gigs and stuff.'

'Oh, yeah, us too.' Moss nodded.

That was a lie. We'd never been to a gig in our lives.

'I'm gonna go and get a drink. Would you girls like anything?'

'Yeah, I'd love one. I'll have whatever you're having.' I'm not going to lie: Moss *simpered*.

'There's literally only squash.'

'Oh, right.' She giggled awkwardly. 'Squash is good.'

'What about you, Elektra?'

'Don't worry, I'm fine, thanks.'

He sauntered to the refreshments table where PTA man was still desperately trying to ignore Flissy and James's PDA.

'Elektra, I was legitimately so awkward,' Moss wailed.

That was a little bit true; also she'd been speaking in a strange American accent and saying odd things, but now was not the time to point any of that out.

'Come on, Mossy, he was flirting so much. You definitely were too.'

'No I wasn't.'

'Yes you were, you harlot.'

'OK, yes, I was attempting to and failing miserably. That's even worse. What if he asks me which gigs we've been to?'

'Chill, that's what Google's for; we're experts at last-minute revision.'

'I can't believe I actually said, "I'll have what you're having."'

'He loved it.'

'He looked at me like I was insane.'

That was kind of true actually. 'Insane in a good way. He practically offered to buy you a drink. That's how all romcoms start.'

'Free squash does not count.'

Maybe she had a point. 'So, what's the plan of attack?'

'I don't know. Of course I don't know. *How* would I know?' There was a distinct note of panic creeping into her voice.

'I'm going to disappear so this thing can intensify.'

'No, Elektra, you can't abandon me. I'm too awkward for this.'

'No you're not. Your flirt game was strong. Just carry on doing what you're doing. You'll be like Flissy by the end of the night.'

'Ewww, can you not?'

'I'm going to go and find Jenny and leave you two alone. Text me regular updates?'

She just nodded; she was still panicking.

'Come find us later and you can tell me everything.'

She nodded again. He was on his way back over.

'Love you. Good luck.'

CHAPTER 10

'When I was little, I didn't understand that other
kids thought I actually was Hermione, really geeky.
It was devastating. I thought no one would ever
fancy me.'

Emma Watson

The next morning, Moss arrived at my doorstep
ready to spill her news from last night, and I paid
her in kind by getting my mum to make blueberry
pancakes.

'Tell me everything,' I said once I'd managed to
get Mum out of the room and out of earshot.

'Nothing happened.' Moss sighed and stabbed a
pancake.

'What? Why not? Torr was definitely into it.'

'Maybe, but, like, I don't really know him yet and
stuff. And then he had to leave early.'

'Ah, that's so annoying.'

'I know,' she said as though it were an infringement of her human rights. 'He had to go to some stupid *gig*.'

She stabbed her pancake again. Between the knifing and the blueberry sauce, they were starting to look like the victims of a violent gangland attack. 'I came to find you guys, but you'd disappeared and you weren't answering your phone.'

'Sorry. I sort of misplaced it during the George Michael singalong and then the guy that Maia was with vomited on me so I bailed and got Mum to pick me up early. It was a fun night till then though.'

Moss's phone buzzed.

'That's Torr, isn't it?' It wasn't really a question. Her smile wasn't subtle.

'*Mayyybeee*.'

'What did he say?'

'"Hey, Moss."' She read out the text in a weird accent that was actually worryingly accurate (sort of East End via Gloucestershire). '"Good to see you last night. Sorry I couldn't stay. We should do something soon."'

I felt quite smug. I'd definitely called this one. I was going to take all the credit when this got to full-on relationship stage.

'But what do I reply? Why did he have to be so vague?'

'He really was not that vague. He's so clearly into you.'

'Elektra, help me. What do I put?'

'You're asking *me* for boy advice?'

'You're the only person in the room.'

Fair. 'Erm, what about something like, "Yeah, was nice. Sounds good." But obviously put it a bit more smoothly.' Texting is *hard*. Neither adults nor guys appreciate the amount of thought and subtle subtext that go into the composition of a text.

'Yes, yes, good, so ...' She paused for about ten minutes, staring at the screen. 'How about, "Was good to see you too. I'm around next week"?'

'Perfect. Go for it.' I'd have said, 'Seize the moment,' but this was taking too long.

'I can't send it. What if this is a terrible mistake?'

'It's definitely not.' Obviously, my extensive experience in this area had made me something of an expert. 'You've just got to shut your eyes and send it.'

'Done. Oh, God, that was definitely a mistake.'

'No it wasn't. Do you want to get with him?'

'No ... Yes ... Not sure. He might be a nice person to try stuff with.'

For some reason, we found this very funny.

'You need a couple name.'

'We so do. Mossorr?'

'Torross?'

'Can't be Taurus. We're both Capricorn. Capricorns are caring and loyal.'

They'd been talking about star signs? Seriously? This was not like Moss. She had it bad. 'What about ... Toss then?'

'Not Toss! *Please* not Toss.'

Her phone buzzed again. We both stared. The tension was palpable.

'Ahhh, he's asked me to meet up with him.' Moss had to bite her lip to stop her embarrassingly huge grin.

'To do what?'

'Unspecified things,' she said and we both started sniggering again. I have never claimed that we were mature.

'Just go.'

'My mum'll freak out. Even if I just go for coffee, you know my mum,' she said and I did.

In many ways, Moss's mum was lovely. She was always nice to me; she made a mean lemon cheesecake; I liked how she dressed (skinny jeans, ankle boots, also she had a pink cocoon coat that I lusted after); she never got mad with Moss about the mess in her bedroom; she let me bring Digby round instead of walking him in the park; and she didn't mind that we all called Moss 'Moss' and not Momoko (mostly because Momoko means 'peach child' and while Moss is many things she's not a 'peach child'). But when it came to the whole achievements thing Moss's mum was fierce. Moss got up an hour earlier than me every single morning to practise the piano. After school on Monday, she had extra maths; after school on Wednesday, she had a tennis lesson (and she was never going to be any good at any sport so that was a total waste of time and money); and for *four hours* on Saturday morning she had Japanese class to please her dad who was originally from Japan.

Even by London standards, that was pretty intense.

I moaned about my parents making me do all my homework and monitoring my phone addiction and not letting me watch any of the weirdly compelling reality shows about seriously fat people, but if my mum got too heavy about studying I would just keep saying I was *stressed* until she backed off in a panic and started to buy me lavender oil and Oreos (my favourite, but normally as welcome as hemlock in my house) and schedule 'down time' back into my life.

Moss's mum was in a whole different category. I would bet 100 *per cent* that she wouldn't think dating (anyone) was a good idea – she'd label it 'a distraction' and say no.

And Moss's dad wouldn't be any help because he lived on the other side of London with a new, very young girlfriend. In fact, she looked about the same age as us (but had way bigger boobs). I tried very hard to hate him for Moss's sake, but he was really funny. I don't think Moss hated him either.

Pretty sure her mum did though.

'You could say you were coming round to mine?'

We weren't in the habit of lying to our parents (much), but sometimes you just had to go for it.

Moss shook her head. 'Nah, it's not worth it; she'll find out. I'll be brave and talk to her. You never know – maybe if I offer to mind Haruka for her for a few afternoons.'

'I'll help you,' I said, which was the mark of a true friend. Moss's little sister, Haruka, looked cute, but she was pretty high maintenance (a bit like Moss really, not that I'd ever tell her that).

'Now you have to get with Archie and then we could double-date.'

'That's not even funny.'

'I wasn't trying to be funny.'

'There's as much chance of Archie asking me out as Prince Harry.'

'Don't be so defeatist. Why don't you ask him? Come on, it's the twenty-first century.' That was easy for Moss to say; she hadn't had to ask Torr out.

'Yeah, sure. I'll just go up to Archie at ACT and randomly ask him if he'd like to go on a date. That wouldn't seriously freak him out.'

'He'd love it. Major ego boost.'

'Yep and major ego shrink for me when he says no.'

'He wouldn't say no.'

'I'm so not going to risk it.'

And I wasn't.

From: Ms Chan, Assistant to Deputy Head, Berkeley Academy
Date: 13 January 16:06
To: Year 10; Year 11; Year 12; Year 13
Subject: Lost property

Dear Girls,

In the wake of this year's social, a surprising number of items have been handed in to me. Highlights (which are available for collection from my office) include:

- 1 pair silver spandex leggings
- 3 shoulder pads
- 1 bottle of perfume, 3 cans of hairspray and too many items of make-up for me to list here
- 2 white iPhone 4s, 1 black iPhone 5 and 1 purple Nokia phone with an 'I <3 my Dalmatian' sticker on the back.

At the risk of being gender normative, I am assuming that the 2 skinny ties, 5 Lynx hygiene products and the single size 11 trainer belong to visitors from St John's and have repatriated them accordingly.

There were also a number of contraband items and it goes without saying that I hope that there is no girl stupid enough to come and claim those.

Best wishes for an *organized* term,

Ms Chan
(Assistant to Mr Tibble)

Berkeley Academy: Believing and Achieving since 1964

From: Stella at the Haden Agency

Date: 16 January 12:16

To: Julia James

Cc: Charlotte at the Haden Agency

Subject: *Straker* (working title) project and Capital Film School (Module 3.2: Working with Children and Animals)

Dear Julia,

Mixed news. Firstly, I'm so sorry for the late notice, but the *Straker* (working title) meeting that was rescheduled for 19 January has been postponed again. Unfortunately, we do not yet have a date for any rearranged meeting. I will of course let you know the moment that we have any further information, but I should warn you that there is a chance that the delay could be quite long and that, given the playing age of the character, could affect Elektra's suitability for the role. You will appreciate that such matters are outside our control!

The good news is that Capital Film School have contacted us looking for child actors to work with their students on term projects. This is not paid work. Nor at the moment do we know who Elektra might be working with or the shoot dates or the shoot location. I appreciate that this might not sound terribly tempting compared to a major production like *Straker*, but student projects are great in-front-of-camera experience. Ideally, Elektra should be building a showreel and this might give her some material. The casting is next Wednesday (21 January) at 5.15 p.m. at the film school. Let me know what you both think.

Best,

Stella

CHAPTER 11

*'Right now I'm eating doughnuts. I've just been
inundated with doughnuts; it's a perk of the job.'*
Jennifer Lawrence

'This is not what I expected London's finest film
school to look like,' said Moss. To be fair, it was
pretty dingy. We were in what appeared to be a
school common room.

A guy put his head round the door. 'Is one of you
Elektra James?'

'I am.'

'Cool. I'm Ed. I'm the director.' Seriously? He did
not look like a director, not even a student director.
'You're meant to have a chaperone with you. We're
not allowed to audition minors without a chaperone
present.'

'That would be me,' said Moss. It was sort of true – Mum had had some crisis (a real one that was temporarily more important than me) and Moss had come with me instead.

'Cool – except the thing is the chaperone's meant to be over eighteen,' said Ed apologetically.

Ah. Moss tugged down her school skirt. 'I am over eighteen. I'm just very short.' I loved Moss.

'Yeah, she looks way younger than she is,' I offered. To be honest, Ed looked like he should have been in Year Twelve himself.

'I'm Elektra's ... older ... cousin?' We were clutching at straws.

'Right. Sure you are,' said Ed. He looked at us and then at his watch. 'Cool. We're all just going to go along with that "older cousin line" then.' He grinned; Ed was quite hot under all the grunginess. He showed us into a tiny room. 'You sit over there and, like, keep an eye on us,' he said, motioning Moss over to a stool in the corner. 'Would you be happy to do a quick read-through, Elektra?'

'Sure,' I said fake casually, like I'd had years of audition experience and not just the dead-child-fail behind me. This was my chance to put into practice all the 'how to succeed at castings' advice I'd gleaned from literally hours of googling. Ed handed me a page of script. I took it gingerly; there was what looked suspiciously like a curry stain on one corner. I skimmed it quickly.

1. EXTERIOR. WAREHOUSE — LONDON
THAMES — DUSK —
A deserted, derelict, industrial warehouse overlooking the River Thames. A shape is seen in the half-light, a bundle on the cold floor. A body, a corpse. The corpse stirs in the gloom and the camera zooms in; it is a young girl in her early teens...

DEAD CHILD
I'm so, so cold.

FATHER
(*Says nothing; hands her a blanket.*)

DEAD CHILD
Father? Is that you, Father?

FATHER
(*Says nothing. Sits with face turned away from the dead child. His shoulders are shaking. He is crying.*)

DEAD CHILD

I'm still so cold. So very cold. Look at
me, Father. Please look at me.

FATHER

(*But he is frozen in grief – silent.*)

DEAD CHILD

What did the stranger mean when he said
everything would be different?

There was more: I had fifteen lines. Fifteen lines
was good.

Fifteen lines was good even when they didn't
make a lot of sense.

'Ready?' asked Ed and I nodded. Sort of. I was
going to have to do all this emoting in front of Moss
who kept letting out nervy little giggles.

It was very hot in the room (also it smelled quite
strongly of beer) so I struggled a bit to find my inner
Frozen and 'Let It Go'.

And now I had to get that song out of my head.

'Do you want me to start off lying down?' I asked.
Moss snorted. My mum wouldn't have snorted.

Ed looked unsure. 'Er ... it's up to you, but it's
cool if you just want to do it all sitting. That's what
the others did.'

I resisted the temptation to ask how many

'others' he'd seen. I was mucking this up. At least now my hands were shaking from nerves so I could work with that. I sat on the floor with my back against the chair legs and took a deep, deep breath. I could do this.

'Cool,' said Ed when I'd finished and then he made me do it again, twice.

He looked over to Moss when we were done. 'It's cool if you want to read too.'

I was quite pleased when she said no.

'What's the film for?' I asked as he showed us out. 'Is it for your degree?'

'Yeah. It's for my Working with Children and Animals module. We have to do a short film with one or the other and I had a bit of a bad experience with an angry Pomeranian when I was younger so I chose kids.'

Great.

'I need cake,' said Moss when we were out of the door.

'You need cake?'

'I really do. That was tense. I think I felt like mums do when they're watching their kids in the nativity play.'

'Most mums don't laugh at their kids.'

'Mine always did. Sorry, it was nerves. I don't

know how you can do that. I'm actually a bit impressed.'

'Aw, thanks, Mossy.' Admittedly, Moss wasn't the one I needed to impress, but I wasn't going to turn down praise. Also my mum had given me 'emergency audition money' and we'd reached a cafe offering hot doughnuts so the day wasn't going to be all bad.

'So how's stuff going with Torr?' I asked when we were sitting down.

Moss tried to look casual and nonchalant, but it really wasn't working. 'We've been texting and I might see him again on Saturday.'

They'd already arranged to meet up twice, but the first time Torr had played it safe and turned up with two of his mates for protection and the second time had been cancelled when Moss's mum had faked an emergency and made Moss stay at home to look after Haruka.

'What time on Saturday?'

'Don't know, he hasn't said.'

I resisted the urge both to point out that she had a say in it too and that we'd planned to hang out that day. 'Cool,' I said (it was catching). 'And it's a full-on date, right?'

She shrugged. 'I'm not entirely sure. It's just the two of us this time. I think.'

She looked a bit stressed which was fair enough.

We were both pretty clueless about this dating business (to give it an optimistic, not to say euphemistic, name).

'You could ask Flissy,' I suggested. 'She'd have some useful expertise.'

'Eurgh, can you imagine how smug she'd be?'

'True. She and James have been going out for so long though.'

'I *know*. How is it that Flissy of all people ended up with an emotionally fulfilling, stable relationship?' asked Moss.

'We don't know that it's emotionally fulfilling.'

'She says it is and I don't think he gets the chance to say anything. Ever.'

'Maybe the secret to relationship success is to date a guy with literally no brain,' I said.

'Are you going to test that theory?'

I gave her the sort of look such a question deserved. Also there wasn't a line of fit, brainless guys vying for my hand.

'Is Archie clever?' she asked, licking sugar off her fingers.

'Sadly, that is not relevant as we're never going to be in a relationship. And yes he is. Probably.' I didn't really know, but he didn't look stupid. 'I'm tragic. I'm the only person in our year not on the Maths Olympiad team that hasn't pulled.'

'C'mon, Elektra. That is so not true.'

I looked at Moss hopefully.

'I think maybe most of the Olympiad team have got lucky by now.'

I was nearly at the 'no sense of humour' stage. It was just humiliating. Even my mum (getting in touch with her inner Mrs Bennet) had started asking a bit desperately if I'd 'snogged' anyone. Statistically, it should have happened by now. I might not have been Moss or Talia, but I wasn't hideous and the bar was set quite low. It wasn't that I hadn't had chances. I mean, boys had pounced, but not the boys I'd wanted to (frankly, pretty desperate boys – brave but still desperate) and I'd ducked. Now I wished I'd just let them pounce. At thirteen, any guy is just grateful that you're there; by fifteen, it felt like you were expected to be expert at it. It's like rollerblading: the longer you leave it, the harder it gets.

'Sarah Walsh and Andrew Bane are going out now,' said Moss (unhelpfully).

'But she looks about ten.'

'And he looks like her brother. They have exactly the same nose. It's just wrong.'

'It's hopeless. I'm never going to leave the house again. I'm going to stay home and eat sweet things and become so fat I have to stay in bed with only Digby and his dog breath for company and you'll have to visit me and tell me what it's like outside.'

'I wouldn't rely on me for an education. I'm nearly as clueless as you.'

'But not quite – thanks for the reminder.'

'Sorry. There's always *Cosmo* for helpful tips.' She fished one out from her bag, headline *Your Breasts Called and They're Feeling Neglected*. (I think my breasts would still have needed parental permission to use the phone.)

'Ew, I don't think I really want to know *Magic Ways to Touch His Ear Lobes*.'

'You're freaked out by ear lobes?' Moss sounded worried for me.

'I just don't see them *that* way. This isn't helping. I don't doubt *Cosmo*'s educational intentions, but these articles all assume I've already snagged the guy. Which, as we've discussed at length, I haven't. But you have, so you're just going to have to find out stuff and report back. Come on, Mossy, it's your duty as a true friend.'

'You need to do your own research.'

'HOW?' I wailed. 'We've just established my hopelessness.'

'You're just a bit rubbish at knowing when someone's into you.'

Actually, that was true, but it was complicated. How was I meant to know? It wasn't like anyone was ever honest; that would be social suicide.

'What about Danny Wright?' went on Moss.

'What about Danny Wright?'

'He was texting you, like, ten times a day. What more of a sign do you want?'

'Danny Wright plays rugby. He was probably only texting me so he could show all his mates or for a bet or something. Also he's always breaking into weird chants that don't sound human. It's confusing.'

'That's anti-rugby-team prejudice, Elektra James.'

'No, that's fact. I'm not buying into this whole rugby team status points thing.' Well, I wasn't going to admit to buying into it. 'Anyway, I have too many opinions for Danny Wright; his texts were boring.'

'You need to stop discriminating based on looks or personality; you're being way too picky. And his texts were only boring because you weren't into him. You wouldn't think it was boring if *Archie* texted you with a bit of rugby banter.'

No I wouldn't. I wouldn't think it was boring if Archie texted me about the fact that his mum had run out of washing-up liquid.

'You actually just sighed.' Moss looked at me despairingly.

'I didn't.'

'You did.'

I probably did.

I might have blushed as well.

My phone barked and Moss answered. 'Hello, this

is Elektra James's personal assistant and chaperone speaking. May I help you? Oh, right ... Sorry ... Sure.' She passed me back the phone, mouthing, '*Sorry.*'

'Hi, Elektra?' It was Charlie. 'I can't reach your mum and that student director person's been on the phone already. He liked you.' She sounded annoyingly surprised.

'He's called Ed. I liked him too.'

'Do you want to do his film then?'

Hell, yes.

From: Charlotte at the Haden Agency
Date: 22 January 14:21.
To: Julia James
Cc: Stella at the Haden Agency
Subject: Capital Film School (Module 3.2: Working with Children and Animals)
Attachments: Script.doc; Map.jpeg

Dear Julia,

Further to my conversation with Elektra yesterday, I can confirm that Edward Price at Capital Film School would like to book Elektra for up to one day's filming on Saturday 7 February. The script is attached. I've highlighted Elektra's lines and she'll need to be off-book.

The location is marked on the attached map. Any problems finding it, please call Edward directly on 07778 345651.

In the meantime, could you please email me Elektra's measurements (height, chest and waist) as a costume will be provided for her? There will be catering on-site. You should also be given a form to fill in for travel and any other legitimate expenses.

Best,

Charlotte

P.S. I got your email about the singing masterclass. Singing is a great skill for an actor, but if Elektra really isn't keen and feels that it's not her thing then it's absolutely fine for her not to attend!

★

CHAPTER 12

'It's mad and bananas and amazing.'
Tom Hiddleston

'This can't be the right place,' said Mum, pulling up in a narrow side street. She looked doubtfully at the directions she'd printed out. 'Can you get out, Elektra, and see if anyone else is here?'

Great, it was still dark and it was freezing. 'It doesn't look like anyone else has been here for about a hundred years,' I said, looking up at the looming Victorian warehouses. I'm not sure why we were surprised; the script had promised we'd be filming in a disused warehouse.

A small scruffy white van with **There is no Planet B** scrawled on the side in luminous paint pulled up alongside us and Ed leaned out of the window. 'Hey, Elektra and Mrs,' he paused, 'er,

Elektra's mum. Cool. Whoa, you're totally on time.' He sounded surprised, like timekeeping was on a module he hadn't studied yet. 'Excellent, yeah.' And he looked at us as though he wasn't very sure what to do with us.

A worried-looking guy got out of the other side of the van and came over.

'Hi, I'm Hadid. I'm the first AD on this shoot.' I wasn't sure what that was, but it sounded important so I did a deferential head dip. 'It's going to take us a bit of time to set up so would you mind just sitting tight for a bit and we'll come and get you when we're good to go?'

'Sure,' I said because my mum looked too cold and fed up to speak. We watched as more people and heaps of equipment than seemed possible were unloaded from the back of the van/Tardis. 'It's so exciting,' I said to Mum as a huge light was carried inside the building.

'I need coffee,' was all that she said.

She kept saying it at five-minute intervals for the next forty minutes until a pretty girl with a nose ring, who introduced herself as Megan, came out to collect us.

The inside of the building was spookier than the outside. There were broken windows and pigeon poo on the floor and the faint smell of pee. It was *perfect*.

Hadid and Ed and two other guys were doing intense things with cables and big lights and barely looked up as we passed.

'You can wait by the fire till they're ready to shoot,' said Megan and I thought my mum was going to kiss her. The fire was a tiny old-fashioned electric fire with fake orange flames, but we huddled round it like it was some sort of Viking hearth. Megan brought us tea in plastic cups and a couple of foldaway chairs. It was like being at some weird (very underfunded) Boy Scout thing.

'If you want food or drink, just ask me – I'm on catering – or help yourselves.' She pointed to a little table heaped high with random packets. There wasn't a vitamin in sight. Excellent. 'Now I need to take Elektra for costume and hair and make-up.'

I'd been looking forward to this. Lead on. It turned out Megan was on catering *and* on costume *and* on hair and make-up. Multitalented and/or Ed's girlfriend. My costume was this skinny little black dress enthusiastically distressed with rips and mud (actual mud so it smelled a bit).

'Wow, it looks even better on you than on the mood board,' said Megan (design too then) when I emerged, all self-conscious, from behind the makeshift screen. 'Make-up now.' She positioned me beside a window and peered at me for about five minutes like I was a thing and not a person. 'Ooooh, you've got a little spot coming … and another one here.' She pushed my nose to one side to get a really good look.

'Sorry.' There wasn't much else I could say.

'It's OK. I'll cover them up for you.' She started dabbing at me with a little sponge.

'Will it show?' I was getting a bit anxious.

'No. To be honest, our camera kit's a bit last millennium so we'll be lucky if everyone's not blurry.'

I was grateful for that. I'd have quite liked a smoky eye or something, but all I got was layers and layers of very pale foundation (on account of being dead).

'You're done,' said Megan finally (it took extra long because she kept touching up her own eyeliner; she was definitely into Ed). 'They're not ready for you so just go keep warm by the fire.' She looked worriedly at my goose-pimply legs (the script demanded bare legs).

A middle-aged man was talking to Mum. 'And then delays on World War Z were endless, weeks hanging around in Glasgow, waiting to be called – but hey, Brad's totally a great guy.'

'Brad Pitt?' I interrupted.

'Sure. Brad's a straight-up guy,' he said (whoa, BAD breath). 'I'm Dan and I've just been having an interesting conversation with your lovely lady mother here about some of the people I've worked with.'

Whatever my 'lovely lady mother' was trying to tell me with her eyes, it wasn't that they were having an 'interesting conversation'.

'Dan's been telling me *all* about his experience working with Kevin Spacey too,' she said.

'And now I'm playing your father.' He laughed like it wasn't funny. 'It's good to stay in touch with the indie stuff ... Tom was just saying the other day that these students can be the big directors of tomorrow.'

'Tom as in ... Tom Cruise?'

'Mmm,' he said in such a sketchy way that I was pretty sure it was another Tom that had been handing out the career advice.

My phone barked (very quietly because Megan had warned me to turn it right down in case they were doing sound checks).

How's it going?? What you doing?? Tell me EVERYTHING. Moss was awake and checking in.

I sent her a pic of my costume. **Verdict?**

I would have gone with asymmetric sleeves, but otherwise yep, you're a pretty well-dressed corpse. You done any filming?

Not yet

What you doing?

Just having a little campfire moment with my mum and new 'dad'. I took a sneaky pic for her.

Not much there for Bertie to worry about then

You have no idea

'Addicted to your phone I see,' said Dan, who seemed to be taking this paternal-interest thing a bit too seriously. 'When we were working on World War Z, there was a total mobile ban except for when Brad wanted to keep in touch with Angie ...' And he was off. It was a happy moment when one of the students called him over to run some solo scene.

'You OK?' Mum asked me (we were sitting very close together because we each had one arm in her cardigan).

'Yes,' I said and I was. Except for the fact that I was too scared to use the only loo because of the spiders, it was kind of cool (as Ed would say).

I was freezing, I was starving, I needed the loo, but it was All Good. I was following in a great tradition of freezing, starving artists. All that was missing was a garret in Paris.

Has anything else happened? Moss an hour later.

Nope, but I've eaten four bags of crisps and most of the biscuits. It's extraordinary there aren't more fat actors. **You still meeting Torr for 'coffee'?**

I am. You make it sound so dodgy. It's genuinely just coffee. Yeah, right. Moss hates coffee. **I'm in Starbucks now. Waiting. He'd better show.**

You're early?!! She was never, ever early. Bit keen.

No. He's LATE. Not keen enough? He'd cancelled last weekend's plans at the last minute and hadn't explained why.

He'll show, I texted. He'd better.

'Right,' shouted Ed, 'we need Elektra and Dan for this one.' I should have gone to the loo when I had the chance. 'OK, guys, so this is the scene where the father – who may or may not be alive – grieves for his dead child and tries to warm her when she wakes – or doesn't wake. Is that all clear?'

No, *obviously* not, but we both nodded. He showed us our marks. This time I *was* going to have to start lying down. It was like lying in a very, very filthy igloo.

'So, do you want me just here?' asked Dan and, for the eighth time, Ed explained patiently that he did indeed want him in the exact same place he'd shown him ten minutes earlier. I would die of hypothermia before he got to the '*hands me a blanket*' bit.

'So, we're going to go straight into a take. Camera ready?' asked Hadid, chalking something on to a genuine clapperboard (an object which made me irrationally happy). 'Ready?' And then. 'Sound ready?'

'Ready,' said the student who was doing the sound.

133

'Scene Three, Take One,' said Hadid, holding the clapperboard in front of the lens.

'Three, two,' Ed was clearly loving this bit, 'one, *action!*'

Hadid clapped the clapperboard and we were off.

'I'm so, so cold,' I started.

It was a long day. Maybe a little bit because Dan needed more takes than I did, but mostly because of technical things happening or failing to happen (there was a stressy half-hour when they couldn't get the walkie-talkies to work). I was pretty sure that there were rules about how long minors should be working on-set, but Ed obviously hadn't read that far in his 'Working with Children and Animals' module. It wasn't until after eleven o'clock at night that he finally shouted: 'That's a wrap. Cool. Thank you very much, everyone.' And we all hugged and kissed (even Dan) as if we'd spent several months together on location.

I could have stayed all night. In fact, I could have stayed several months. It was a long day, but I loved it. I wanted more days like that. Although maybe in the Bahamas next time.

Mum was so tired going home that she almost crashed the car. To be honest, she quite often almost crashes the car, but this was, even by her standards, a close shave. I imagined the headlines: *PROMISING*

YOUNG ACTRESS PULPED ON THE HAMMERSMITH FLYOVER. HOTSHOT BREAKTHROUGH DIRECTOR EDWARD PRICE DEVASTATED BY LOSS OF HIS MUSE ...

Dad took one look at her face when we fell through the door and handed her an exceptionally large glass of red wine. 'You look exhausted. I'm sorry, I should have taken her.'

Go ahead; talk about me as if I were a parcel.

'No, no, it was fine. I wouldn't have wanted you to miss Chelsea v. Arsenal.' Weirdly, I don't even think Mum was being sarcastic. 'Who won?'

'Arsenal, late goal. Chelsea were robbed by the referee.'

Of course they were. We tried to look sympathetic. I think we failed.

'We both had a hard day then,' said Mum. 'I don't think I'll ever be warm again.'

Dad took off his big black jumper (all his jumpers are big and black: it's an architect thing) and she pulled it on over her own clothes and gave him a hug. They weren't very huggy people (thank God) so I think she just wanted to warm up. Fair enough, but they were ignoring me.

'Excuse me, *I* was the one who was working. Mum just spent the day reading her book. And I was practically naked all day so I should have got the jumper.'

'Well, did *you* have a hard day?' Dad asked, turning to me. He didn't offer me any wine, which was harsh, but he did throw me the blanket from the back of the sofa. It smelled of Digby, which was not as unpleasant as it sounds.

'I had an *amaaazing* day. What's for supper?'

'It's half past midnight.'

'Yep, that's probably why I'm starving.'

'Haven't you eaten anything?'

'Just crisps.' Many, many crisps. And biscuits. And chocolate.

'Then you need pizza. Now.'

Better. Still not wine but better. I was going to tell Dad all about my day on the set – what I actually did for my moments on film, my ability to play dead like a bona-fide corpse, my perfect response to direction, my absolute embodiment of the character, etc. etc. etc. In other words, I was going to big myself up because it was just my dad and even if he didn't believe every word I said (or listen to half of them) he wouldn't hate me for bragging. But then my phone barked.

Hey, Elektra

I didn't recognize the number.

Sorry, who's this?

Archie, and then a second later: **from ACT**, like I wouldn't know.

Hey, Archie (I know, I know, weak response.)

136

We all missed you today

Lens had been running a Saturday workshop on stage combat for our Thursday class.

That's nice

I was keeping it neutral. After all, he hadn't said, 'I missed you today' – 'we all missed you' was probably just typical Archie being polite and yet . . .

Even Christian?

I was definitely going to keep the conversation alive.

OK, Christian didn't miss you
Big Brian?
Big Brian definitely didn't miss you
Haha, so what are you up to?

An open question. Moss had drilled me; I knew what to do. I had to give Archie something to work with.

Not much. I just wanted to let you know that next Thursday's class is starting 30 mins later.

Oh, maybe not. Disappointing.

WAITING

• Time (awake) spent at school: 63.1 per cent; time at school spent thinking about acting: 52.5 per cent.

• A bit distracted by a school trip to Hadrian's Wall (very, very cold and I was sick on the coach both ways).

• Number of auditions since Dead Drop and Ed's film: 3 (random child in some 1920s drama; role as a domestic servant in a Victorian mockumentary; child number 3 in the background in a sausages advert); strike rate: 0.

All percentages are approximate, i.e. made up.

From: Stella at the Haden Agency
Date: 6 March 10:45
To: Julia James
Cc: Charlotte at the Haden Agency
Subject: *Fortuneswell* (part of Mary)
Attachments: Character scenes.doc; production details.doc

Dear Julia,

Would Elektra be free for a meeting on Saturday 14 March at
3 p.m. at the American International Church, Tottenham Court
Road with Sally Upton (casting director, Upfront Casting) and her
assistant, Tracey Broady? It's a weekend so Elektra won't have
to miss any school to attend. Please let me know *as soon as
possible* if there are any problems.

This sounds like a fantastic project. It's a costume drama set in rural
Dorset (production details attached). A family faces challenges
when the father goes off to fight. We've suggested Elektra for the
role of Mary, the second oldest of four daughters. It's a great role
as you'll see from the character scenes attached. Elektra should be
very familiar with these scenes before the meeting.

Kind regards,

Stella

P.S. After an unfortunate incident involving one of our older clients,
we're reminding all our clients to make sure there is nothing
inappropriate on their social media and to check their privacy settings.

★
CHAPTER 13

'*Everyone in high school is starting to do "that"
now. But not yet, not for me.*'

Elle Fanning

Thank God it was Thursday. Thank God even
more that it was five thirty and I could escape
to ACT. Actually, it was only five thirteen, but I
needed my fix. It had been a really bad day for a
lot of reasons:

1. All the usual Thursday at school reasons
   (mostly timetable related; any day that
   starts with double maths is going to be a
   stretch for me).
2. The specific *this* Thursday at school reason
   (detention for losing both my English set
   texts which was harsh because I'm pretty

sure that they'll both turn up in the same place, probably the day after term ends).

3. A stupid argument with Moss over whether Torr should come with us to Starbucks after school. Obviously not, because a) they'd sit there wrapped round each other and I'd have to pretend not to be embarrassed by their PDAs and b) he would want to talk about politics in the Middle East.

4. An audition for a part I would have been *perfect* for was cancelled (second lead schoolgirl in a mystery set in a boarding school in the 1950s).

5. I'd had a row with my mum because I'd forgotten Granny Gwen's birthday. This was completely unfair because a) how was I meant to remember without Mum reminding me which she says she did, but which she didn't and b) Granny Gwen barely remembers *my* birthday (I get the same card with sparkly kittens on it every single year and I'm not entirely convinced it's not a bereavement card).

So, even if Lens made us all spend the *entire hour* warming up to Britney, being at ACT was a *guaranteed* improvement on the rest of the day. I went to wait in the green room (which was painted yellow not green and which (always) smelled of salt and vinegar crisps and hairspray). Daisy was there, reading *The Stage*.

'Did Stella put you up for *Fortuneswell?*' I asked.

Daisy and me didn't usually go to the same auditions because we looked so different. I was head and shoulders taller than her for starters. But *Fortuneswell* was looking for four girls. It was a new drama – well, the casting call said it was a new drama, but as far as I could see it was just *Little Women* set in Dorset, moved back a hundred years and with Perfect Pa going off to fight Napoleon instead of the Southern States. I was going up for the part of Mary (who was really just an olde English version of Jo: tall, bookish, gawky but with less good hair).

'Yep, the Sophie part,' she said.

The Sophie part was basically Beth. 'Lucky – you'd get a death-bed scene.' I wasn't thrilled about corpse opportunities, but I did long for a really good death-bed scene. 'Are you excited?'

'Sure,' she said and smiled, but she didn't exactly sound excited. I *was* excited, not only because I still got tragically hyped about every audition (which is a triumph of hope over limited experience), but because even if it wasn't a very original storyline it was a good one. Also there would be *period costumes*.

'Are you off-book?'

She nodded. 'Off-book' was just a bit of jargon that

meant you'd memorized all your lines (I got more of a thrill out of using jargon than was dignified). It was typical of Daisy to have the lines down days before the audition. It was typical of me that I would still be neurotically learning them the night before.

'Stella put you up for the *Straker* role too, didn't she?' Daisy asked.

'How do you know about *Straker*?'

'Upside-down reading in Stella's office,' she confessed. 'Don't worry, I won't tell anyone about it.'

I could trust Daisy. 'What about you?'

'No, I don't look fifteen.'

That was true.

'How did the meeting go?'

'Not so well,' I said and because she knew what it was like she didn't ask me anything else. After multiple postponements, last week I'd finally had the first meeting with the casting director to read through the 'eat the bugs' scene. I'd been super excited (leaving aside the whole maggots angle), but it hadn't been great. There'd been a conveyor belt of girls who all looked pretty much the same as me and I'd had about one and half minutes to give them my whole 'I'm terrified but don't want to die of starvation' thing. I wasn't optimistic.

'Baby One More Time' started to power through the (thin) walls. Class was starting.

*

Lens clapped his hands. 'OK, gang, everyone's here, you're all warmed up and we're going to do something a bit different with script work. So I need two volunteers.'

I stuck up my hand – might as well just unleash the keen. Script work was my favourite.

'OK ... Elektra and ...' He looked around the room. 'Archie.'

Oh. Great. I mean, half of me genuinely thought that was great because, well, *cheekbones*. But the other half of me was in full flight mode. I needed to man up. This was a good thing. Tons of co-stars ended up together: Ashton Kutcher and Mila Kunis, Emma Stone and Andrew Garfield, Nicholas Hoult and Jennifer Lawrence (OK, maybe not 'forever after'). My complex inner monologue was interrupted by Lens handing me a script.

'Take five minutes to read it through and think about the characters. Let's keep it old school – you play A, Elektra.'

Looking at the script, it took me less than one minute to start panicking and less than two to regret volunteering as tribute.

A
Babe, there's something I need to tell you.

B

You look serious. What is it?

A

I don't know how to start to tell you
this ... (*long, emotional pause*)

B

You're scaring me. Something's happened.
What's happened? (*beat*) Hey, don't look
like that — it can't be that bad.

A

I'm pregnant. (*further long, emotional pause*)

B

Right.

A

Right? Right? That's all you have to say?

B

I'm sorry, it's just very (*beat*) unexpected.

A

Look, I know it's early in our
relationship, but ...

B

But what? You want to keep it?

A

(*beat*) Yes. I think I do. (*long, tense pause*) You'll stay? We can be some sort of family.

B

It's a lot to take in.

A

I know, I know. But it's a baby. Your baby is growing inside me. Feel my stomach. (*B doesn't move.*) Feel it!

(*B cups her pregnant belly.*)

So, last week I had my first proper conversation with Archie (and yes, a thirteen-line text exchange counts) and this week he was going to be 'cupping my pregnant belly'. This was not the kind of escalation I'd been planning in our relationship.

'So, how this is going to work is that Elektra and Archie are going to try this scene however they want. There is some direction in the script – which I wrote by the way ...' Lens paused then sighed. 'That pause was for a round of applause, but never mind. Then we're all – yes, all of us so I'd really appreciate it if you'd put your phone down, Christian – going to give them more direction and we're going to see how many different ways we can take this. The scene's quite ambiguous so there are lots of possible interpretations.'

What was he talking about? The scene was really, really not ambiguous. That was the problem.

'Right, let's get going. Come up in front, our A and B.'

Archie and I made awkward eye contact. I was struggling to get into the mindset of a pregnant teen.

We gave it a go.

Me: (deadly serious to try and distract from my deadly serious levels of embarrassment) 'Babe, there's something I need to tell you.'

Archie looked at me, sweet and concerned. Focus, Elektra, focus – he's a really good actor. He touched my arm – gently, reassuring me (no, reassuring A; either way it was nice). Once I'd passed the 'I'm pregnant' line and I hadn't fainted or vomited (although that would have been very 'method'), I started to relax into it. And making eye contact with Archie when Archie was B was easy. Every pause was without doubt 'emotional'.

'It's a lot to take in ...' Archie looked properly distraught (which I – sorry, which A – found borderline offensive).

Then Brian laughed.

'Feel it!' I carried on. Christian started cackling too and one or two others joined in. The corner of Archie's mouth twitched as he came nearer and stroked my 'pregnant belly' (which was looking depressingly realistic thanks to my earlier cake consumption).

'OK and let's pause,' said Lens because the only tension left was the sort that comes from trying not to laugh. 'Very good, very good. I believed in you as a couple in that situation.'

'A *couple*'? Thanks, Lens – that killed any hope of more eye contact.

'Right, ideas for different ways of playing it. Issam?'

Issam shrugged. 'Dunno. Maybe Archie could have looked a bit more scared from the beginning? I mean it's, like, terrifying.'

Well, yes.

'Yes, even more fear from the outset, that would change the scene. Other ideas for how our couple could have done things differently?'

Brian muttered something under his breath that had more to do with A and B's life choices than any stage direction. Lens stared him down. More laughter. I went red (redder). I don't know how Archie was reacting because I wasn't looking at him. I'd probably never look at him again.

'Maybe Archie could make the hold at the end more tender?' suggested Daisy.

Noooooo. Daisy was meant to be my ally.

'Yes! Good suggestion. Why don't you come up behind Elektra this time, Archie, and put your hands round her stomach that way? So you're holding her? *Tenderly.* Yes, Daisy, I *like* this.'

Oh, God, now Lens was in full swing. I also had a bad feeling that this was being snapchatted to half of London.

'We are no longer friends,' I said to Daisy when Lens finally switched up the parts of A and B (to Issam and Christian which was going to be interesting). 'Seriously, you deserve to be paired with Brian for doing that.'

'Ha, I gifted you that. You LOVED it.'

'I did n—' I started.

'Don't even try to deny it. Archie looked like he was also *very much* enjoying it.' We both looked over at Archie, who was having a very self-conscious, banterous conversation with some of the guys. In fact, I could stare as much as I wanted because I was pretty sure he was not going to look in my direction. Ever.

'He's just a brilliant actor,' I said.

'That too,' said Daisy. And then we couldn't talk about it any more because Christian had got to the 'I'm pregnant' line and, I'm not going to lie, it was really hard not to laugh.

CHAPTER 14

'*I don't really want to be an actor.*'

Asa Butterfield (2008)

'*I don't want to let acting dominate my life, not until I'm about twenty.*'

Asa Butterfield (2011)

'I'll take her,' said my dad in the same way someone would have said, 'I'll dig that grave,' or, 'I'd love to pay that tax bill.'

'Can't I go on my own?' I asked. 'It's only, like, four stops on the Tube.' The *Fortuneswell* auditions were being held above a church hall on Tottenham Court Road (this acting business was getting me into a surprising number of religious locations).

'No, under sixteen you're meant to be accompanied,' said my mother who by now was a bit of an expert on this whole auditioning thing.

'They're not going to know. I'll just attach myself to some random adult.'

'That sort of comment is *why* you can't go on your own,' said Mum, who was in a filthy mood (which probably had something to do with the washing machine having so thoroughly flooded the kitchen that this was like a conversation in a lifeboat). 'Either you go or,' she looked at Dad, 'you stay and deal with the repair man.'

'Let's go, Elektra,' said Dad.

Daisy had already gone in by the time I got there. The waiting room was really cold, but then I suppose if the people looking after the church had had money to spare on heating they wouldn't have been renting out its rooms for show business. It was the right place for it though, dispensing sermons on the American dream alongside providing audition space for the Hollywood dream. You could tell who was going in for auditions and who was going to church: the actors were the ones who really looked like they were praying. Plus, it was conveniently close to the London Scientology headquarters so if Tom Cruise was thinking about casting you in his movie and you were really desperate you could sign up for a billion years there and then.

By the time Daisy came out, I'd abandoned the

waiting room for the corridor. There were more girls in the waiting room than there were chairs (and because they were all so pretty I was getting insecure and wanted to sit as far from them as I could). The minute they'd told us they were running late, Dad had gone for a 'little walk' (i.e. he'd gone to sit in a decent cafe and check his phone and do some work). Daisy came right past me and it was obvious even in my distracted state that she was upset.

'Hey, Daisy. Are you all right? Were they mean to you?'

She shook her head, but she was close to tears.

'Let's go outside for a bit. They just told me that I've got at least half an hour before I'm called.'

We went outside, shooed away some filthy pigeons and sat on a low wall. A couple of other girls stared at us before they went inside, trying to work out which parts we were up for. It was a bit hostile. We ignored them. Daisy was just sitting there, looking blank and miserable and scuffing the toe of her shoe against the ground like a five-year-old. Daisy was always very neat and very sweet so something was very wrong.

'What's up?' I asked her. 'Was it a total fail?' That sounds mean, but it wasn't meant that way and she knew it. It was empathy.

She shrugged. 'It was OK, I suppose. They said I

was "great", but hey, we all know that doesn't mean anything.'

'But that's good, isn't it? Well, it's not bad anyway.'

'I suppose.'

There was a long pause and I wished I had chocolate or something because whatever she said she obviously needed cheering up. Her eyes were welling with tears and the tip of her nose was suspiciously red. Even her blonde curls looked sort of flatter and sadder than usual.

'The thing is, Elektra ... I hate it.'

'Hate what? Auditioning? *Everyone* hates auditioning. There's *nothing* to like about auditions. We'll just have to get so famous we don't have to bother any more. Give it a few years and we'll only turn up for "courtesy meetings" and Scorsese will be begging us to appear in his movies.' I was hoping to make her laugh, but Daisy was crying for real now in that silent, apologetic, desperate way of someone who doesn't like to make a fuss.

'No, you don't understand, I hate it *all*. I *hate* the auditions and learning the lines and forgetting lines and worrying about being late and everybody being nervous. I *hate* not getting callbacks, but I *hate getting* callbacks too. I *hate* worrying about getting a spot before filming or putting on weight and standing in the wrong place and saying the wrong thing and ... oh, I don't know ... just being ... disappointing.'

I didn't know what to say. Daisy was so *good* at all this; how could she feel so bad.

Also she was very slim and never got spots.

I put my arm round her; she was all sweaty from crying so hard. I had a crumpled tissue in my pocket, hopefully not snotty, so I gave it to her and just sort of hugged her.

Another girl walked past and looked smug to see Daisy upset. She probably thought it was one less girl for her to compete with.

'But Daisy, you're really good. You're the best girl in our ACT class by miles; everyone says so.'

'I don't really mind the *acting*,' she sniffled. 'It's the rest of it. I hate it, I really do. It feels like it's taken over my life and it's just not fun any more.' She started the silent sobbing again.

'But you're always getting jobs and casting people love you. You're like a total professional.'

She looked at me sadly. 'I do voice-overs for frozen-food adverts and cleaning products, and training videos for companies and way too many videos for parenting channels. I'm always working, but the jobs I get are pretty rubbish.'

I hadn't thought about that. All I'd noticed was that she got work. I'd been kind of jealous. I hadn't stopped to think what the jobs were.

'Well, you get to miss lots of school,' I offered.

'Yes,' she said. 'That's true. And that's why I'm in the bottom sets for maths and science.'

'Then stop,' I said simply.

She looked at me as if I were mad.

'I mean it. Do something else. You could be a dancer or a singer or – I don't know – even a model.' Maybe not a model. she was probably way too short, but I found that telling girls they could be a model usually had a cheering effect.

'But that's it, Elektra, I don't want to do "something else" – "something else" will just be another *thing* with schedules and classes and having to be better than other people at "something else" or at least look better than them. I just want to hang out and do *ordinary* stuff.'

I was confused.

Part of me thought that she was simply mad. Daisy was getting parts so why did she just want to do the ordinary stuff? How boring would that be?

And how could Daisy bear *not* to do the acting stuff? I was still high from being part of Ed's student short film and that had been weeks ago. But it was horrible that she was so sad. (Although I couldn't help thinking that if the casting director could see Daisy now they'd book her on the spot for the 'Sophie/Beth' character because she looked really pretty when she cried.)

No, not helpful, Elektra. I pulled myself together. 'Then *stop*,' I said again.

'My parents would freak out,' she shuddered. 'They've spent so much money on this. Headshots that cost a fortune and all the acting classes and singing classes and dancing classes and even the travel and stuff. I'm only just starting to make money from this by taking those rubbish jobs.'

I felt ashamed then. Because I hadn't thought about the money at all. For an uncomfortable moment, I wondered how Daisy saw me – me in my big house with my architect dad (even if he's mostly just doing kitchens) and my shopping-addicted (even if she denies it), stay-at-home mum and my occasional piece of designer clothing (even if it is bought for me by a mad French step-grandmother). I'd never *have to* miss school to do a training video or a dog-food commercial to earn some money. Well, probably not ever. I gave Daisy another hug, a bit to cheer her up and a bit so that if she thought I was spoiled at least she would think I was spoiled *and* nice.

'You should go,' said Daisy. 'Your half-hour's nearly up.' Classic Daisy; she'd never be late. Although I felt guilty leaving her in such a state, I was on my feet and in that building in seconds.

I was red and rushed when I got into the taping room. I didn't even have the pages of script they'd sent me with my lines ('sides' they're called) with me. I knew them by heart, but felt a bit naked not having them in my hand like a little comfort blanket. I didn't know which of the two women in the room was Sally Upton (the casting director) so I just gave them both my best, 'hire me, I'm really nice to work with' smile. I don't think they even noticed; they were making notes and whispering – obviously, the girl before me had given them something to talk about. I prayed she'd been up for a different role.

'OK, shall we just get on with it?' said the older of the women, finally looking up.

Great, a bad-tempered, bored casting director was all I needed. I wondered how many teenage girls she'd already seen. Plainly too many.

'Can you make your accent a bit more neutral, please?' said Mrs Upton when I was halfway through.

What did that *mean*? How could I possibly sound too posh for an upstairs role in an English period drama? What did that leave me? Biopics of eighteenth-century princesses? Bit niche. 'Would you like me to start over?'

'No, just pick up from where you were.'

I could feel that I was still all red and my neck was worryingly itchy so, as well as sounding wrong, I suspect I wasn't looking my best. I tried to remember where I'd broken off, but I was all over the place. I was pretty sure Daisy never made this sort of mess of an audition and she was the one crying outside. 'Um . . . sorry, could I just look at the script for a second?'

The woman handed it over. 'When you're ready.'

Clearly, whatever I did, she would just like me to do it quickly so I could leave, she could see the remaining girls and get some coffee or vodka or whatever it was she needed to get her through the rest of the day.

I began again.

MARY

(*throwing aside her embroidery*) But Mama, I'm *bored*. You don't allow me to read any more and I'm not one to lounge and lark around. I must and I shall be useful. There must be something I can do for someone and if that someone is happy to give me money for being useful to them then that is surely a good thing, not a shaming thing . . .

OK, that was what I was meant to say. What I actually said was something more like:

But Mama, I'm bored. You don't allow me to read any more and I'm not one to lark and . . . lark and . . .

I started over, got that bit right and then,

> I must and I shall be . . . happy? No,
> erm . . . useful?

I started over again and got all the way to the end of that bit. I was pretty sure I had a sweat moustache.

Mrs Upton was reading the mother's part for me (in a voice so neutral that it was beige).

MAMA
You shall spoil your eyesight and need
spectacles like that unfortunate girl
Rebecca.

MARY
(*muttering under her breath*) At least
Rebecca has something to do all day
long . . .

I bet if I looked hard enough I could probably find the actual page in Little Women that they'd ripped that scene off from.

I didn't think I was doing anything different and I was pretty confident that at least Mary's irritation was going to come over as genuine, but she didn't interrupt again. It was over in a couple of minutes.

'Thank you,' said Mrs Upton in the very same colourless voice and went back to her note-taking.

The other woman, who hadn't said a word, smiled warmly at me as I left. A pity smile.

Daisy had gone and Dad wasn't in the waiting room.

Where are you? I texted him.

Across the road in the cafe. Are you done?

Yes. I waited for him to launch into the whole 'how did it go' line of questioning.

Good. About time. I am dying of boredom.

He was a really poor chaperone. Perfect.

From: Stella at the Haden Agency
Date: 17 March 18:04
To: Julia James
Cc: Charlotte at the Haden Agency
Subject: OmniNut voice-over
Attachments: Draft agreement between E. J. and OmniNut Ltd. doc; map.jpeg

Dear Julia,

OmniNut Ltd liked the voice clips we sent over and would love to book Elektra for the voice work for their upcoming commercial on Tuesday 24 March. You'll see from the attachments that this sort of work is well paid (!) and we're sure Elektra will enjoy it too. The agreement is in standard terms so if you're happy just sign it and send it back. The studio is a little out of the way so we've enclosed a map. As this is a school day, we'll need a permission letter from Elektra's school.

Kind regards,

Stella

P.S. So pleased you're over that flu, Julia. ☺

From: Mrs Haroun, Head Teacher, Berkeley Academy

Date: 18 March 16:13

To: Julia James

Subject: Elektra James's absence from school, Tuesday 24 March

Attachments: Permission letter.doc

Dear Mrs James,

Further to our conversation, I attach a letter on the school's headed notepaper in the form we discussed authorizing Elektra's absence from lessons on Tuesday 24 March.

Whilst on this occasion I am happy to grant permission, can I please stress that it would be helpful to have more advance notice next time (should there be a next time). Whilst we are of course happy to support all our girls in their fulfilling out-of-school activities and whilst we value the dramatic arts, we do take our absence policy very seriously.

Kind regards,

Maryam Haroun
Head Teacher, Berkeley Academy

P.S. Good Luck, Elektra, and let us know how it goes!

Berkeley Academy: Believing and Achieving since 1964

★ CHAPTER 15

'You can just be the condiment. It's really kind of freeing, just being a sidekick weirdo.'

Alex Pettyfer

'Did you ask Moss to take notes for you in lessons today?' asked Mum.

'Mmmm,' I said. No. I'd forgotten and anyway Moss's notes would be a bit useless (she has a very good memory and writes nothing down). I'd copy off Maia if I had to.

'And what about homework?'

'What about it?'

'Will Moss let you know what needs to be handed in for tomorrow?'

'Sure,' I said. No. One of the best things about having a Tuesday off school to voice a squirrel was that nobody (except for my mum and maybe

Madame Verte) would expect me to hand in homework on Wednesday.

You around, Moss? I texted. No answer. **I'm on my way to be the new voice of nuts. It's taking AGES to get there.** No answer.

'Have you had the results back of that biology test?'

'No.' Yes. **Moss? Mum's interrogating me about school. Any minute it's going to get worse and she'll interrogate me about my life. HELP ME.** Five minutes later. **Text meeee.** No answer.

'Is Jenny still going out with that nice boy?' asked Mum.

A deceptively simple question but a) Jenny hadn't 'gone out' with anyone, b) Jenny had got with two boys in the last month and I wouldn't have described either of them as a 'nice boy', c) Mum knew Jenny's mum so saying anything at all was risky and d) any moment now Mum would ask me why I wasn't 'going out' with anyone.

'Mmmm,' I said non-committally.

'Any boys on *your* horizon?'

I felt a little car sick. 'No, not a single one.'

'Or girls?' she said.

'No, no girls either.'

MOSSS! Save me!

'Can you check if it's the next junction, Elektra?' Saved not by Moss but by navigation duties.

'It is,' I replied. I was almost confident because Mum had asked me to check at every single junction for the last forty minutes. We turned off into a horrible tangle of one-way roads going through a big industrial estate. By now, we were both a bit sweaty as Mum drove up to the gates of what we hoped was the right unit. There was a guard, but he was too busy watching *Desperate Housewives* to check who we were and he just waved us straight through.

'We could literally be international drug smugglers,' I said.

'Yes ... but that's a really good episode,' replied Mum.

'Fair. Anyway, I doubt many international drug smugglers visit small industrial complexes in Hertfordshire. And cartels comprising a mother and daughter team from North London are probably a bit niche.'

'That's what you think. And that's why it would make the perfect cover. No one would ever suspect us; you're too disorganized and I seem too uptight to traffic large amounts of hard drugs.' Seem? 'We could have family in Columbia that we needed to visit frequently.'

She had this way too worked out and a double life as a large-scale drug smuggler would explain a lot of her neuroses. We parked up outside what was essentially a metal box with a big monochrome plaque reading DAYBREAK SOUND SOLUTIONS next to the door. A depressed-looking teenager in incredibly tight jeans finally opened the door. He didn't say anything, just started backing towards the office (slowly because of the debilitating tightness of the jeans).

'We're here for the voice-over,' I said.

He looked at us completely blankly. '*Okaaaay.*'

'For the squirrel commercial?' my mum prompted.

Now he was blank *and* judging us. 'OK.'

'Do you know where we go?'

'I'm work experience,' he drawled and hobbled back into the office. This clearly wasn't how he'd imagined the cool 'media internship' some relative (I'm guessing) had promised him. He waved us into a room helpfully labelled *waiting* and disappeared. We sat down on a clear plastic sofa (my dad would have loved it: very Scandi, absolutely colourless and brutally uncomfortable) and hoped for the best.

My phone barked. It was Archie. **Hey, E, what's up?**

At a voice-over thing

This was ridiculously exciting because a) Archie had sent me an apparently random text and b) I had something cool to say. What were the odds?

Sweet. What for?

Utterly Nutterly Nuts. Presumably, as contrasted to other nuts that were in some way not nutterly. Sub-nutterly? Less cool. I had time to make Mum a cup of tea and to eat two biscuits (the catering fairies had left a tray labelled *help yourself*) before my phone barked again.

Decent script?

Haven't seen it. But my character is called Squirrelina so I am optimistic.

Hahaha

Second most important squirrel in the advert

I'm impressed

You should be. This was borderline drama banter.

A very stressed man with absolutely no hair and a very abundant beard jogged into the waiting room. 'Elektra?'

'Yes.' I stuck my hand up. 'Hi, that's me'.

Got to go, I texted quickly.

'Great, I'm Martin, the director.' He gave me a very assertive handshake. 'And is this Mummy?'

Mum looked like she was about to throw up. 'Yes I am ... "Mummy".'

'Great, well, Mummy, if you want to just wait out here, we'll have Elektra done in no time.'

He made it sound like I was going to have an HPV jab, not become the voice of the second most important squirrel in the advert.

I followed the creepy bearded man (as you do) into the recording studio. The ceilings and walls were all covered in light grey padding and there were spaceship style control panels with big computer screens down one wall.

Two guys in T-shirts with *sound guy* written on the back (so that cleared that up – I had a feeling if I stood still long enough around here someone would label me too) and baseball caps introduced themselves and I straight away forgot their names.

'And the client is here too,' said Martin, pointing at a large speakerphone.

A disembodied voice boomed, 'Pleased to meet you, Elektra.'

'You too,' I said, which just sounded weird.

'So, let's give you five minutes to read the script,' said Martin, pressing a single page into my hand, but then carrying on talking at me so that I could barely read it. 'We're all very excited about this project and I think that we can really make the audience, the potential *buyers*,' he looked at the speakerphone, 'feel a connection with Squirrelina, yes? Great. Well, why don't we go for a read-through? I'll be reading the other parts for now.

Squirrelina, I have a present for you!
(Martin was getting into character.)

Oh, Colonel Kernel, do you really? A present? For me? (I tried my best to get in touch with my inner squirrel.)

Yes, he stole it from those silly humans.

Naughty Colonel Kernel! (I couldn't quite believe Squirrelina was actually flirting with a guy called Colonel Kernel. She was a strong, independent woman. She could no doubt provide her own nutty treats. She really needed to raise her standards. My script directed me to make a loud crunching sound followed by a noise of appreciation.) **It's just so utterly nutterly!!**

Well, as we say in the Squirrel Special Services, Nuts Nuts No Ifs No Buts.

Nuts Nuts No Ifs No Buts! I like it!

'Good job.' Martin nodded. 'You just really got her.'

The sound guys tried not to laugh.

'Can we try it again with her voice a little bit higher and more musical so she sounds a bit sweeter and more girly, yes?' suggested the client-in-the-phone. 'Also her "gentle crunching noise" sounded like she was crushing bones so maybe tone it down a tad.' There was the distinct sound of a loo flushing in the background; I struggled not to snigger.

'*Righhht*,' said Martin. 'And could you give me a bit more variation on the first line because Squirrelina is genuinely surprised by the present? And if you could build up "utterly nutterly"? Make those double exclamation marks really count?'

'So we really feel it's a moment of taste epiphany, yes?' contributed client-in-the-phone.

'Er, yes, "taste epiphany", sure.'

'Amazing,' said Martin. 'Also it would be great if we could give "Nuts Nuts No Ifs No Buts" a bit of a wondrous quality; take your time over it like you've just discovered this amazing new idea, yes?'

By the end of the read-through, I was starting to feel a real affinity for Squirrelina. Granted, she wasn't exactly a feminist icon or a particularly complex character, but she seemed like a genuinely sweet girl/squirrel. And you have to hand it to her: she knew how to wrap Colonel Kernel round her little finger. I didn't actually know if squirrels had little fingers. I'd google it later.

'Right, let's get her into the box,' said the older of the two sound guys (which is not a good sentence to hear when you're under pressure).

The 'box' was just a small soundproofed room to the side of the studio, divided off by a glass wall.

'OK, Elektra, can we have you standing right up close to the microphone?' The younger sound guy was setting me up. 'Literally so your face is nearly touching that gauze circle in front of it. No, no, that's not gonna work – you're too tall.' He adjusted the microphone an embarrassing amount. And I'd thought voice work would be the one time my height wasn't an issue. 'Headphones comfy?'

I nodded; he gave a thumbs up to everyone on the other side of the glass and left me on my own. I looked at them through the glass and they looked back at me. Martin gave me a little wave and I waved back. I hoped I was waving not drowning. I'd never think goldfish had it easy again.

'Right, shall we just go for one? I'll give you the cue,' said the older-sound-guy through my headphones and he did and off I went.

'OK, Elektra, that's risking coming in at thirty-three seconds so we're going to need to lose three somewhere. Could you maybe speed up the "No Ifs No Buts" bit?'

I must have done it ten times before I was released out of my glass box.

'So, I think we're all done on this section. What time is Squirrel Three coming in?' asked younger-sound-guy.

171

Martin looked at him reproachfully. '*Private Pine Nut* is due at twelve thirty.'

'Great, so let's break for lunch now.'

'Yes, thank you so much, Elektra. You're all done. Great session – you were fabulous,' said Martin and younger-sound-guy ferried me back to the waiting room.

'How did it go?' asked my mum (as she now so often did).

'Good but also weird. Like really weird.'

'Why?'

'Because I was playing a post-feminist talking squirrel called Squirrelina.'

'Ah, yes, that was a stupid question.'

'Do you know what was even weirder? I forgot to be nervous.' And I had. Strange.

'Good. Well, thank goodness you're done. I've been so bored. The magazine selection was disappointingly arty and I've still got *Desperate Housewives* envy.'

'Right now I feel a very strong genetic link to you. Netflix marathon when we get home?'

'You've got the stamina for a Netflix marathon?'

'I do. I am the Colonel Kernel of Netflix marathons.'

My mother looked at me like I'd gone slightly mad.

I didn't blame her.

From: Stella at the Haden Agency
Date: 26 March 15:32
To: Julia James
Cc: Charlotte at the Haden Agency
Subject: *Open Outcry* and *Straker* (working title) projects
Attachments: Agreement.doc; outline.doc; character scenes.doc; map.jpeg

Dear Julia,

Further to our telephone conversation today, here are the documents on the *Open Outcry* project (16 April, location marked on map). Call me if there is anything more you or Elektra need to know. It will certainly be a fun way to round off the Easter hols!

Nothing concrete to report on *Straker* I'm afraid. The casting team have confirmed that they did receive the additional scenes we put on tape in the office at the end of March and so all we can do is wait. There's a lot of *waiting* in this business. (But great job on OmniNut!)

Kind regards etc.

Stella

P.S. Your planned getaway in Scotland sounds wonderful! I need a technology detox myself!

CHAPTER 16

'*I do want to push the boundaries, try stupid trends and all that experimental stuff that teenagers do. But I don't want to mess up.*'

Chloë Moretz

I literally had to doorstep Moss to see her. I got it: between her mum trying to get her trained up to perfection and having to be available at every possible free moment in case Torr wanted to meet up, she was really, really *busy*. But a) I had news for her and b) I'd miss her when I was dragged off to my midge-infested, rain-bogged holiday destination in darkest Scotland.

'Come up!' she yelled when Haruka (wearing a particularly fine bee costume) let me in so I did, then picked my way through the heaps of discarded clothes on the floor and curled up beside Moss on the island of the bed. It was the only place to sit. Also beds are lovely.

'Help me, Elektra!'

Moss was better than me at fashion, but she was clearly too stressed to think straight.

'Date with Torr?' I asked, pointing at a top that would display enough cleavage to be interesting, but not so much that her mum would make her change.

'I think so.'

'Now? Here?'

Moss looked pointedly at the row of stuffed animals lined up under the window. 'No, Elektra, not here.'

'Where?'

'I don't actually know yet,' said Moss, toying with her phone. 'He hasn't replied since he suggested it earlier. So I started getting ready straight after school, but then I felt like a freak so I got un-ready again and now I need to start over.'

She was currently wearing sweat pants with *I'm Not Normal* written across the bum.

'Mossy? Are you wearing red lipstick?'

She looked embarrassed. 'A bit.'

'I thought we'd already established we were never going to be sophisticated enough to wear red lipstick?'

'I'm allowed to make my own call on that.'

'Sure.' *Ouch.* 'It's been ages,' I said.

'What?' she asked, trying to choose between two pairs of identical skinny jeans.

'You and Torr.' And it really had. Anything over a fortnight was considered practically an engagement at our school. 'You're like Flissy and James. That'll be you on the gymnastics bench at the next social.' Flissy and James were still together, but there was a possibility that this was because he didn't know enough words to break up with her.

Moss laughed (and it wasn't a sarcastic laugh which was worrying).

'I can't believe you're legitimately dating.'

'We're not. We haven't had the "exclusive" conversation so I still don't know what it really *is*.'

'Torr hasn't got time to fit in anyone else. You've been to see two films with subtitles in the last week. It's weird.'

'Nothing weird about that,' she said defensively.

'There is if you're somebody who hates pretty much all films except *Mean Girls* and *Love Actually*.'

She shrugged. 'Torr wanted to see them.'

'Torr wanted' was fast becoming one of her favourite phrases.

'But, I mean, I really liked them as well.'

'Seriously? Even the Swedish one with the "original" sound score and no happy characters?' I'd read the reviews: they were not good.

She shrugged again. 'Obviously not as good as *Mean Girls*.'

'To be fair, few films are,' I said.

'Torr didn't want to go on his own,' she said.

That was actually quite cute. 'Do you want an Utterly Nutterly nut?' I asked her, changing the subject. They'd sent me a big pack as a thank you.

She looked doubtful. 'What are they like?'

'Like normal nuts, but with a delicious caramel coating.'

'Yeah, I can read that on the packet. What are they actually like?'

'I'm not a huge fan.'

They were really, really disgusting. It's a good job I hadn't tasted them before the voice-over session. I'd have had to really engage my acting skills then. Poor Squirrelina.

Moss kept checking her phone and then putting it down a little further away. She was not chill about the date thing.

'Are you definitely still seeing Torr today?' I asked after a bit. This was killing me. I was usually up for any amount of relationship analysis, but I was bursting with news and I couldn't find the right moment with Moss being so distracted.

'He's just working out what he's doing.'

Her phone buzzed. She grabbed it and read the message. Her shoulders drooped. 'Oh, right. I think he's got something on now.'

'Classic guy.'

'He's not. You don't know him. And, no offence,

but you're not exactly an expert. He's just really busy with family stuff.'

'Wow, OK.' But she looked upset as well as defensive and I didn't like that. 'Look, let's ditch the Nutterlys, crack out the crisps and watch some *Gossip Girl*. Who needs a real guy when you've got Chuck Bass?' A line of reasoning that had always worked in the past.

Ten minutes into the episode (and despite excellent distraction efforts from Chuck and Blair) I couldn't wait any longer. 'You know that casting where I turned up and nothing happened and I *despaired*?'

'Which one?' asked Moss.

'The one I was super happy about because I missed the simultaneous equations test.'

'I thought that was just an excuse because you hadn't prepped for it.'

'Well, I hadn't, but no it wasn't. It was an audition. An audition for a part. A part ...' I paused for dramatic effect. 'A part for which I am *apparently perfect. Perfect*. How many times can I repeat that without sounding tragic?'

'At least once more,' said Moss, which was particularly generous under the circumstances.

'Me. Perfect.' I let out a tiny sigh of satisfaction. 'OK, it's a *very* small part, but it's in a proper *film* and I don't have any words, but ...'

'But it's *massive*,' she said, which was the right thing to say, and then she let me tell her all about it with repetitions and deviations and lots of stopping to gasp at the sheer amazingness of it all (admittedly, she kept checking her phone, but that was OK).

The film was called *Open Outcry*. It was a psychological thriller set in buzzing, rich, immoral, modern-day London – one of the bad financier/ good detective genre. The bad financier, the good detective and his super-hot, much-younger love interest were all being played by really famous actors: Daniel Craig, David Tennant and some new girl actor fresh out of RADA called Lucrezia (OK, she wasn't famous – yet – but she was cool enough to have Lucrezia as a stage name). Yep, a *James Bond*, a *Doctor Who* and a girl with great hair were my *co-stars* (I said that quite a few times: my *co-stars*). I was only in one scene as one of a bunch of schoolchildren crossing a street, but I was singled out by tripping in front of a car only to be pulled out of the way by the evil (but disturbingly sexy) financier who's en route to destroying the world. In just a few moments, I would set him up as a complex character, gain him temporary audience sympathy and generally endow the plot with depth and subtlety – pretty pivotal stuff. No actual lines, but it did call for an expression of *deep* emotion to be captured in a close-up shot. Actually, forget all of that; what mattered was that I would have a scene with Daniel Craig.

'I'm going to get *touched* by James Bond!'

'That sounds wrong.'

'Status currency. I'll be famous – boys will want to touch the girl who's been touched by James Bond.'

'That sounds wrong too,' said Moss. 'Hah, Flissy will ask you to join her crew.'

'They say fame has a downside. I won't tell her. It gets better.'

'Better than Daniel Craig?'

'Yep. Guess who's playing one of the schoolchildren?'

'That's not the hardest question you've ever asked me. Archie, right?'

I nodded. 'And we had a *real-life* conversation.' Sort of. Archie had been talking about the film to another boy in our ACT class and I'd been sitting nearby and Archie had kind of included me – well, he'd spoken quite loudly (which he hadn't needed to because I'd been listening in anyway) and smiled at me. Then he'd come up to me and asked if it was true that I'd been cast as 'The Schoolgirl' in *Open Outcry* and I'd modestly said I had and he'd said, 'Cool.' I was going to tell Moss all about this major change in our relationship, but her phone buzzed.

'Torr?' I asked, which was a redundant question because she was doing that thing where you look at your phone with *exactly* the same expression as if whoever's contacting you were right there (which on this occasion was making me feel a bit uncomfortable).

'Actually, I think Torr might be free for a bit right now.'

Ah.

Ten minutes of emergency styling and I left her to it.

WAITING

• Easter holidays – not even a bit distracted by ten days in a location in Scotland so remote there was no Wi-Fi. Absolutely zero to report on anything. Basically, it was like I didn't exist.

• Time spent fantasizing about Daniel Craig: 73.2 per cent.

CHAPTER 17

'[James Bond] might be chauvinistic occasionally, but the women he likes are strong, intelligent and are equal to him.'

Daniel Craig

I didn't sleep the night before the *Open Outcry* shoot. Mostly, I just lay awake, worrying that I would look tired. Mum kept coming into the room and asking in a whispery voice (being her, it was still pretty loud) if I was asleep yet. I even resorted to the relaxation CD that she'd bought me when I was doing secondary-school entrance tests.

```
'Imagine blowing up a big, big red
balloon. Put all your troubles in the
big red balloon ... let go of the big
red balloon and watch it float up and up,
```

drift off out of sight, carrying all your
troubles away ...'

It didn't help. I just lay awake for hours, worrying about an enormous big red barrage balloon of (unsolved) worries floating up from my house. It was a disturbing image. Also the 'soothing' voice was annoying.

My call time was a frankly cruel seven a.m. and the location was an hour away so that, combined with my sleepless night, meant I was exhausted and, more importantly (given this was a purely non-speaking role), I looked *hideous*. I supposed there'd be make-up people, but they'd have to be miracle workers to cover up the purple shadows under my eyes.

The location was just an ordinary street in a quiet (usually quiet, not so much when an entire film crew shows up) bit of South London which had been cordoned off with huge red Road Closed signs everywhere. In the script, it said that the scene I was in took place in the middle of the City in among glittery skyscrapers, basically streets paved with gold, but this was just a pretty ordinary street with a school, an office block and some red-brick houses. Maybe they'd changed the script? Or maybe they'd just work some sort of film magic. There were about ten huge trucks parked nearby and lots of chunky men wearing chunky black clothes and chunkier black boots sitting smoking outside the school hall.

The hall was where they'd set up base camp and it smelled of sports kit and damp and (oddly) bacon. There were loads of kids there already and it was really noisy. There were two hot blondes at the door who looked scarily similar with their hair twisted up into messy buns right on top of their heads (which I only mention because it's a hairstyle that seems to make other girls look effortlessly cool, but which I seem unable to achieve without either looking like a cow has pooed on my head or I'm sporting a very small reproduction of the leaning tower of Pisa). They wielded clipboards and had earpieces (which oddly didn't get in the way of the hair) and had loud, posh voices and seemed to be in charge of all of us.

I filled in a form with my name and all sorts of details that they must have already had and handed it to one of the girls who didn't even look up as she took it. She was too busy talking to her friend. She had a real posh girl's lisp, but, from the little I managed to make out, they were obviously still recovering from a legendary night out. ('Thecily was *tho* pithed last night. It was hilariouth. Tham had to hold back her hair when she was thick all over hith coat . . .')

My mum, who was all fluttery and nervous (why? Nobody was going to ask her to do anything except sit and gossip with all the other parents), tried to encourage me to eat one of the bacon sandwiches that they were handing out at a long counter at the far end of the hall, but I felt a bit sick and for once the smell wasn't doing it for me.

'Well, go and get a banana or something.'

'I'm not hungry.'

'You need to eat something,' she said (as she so often did).

'I can't.' (I didn't say that very often about eating.)

'You should: it would be really embarrassing to faint.'

She had a point; I would do just about anything to avoid public embarrassment and there's something about someone just raising the possibility of fainting that always makes me feel a little peculiar. I went over to the catering table and joined the queue.

'Hey, Elektra.' I turned round to find Archie in the queue behind me. 'So, are you nervous about your starring role?'

No point pretending so I nodded.

He looked good. Obviously, no sleepless night for him. He was just wearing jeans and some random T-shirt and a big parka, but the jeans were really nice jeans … Yep, Elektra, maybe concentrate on his face. He's too fit to look at for long: concentrate on the floor. Trip over your own feet. Pretend to be doing a small and interpretive dance move to show your inner confidence for the shoot. Smooth.

'Don't worry, you'll be great. Anyway, it'll be over before you know it.'

He didn't know how prophetic that was. I just thought it was sweet. Was there a chance that Archie was that rarest of combinations, hot and nice? Probably not, but he was definitely hot which was enough to be going on with.

We got to the front of the queue and he collected three bacon sandwiches and gave me one. Boys were hollow. Not fair. I didn't ask for a banana (obviously).

'Do you want a drink?'

'I'll get them – you haven't got any hands left. What do you want?'

He nodded at an apple juice and I picked up two cartons and we went and slid down against a wall to make our own little picnic area. I handed him the juice.

'Bloody hell, Elektra, your hands are freezing.' He caught them up in his. 'Let me warm them up for you,' and he folded them into his parka, warm from the fleecy lining and from his body.

At this point, my hands might have been cold,

but you could have fried an egg on my face. I mumbled, 'Thanks,' and sat there stiffly, utterly unable to enjoy the moment.

And it was a moment.

It took me a good five minutes to calm down from the whole hand thing and be able to string together a sentence. But after we'd sat there for a bit I did start to get used to Archie, like some weird sort of reverse aversion therapy (attraction therapy?). And no question he was speaking to me. We were having a proper conversation. There were plenty of other girls there and most of them were trying to get his attention (which was fair enough), but he was talking to *me*. It was all just chat about ACT and school and stuff and I was trying hard to reply like a rational person while also working out whether he was sending me any deep meanings at the same time. It was good.

Stressful but good.

There was a lot of milling around going on. All the filming was happening outside, but the huddle of kids here for the schoolchildren scene were being kept strictly inside and didn't have a clue what was going on. Every so often, there was a sort of reverential hush because one of the celeb actors would come into the room and try really hard to look ordinary and we'd try really hard not to stare at them and no one would succeed.

But after a little while I started to get a bit jumpy. I might not have had any lines as such, but I was the most important kid in this scene and I'd expected a director (even just the *third* assistant director), someone/anyone to tell me what was going to happen and well, if I'm honest, kind of make a teeny fuss of me. It's not like I'd expected a dressing room with my name on the door, but I'd thought someone would be checking out what I was wearing and whether my chosen '*age-appropriate casual wear*' (jeans/sloppy navy sweater – basic enough not to distract from my own utter fabulousness) met the brief they'd mailed over. And surely they weren't going to let me loose in front of the cameras without doing something about my face. I knew the best actors were meant to be free of petty narcissism (really? Really?), but I'd be in *high definition* and on *big screens*. What if I'd had a massive spot that needed concealing? That sort of thing could have messed up the aesthetic for a whole scene.

But nobody was checking me over, nobody was masking the shadows under my eyes, nobody was saying anything to me. I was just hanging around with all the others – the extras. It wasn't all bad; firstly, because I didn't actually have a spot, massive or otherwise, and secondly because of, well, Archie. But I just had this worried feeling that all was not quite as it should be.

'What's that mark on your arm?' asked Archie.

I blushed – for two reasons – firstly, because the mark was where I'd scrubbed at my arm really hard that morning when my dad had noticed that I had *Elektra <3 s Archie* scribbled on it in black ink, worse, permanent marker (Maia has a thing for writing inappropriate *and untrue* things on other people) and secondly because Archie *touched* my arm when he said it.

'It's just a mark,' I managed to say, concealing the tiny mental breakdown I was suffering as a result of The Touch and The Hands. 'Erm ... it was just my homework pages for maths. I didn't have my homework diary so I just, you know, scribbled it on the nearest thing to hand ... which was my hand – well, arm.' I prayed he couldn't see the faint outline of the heart as clearly as I could.

'I do that too,' he said and it took me a moment to realize he didn't mean draw hearts on his arm. He was definitely being super friendly – if I could have stood to walk away (and if they hadn't made us switch off our phones), I would have texted Moss immediately.

'Happy birthday for yesterday,' I said, desperately trying to move the conversation on to safer ground.

'How did you know it was my birthday?' he said, looking confused.

'Facebook.' Oh, God, now he'd think (know) I was a stalker. Also there'd been some seriously wrong posts about how his life was going to change in all sorts of ways now he was sixteen.

'You're blushing.'

Of course I was blushing. 'It's just hot in here.'

He raised an eyebrow and for one fleeting (and worrying) moment reminded me of my dad.

I looked around the room again, partly because I was not cool with all the eye contact without a script to hide behind and partly to see if there was any sign of someone coming to get me for my big moment.

It took a bit of time for the horror of what was happening to dawn on me.

The Clipboard Girls seemed to be paying a lot of attention to a girl at the front of the room, even having her make-up done in an area separated off from the rest of us by a row of chairs. A crew member's kid? Whoever the girl was, it looked like she was getting special treatment.

Unlike me, because now I was being herded along with all the other kids outside.

'Elektra, shouldn't you be ... ?' began Archie but, before I could answer, a big guy with a ginger beard and an earpiece called out: 'Can the girl in the big navy jumper stand back a bit?'

Stand back? 'Sorry? Me?'

'Yes, you. Could you stand back?'

He really did mean stand back, not stand out.

The girl who was getting special attention was now talking – actually talking – to Daniel Craig and she wasn't getting his autograph. This did not look good. No? Surely not? *Please* don't let this be happening.

'Quiet on set ...'

CHAPTER 18

'I think of impending doom all the time.'
Robert Pattinson

'I'm sorry,' I said.

I can't quite believe I was apologizing to them, the two blonde Clipboard Girls *who'd screwed up my movie debut*.

What was I sorry for?

Sorry for having a stupid name?

Sorry for not screaming out after the first take and instead just starting to sob silently by the third and final one.

Sorry for leaving it to my mum *and Archie* (I could crawl away and die) to suggest there might have been a teeny bit of a mix-up.

Sorry for not getting in the face of the other

malicious, duplicitous girl called Elektra before she *stole my role?*

Yes, it did seem like a genuine misunderstanding and I know it wasn't really her fault, but the fact that she was in tears too and getting as much sympathy as me was really doing my head in. How had this happened?

Chloë Moretz wouldn't have apologized – Chloë Moretz would have kicked ass. But then this wouldn't have happened to her.

What are the odds of there being two girls called *Elektra* in a group of not more than thirty kids? Infinitesimal I'd have thought. But the odds of unlucky things happening don't seem to work with me – I mean, what were the odds of being called Elektra in the first place? How many parents look down at their tiny pink bundle of newborn girl and think, 'Honey, let's name her after a Greek woman who plotted to murder her mother'? And my middle name's *Ophelia* – the unfortunate maiden who loved Hamlet, went mad and killed herself. Upbeat choices.

Speaking of trauma . . . I was now angry, upset, still tired, still jealous and still hungry (I hadn't been able to eat the bacon sandwich in front of Archie in a bout of paranoid fear in case my eating wasn't attractive enough). I just wanted to get out of there. I wanted to run away home and hide under my duvet. I definitely didn't want to listen to any more lisped excuses. They weren't going to reshoot, my feelings just weren't worth that much money and anyway they would have problems with the light if they shot any later so there really wasn't anything they could say to make me feel better. The nicer they were, the more I just wanted to *howl*. And all this was going on in front of *everyone*. They'd moved us all back inside and that huge hall that had seemed so horribly noisy before was spookily quiet now as everyone listened in.

I definitely wasn't the girl in the background any more. Serious humiliation.

When we got home, I had to listen to Mum explain it all to Dad (why hadn't she just texted him earlier like a normal person?) and all I wanted to do was curl up in the dog basket and wail.

I phoned Moss again. I really, really needed to talk to her, mostly because she was the only person who would have the sense not to say very much at all, but definitely not to say that it didn't matter. Still no answer. I'd tried, like, seven times and all I'd got was her irritating voicemail – '*Hi, this is Mossy and I'm not* …' muffled voice in the background, definitely Torr, breaks off laughing, '… *here right* …' breaks off laughing. To be fair, she wasn't with Torr for once, she was at some stupid 'How to succeed at Politics' course (tag line *For the high-achieving teenager who is determined to go all the way* – did nobody think that one through?) that her mad mother had made her go on because she thought that it would guarantee that Moss would end up as some sort of world leader. But if she had been around she would probably have been with Torr. Either way, she wasn't available. Again. So I went to bed with just Digby for company.

I hadn't gone to bed at eight thirty since I was about nine. It was weird. I could hear people talking as they walked past under my window. I just lay there on the bed, feeling sorry for myself, and intermittently refreshing my phone in case Moss was back online.

Pathetic.

There was a little tap on the door and my mum came in. 'I just came in to say goodnight,' she said, which I knew wasn't true. She'd given up coming in to say goodnight about a year ago because she couldn't stay awake long enough (and a little because she knew I needed her not to). 'Squish up, both of you.' She clambered into the bed beside me, nudging Digby out of the way (which pissed him off), and put her arm round me. 'You can cry if you want to.'

'It's OK, I've cried enough for one day.' And I never cry. Well, not on the outside.

'Dad says he'll come up if you want him to.'

We both looked around at my room, which had sort of exploded when I'd got ready at dawn. It was a brave offer but no. I shook my head.

'I could give you a present if you want. Eulalie sent something over that looks especially shiny.' By which she meant too expensive and quite possibly vulgar. On any other occasion, I would have had the ribbon off in under a second.

'A present to congratulate me on my first film role?'

She didn't say anything so I knew I was right.

I shook my head. 'Maybe you should give it to the other Elektra.' That was a bit unnecessary, but this was not my finest hour. 'Sorry, I'm not in the mood.'

'Not even for one of Eulalie's over-the-top *cadeaux*?'

'Nope.'

'She sent it in a cab so that you'd get it today.'

I shook my head.

'How about a piece of my cake then?'

'Nope, not even your cake can help this situation.'

'That bad?' Her chocolate cake was epic.

'That bad.'

'It'll all keep,' she said and we lay there for a bit and although she was being nice I just wanted her to go away. I was weirdly sweaty and I just needed a bit of space. 'Stella phoned,' she said.

'Is she upset with me?' This was so embarrassing. Another wave of heat.

'Of course she isn't! She just feels bad for you. She says to tell you that everyone's really sorry and that you'll still be paid.'

I didn't care about the money and I definitely didn't want people to feel sorry for me.

'That boy was cute.'

'Which *boy*?' Like I didn't know who she meant. She knows too much. I don't always understand *how* she knows as much as she does, but she just does.

'You know which boy I mean; the one who gave you his handkerchief. I didn't think boys carried hankies any more.'

'It wasn't a hanky, it was a napkin.'

I love you.

Go away.

Please.

Things I didn't say.

'It was still very nice of him,' Mum said.

'Yep.' I didn't really want to have this conversation.

'So what's his name?'

'Oh, he's just a guy from ACT. I don't really know him.' Well, that would certainly be true now I'd made such a colossal tit of myself in front of him.

'There'll be other parts,' she said for about the fiftieth time.

'I know,' I replied for about the fiftieth time, although I still didn't believe it. And there wouldn't be other parts in a film with James Bond. And Archie Mortimer.

After a bit, I sort of pretended to have fallen sleep and Mum crept out in that exaggerated tiptoe way that people do when they're trying not to wake up babies. Digby jumped back on to the bed, did that going round and round thing for a minute or two and then settled down fatly on my feet. At least one of us was happy.

I was still wide awake.

My phone barked: **The other Elektra was rubbish. Archie x**

Dear Elektra,

Charlotte and I just wanted to say that we heard what happened at *Open Outcry* and it shouldn't have happened and we're sorry. Come and have coffee and cake soon and we'll tell you some much worse stories about things going wrong on set (but you have to promise to keep them secret!). The people on set said you handled the situation like a pro, so well done you because this was <u>one hundred per cent</u> their fault.

Onwards now – there will be other opportunities.

Big hugs from both of us x

★
CHAPTER 19

'There's always a part of you that wants to please your parents.'

Max Irons

'She says she's *fine*, Bertie, but you know what she's like.'

'Yes, I got the "it's *fine*" line too. Plainly, it's not fine, but *how* not fine it is I'm not sure.'

'She's done nothing but mooch about for the last two days.'

'To be fair, she usually mooches about during the holidays. I don't think we need to panic,' said Dad.

'I just wish she'd talk to us about it.'

'There were always going to be some knocks along the way.'

I was sitting (very quietly) on the stairs, listening

to my parents talking about me. I appreciate that this sounds quite furtive, but I was an only child.

'This *Shouting Out* film is a very hard knock.'

Was that *Eulalie*? When did she arrive? They were literally having a conference about me.

'She's tired too,' my mum went on.

I was tired, but it is really annoying to hear someone say that.

'She looks dreadful.'

Brilliant. Thanks, Mum.

'She's had all the stress and none of the upside.'

True. I started to feel quite sorry for myself.

'I'm worried it'll start to affect her schoolwork. I'm pretty sure she's behind on her coursework and she's back to school again tomorrow.'

I was and sadly I was. I'd had better Easter holidays. The conversation was getting dangerous. Digby padded down from my room (he'd been having a lie-in on my bed) and came and leaned against me. It was comforting.

'We need to keep an eye on it,' said Dad.

I wasn't sure if 'it' was my homework or my acting. Either way, this wasn't good.

'Maybe we just need to say "enough",' said Mum.

No way. I was not going out on a low.

Open Outcry was a massive low.

'She enjoyed the Utterly Nutterly thing,' said Dad. That seemed a long time ago. 'Maybe she'll get repeat nuts work or, I don't know, get promoted to crisps or something and that'll cheer her up.'

'Cheer who up?' I asked 'innocently', walking into the kitchen. Eulalie wasn't there which was confusing.

'You,' said Mum in her concerned voice (I hated that voice).

'I'm *fine*,' I said and they both looked at each other. 'I really am. You're not worried about me, are you?' I didn't give them time to answer. 'Because I'm *fine*.' Maybe I needed to stop saying that.

'But are you being really fine?' said Eulalie's voice from the laptop. I angled the screen and there she was, skyping in a negligee. 'There will be other chances, *chérie*. This *Shout Out* film, he will certainly be a disaster.'

'*Open Outcry* not *Shout Out*,' I corrected. Eulalie struggled with names unless they belonged to handsome men.

'*Shout Out/Open Cryout*, it is the same. Nobody will ever hear of him. He will sink without trace.' It wasn't just the accent: she struggled with English pronouns too. 'You will be having a much better role soon. I know this for sure. Maybe one with words. Or a costume?'

Eulalie had disapproved of the clothing brief for *Open Outcry*. She was the only woman in the world who thought I'd look good in a corset.

'What about the *Streaker* film?'

'*Straker*. They just keep postponing everything. I don't think it'll ever happen.'

'Maybe they make again *Funny Face* or *Roman Holiday*?'

Roman Holiday had been a high point of my Gregory Peck studies. Eulalie was also the only person in the world who thought that I looked like Audrey Hepburn. I looked nothing like Audrey Hepburn. She disappeared from the computer screen, but I knew she'd be back and she was in just a minute, waving a fresh glass of champagne at me. 'I would offer you some if this stupid technology allowed it.' Her head loomed perilously close to the camera so that she looked a bit like a very glamorous puppet.

'Champagne at nine o'clock,' muttered my mother as if Eulalie were doing hard drugs.

'I wasn't hearing you, Julia,' said Eulalie, who obviously had.

I wasn't expecting them to remake *Funny Face* or *Roman Holiday* – more to the point, if they did, I wasn't expecting a call, but some good news would be welcome. *Any* good news. Another Utterly Nutterly commercial would be OK (I was pretty sure I could develop Squirrelina as a character – maybe get her out there meeting some civilian squirrels). A crisps role would indeed be even better. Whatever else this acting stuff was doing for me, it was turning me into a realist. I'd 'refined' my original list of roles I wouldn't take:

(STILL) Out of the Question

1. Any role that involves total ~~or partial~~ nudity.
2. Any role that involves anything more than kissing. (Maybe I'd decide on a case-by-case basis, but I wasn't brave/desperate/stupid enough to strike this one yet.)
3. Any role where the love interest is a man who is old enough to be my father.
4. Any role in a commercial advertising ~~a 'female sanitary' product (especially if it has a sporty theme)~~; incontinence products; ~~head-lice treatments; wart treatments; zit cream;~~ or anything medical to do with bottoms.
5. Any role in a horror movie.
6. Any role that involves real spiders, large ~~or small, household~~ or Amazonian, venomous ~~or herbivorous~~.
7. ~~Any role that involves bugs. (Including beetles – except lady birds – , any grubs or larvae and maggots and basically anything that wriggles.)~~ (By now I was prepared to EAT the bugs.)

8. Any role that involves snakes, garden or venomous, etc.
9. ~~Any role that involves heights, by which I obviously mean any height in excess of my own.~~
10. ~~Any role that involves singing or dancing.~~ (Well, if they were stupid enough to cast me.)

I wanted to act. Acting made me *happy* – well, the 'doing it' bits anyway and that was enough to make the horrid bits worth it. I was still in this. But now I was in it as a realist. I watched a spider scurry across the floor and I barely flinched (it was very small). What doesn't kill you makes you stronger (maybe).

'Have you got plans for today?' asked my mum, switching off Eulalie (which sounds like a really bad thing to do to your stepmother). 'Why don't you go round and see Moss?'

'I don't think she's around.'

'She's back from her course. I saw her mum in Sainsbury's.'

And I bet they had a really good gossip about us both. I knew Moss was back. She'd phoned me when she got all my messages and she'd been *lovely* and said all the right things (i.e. not very much, but she'd made me laugh), but she was seeing Torr this morning (they'd been apart for *three* whole days) and although she'd asked me to come too I wasn't in the mood for third wheeling. 'I might see her later,' I said vaguely, but I probably wouldn't.

'You can help me bake,' Mum said a bit too brightly. 'We could make cupcakes.'

Great. Retro holiday activities. No wonder I wasn't rushing to give up the acting.

CHAPTER 20

'I'm glad I could do those films and I was glad to leave school. I couldn't relate to kids my own age. They are mean and don't give you any chance.'
Kristen Stewart

'*Babes*, poor you.' The 'sympathy' was pouring out of Flissy as she met me at the door of our form room at lunchtime. I was suspicious right away: even if it was the first day of a new term, Flissy did not meet me at the door of our form room; usually, she slammed the door in my face.

'Sorry?' I asked, but I had a bad feeling.

'I heard what happened.'

I clung to the one per cent chance she wasn't talking about *Open Outcry*. 'Nothing happened,' I said and I tried to push past her.

'You're being so *brave*. I would just have *died* of mortification.'

The one per cent followed the other ninety-nine into the pit of despair.

'What happened in the holidays at your *filming*,' she went on for the benefit of everyone who was listening (which unfortunately was most of the class). 'Or what didn't happen.' She laughed and lounged across the whole doorway so that I couldn't get past.

'Who told you?' I asked.

'A friend.'

She had friends? Wow. 'Who?' I asked because I knew for sure that it hadn't started with Moss. I tried again to get past Flissy and reach the safe zone next to Moss and Jenny and Maia who were watching with horror. I failed.

'A girl I do dance classes with was in it as an extra – an extra just like you now I come to think about it. She knows we go to the same school so she thought I'd want to know.'

'The rest of us weren't that interested,' said Moss (which was supportive, but not that cheering because Flissy had obviously told everyone).

Of course Flissy had found out. Over eight and a half million people live in London so statistically the percentage I know must be irrelevant and yet *every single time* I do something embarrassing it gets back to someone I know.

'Oh, it wasn't a big deal. I didn't care. It was just a tiny part. I didn't even have any lines—'

'Really? When you were talking about it at the end of last term, you made it sound like such a big role. That's ... awkward. Anyway, you must still be *so* disappointed and *embarrassed*.'

Karma is a seriously mean girl. I should never have told anyone about *Open Outcry*. I'd worked out fast enough that talking about acting with anyone that didn't do it was a bad idea. At best, people thought I was a weird drama geek (to be fair I was), at worst, that I was up myself and showing off. I hadn't specifically told Flissy, but I hadn't restricted the information to the circle of trust (Moss, Jenny and Maia) either. And even though Flissy and I don't talk to each other somehow we always know what the other one is up to. Mum, who went through a phase of reading teen psychology books (but somehow never learned about the need for healthy detachment), keeps saying we'll end up friends. She's wrong. She also keeps saying that there must be more to Flissy than mean girl. She's wrong about that too.

What I would have given right now to have been beneath Flissy's notice.

'Well, I got paid. And there'll be other parts.' I sounded like my mum (and she hadn't had much luck with that line).

'Of course there will,' Flissy gushed. 'Apparently, everyone was *really sorry* for you. Maybe you'll get a *pity* casting.'

I hated her, I really did.

I should have left it at that. 'What else did your "friend" tell you?'

'That you cried.' Long pause. 'And that you sobbed all over Archie Mortimer and he had to be nice to you.' She smirked, not even bothering with the fake sympathy expressions any more.

I felt the tips of my ears go hot and red. 'You know Archie?'

'Yeah.' She shrugged as if to suggest that she knew every hot guy in North London (maybe she did).

'How do you know him?' (Why did I ask? Why?)

'He got off with Talia at Fran's Halloween party.'

At Halloween, I had *voluntarily* worn a spider costume, this time complete with weird legs made from tights, and gone trick or treating with Moss and Haruka. An image of Talia in some wrong sort of costume involving fishnets and little else crossed my mind and stayed there.

'So ... so Archie's dating Talia?' I tried to get past Flissy again, but she blocked me.

She shrugged. 'It was just a get with at a party. It wasn't like "true love".' She sniggered. 'It's what people do at *parties*. Do you go to many parties,

Elektra?' And she sniggered again. 'Maybe you'll get to go to all the A-list acting parties now – with, like, Daniel Craig and people. Oh, no, wait! That's not going to happen, is it? Shame.'

Look, a saint would have snapped. A saint probably wouldn't have slapped her though. But I'm not a saint so I slapped her.

Sort of.

In my head, it was a full-on, open-palmed, efficient single slap to her perfect, over-made-up face. In my head, it was a movie moment of exquisite revenge. There'd be shocked gasps of admiration, Flissy would step aside and I'd pass with my head held high and pride restored. Or something like that.

But no. I missed her by a mile.

I'd yet to master the high five so why I thought I could pull off the full-on bitch slap I have no idea. I should have gone to that combat class.

Also I think I had my eyes closed.

At least there was no teacher there to witness it (even my flouncy, failed, girly attempt would have got me into serious trouble) so I was going to get off scot free, right? Well, no. Much worse. Some random girl had been filming on her iPhone.

There's always some random girl filming on her phone. Always.

*

'It's not all bad,' pointed out Moss as she handed me yet another tissue and we examined the footage it had taken someone *seven minutes* to upload to Facebook. 'Flissy comes off way worse than you.' Moss had rescued me out of the doorway and into the corridor. We sat with our backs against the too-hot radiators and everybody took one look at my face and left us alone.

'At least Flissy just comes over like a horrible person. I look like a complete fail at life.'

'Nah, everyone hates Flissy. People will be pleased that someone finally fought back.'

'*Tried* to fight back.'

'Your technique does need a bit of work. I'd have another go if I were you.' No. That was not happening. 'At least you surprised her – look at her mouth hanging open when it's over.' She froze the screen at a particularly unflattering-to-Flissy frame. 'It's even wider than normal so you can tell how stupid she is.'

I'm not sure Flissy is stupid. One minute she'll be saying something spectacularly thick ('Taiwan's a factory in China where they make fake Vuitton bags' being this week's genuine example) and the next minute she'll be coming out with some whip-fast verbal takedown. It's confusing.

'She's not as pretty as Talia,' I said pettily.

'*Nobody* is as pretty as Talia.'

That's true and I don't know if it made her getting with Archie better or worse. It wasn't hard to visualize them together; in fact, it was going to be hard to stop visualizing them together. Talia will probably get spotted by a model agency any day now and they'll *beg* her to do the Burberry campaign or something because she's got that rich, useless look. I couldn't stop watching the video. It wouldn't have been so bad if it hadn't had audio, but you could hear every word because the entire class was holding its breath. No sound and I could have lied about what happened and nobody would have cared. But basically the whole world could not only watch, but also listen to me being crushed over *Open Outcry* and melting down over Archie Mortimer.

Moss's phone buzzed. She looked at the screen.

'Was that Torr?' It was always Torr.

'Yep.'

'Tell me that he hasn't seen it.'

She didn't say anything.

'He's seen it. What did he say?' And I grabbed her phone.

Hahaha Classic Elektra

Great. It wasn't just funny that I'd completely humiliated myself, it was *typical* that I'd humiliated myself. And this from a guy I'd met all of three times (and it's fair to say I hadn't been the focus of his attention). Also Moss had nearly laughed when she'd read it. I took another tissue and watched the likes mount up – 80, 85, 92 ... Well, it was lunchtime; people had nothing better to do. In less than twenty-five minutes, it had approximately fifty more likes than any other status I was tagged in, but it was the Comments (mostly directed at Archie) that destroyed me. Here's a sample:

Good result, bro (Archie was predictably tagged), **two girls at war. Respect** (19 likes)
Take this down (Posted by Moss. 6 likes so far – and nearly all of them from girls in our form which was courageous.)
This is hilarious (27 likes)
Tough choices, dude (3 likes)
Who's the flat-chested one? (1 like – This one didn't bother me as much as you might think because it was posted by Ben Gardener who is this guy who basically has internet Tourette's. He just goes around spraying abuse pretty much at random. Also I was flat-chested. Also only Flissy had liked it – so far.)
You pulled Talia Spearman?!!!!! Nice one, mate (43 likes)
Who hasn't? (12 likes – all from girls. Like I said, Talia was gorgeous.)

And there were others that I just can't repeat.

★ CHAPTER 21

'How fantastic that when I was making all my mistakes people weren't really noticing.'

Jessica Chastain

'Hi, Elektra.' Nelly smiled at me. She ran the office at ACT and hassled us when we missed more than two classes in a row. 'What have you lost this time?'

'*Nothing* – I'm a reformed character.' She looked doubtful. 'It's just that Daisy wasn't in class today,' I said. It was the first ACT class of the summer term. Nobody ever missed first class back because a) there was cake and b) there was gossip. In the wake of *Open Outcry*, maybe I should have missed it.

'She wasn't?'

'No and she missed the last class last term.' Nobody ever missed the last class of term because of, well, cake. Daisy hadn't been at a class since *Fortuneswell* and I wanted to check she was all right. 'Do you know if anything's the matter?'

'I'm sure Daisy's fine,' said Nelly in a voice that meant that even if she knew anything she wasn't going to tell me.

'I've lost her mobile number and I just want to check she's OK.'

'I'm sorry, I'm not allowed to give out students' phone numbers.'

'But it's me, Nelly. It's not like I'm some dodgy stranger.'

'I'm *really* not allowed, Lecky. Message her.'

'She's not on Facebook.'

'Respect. Well, I could give her *your* number if you want?'

I wrote down my mobile number on the edge of her pad. I too had a new mobile number because it was a new phone. A shiny new iPhone, my *Open Outcry* pressie from Eulalie, inscribed on the back, '*Mieux vaut faire, et se repentir/Que se repentir, et rien faire.*' Basically, this translates as YOLO and was the only good thing to have come out of that whole painful episode. Now we could skype on the go. I wasn't sure where my actual phone was at that precise moment (slight but familiar panic), but I knew the number off by heart. 'You won't forget to give it to her, will you?' There was something messy and fun about Nelly that made it hard to trust her powers of organization.

'I promise. Any message you want me to give her?'

I shook my head. 'Not really. Just tell her to call me.'

'OK.' Nelly didn't ask me to explain. Unlike most adults, she was good like that.

'Good class today?' she asked. She always wanted to know what we were doing. I think she longed to be downstairs on the stage with all of us and not up here on her own behind a wobbling tower of paperwork.

'Good. We improvised a *Game of Thrones/Gossip Girl* mash-up.' I didn't mention that I'd spent most of the class trying to avoid eye contact with Archie.

'Sounds interesting.'

'It came to life when Chuck Bass was taken down by the Sons of the Harpy.'

'Who was playing Chuck? I love Chuck.'

'Me too.'

We took a silent moment to dwell on his awesomeness. 'Christian.'

'Oh, dear,' she said.

'His casting provided strong motivation for the Harpies.' I stole an enormous toffee from the bag on her desk. I was still chewing it when I went out.

'Elektra.'

I jumped. The last person I'd expected to see hanging around so late after class finished was Archie. I blushed (obviously).

'Here.' He handed me my coat. 'You left it in class.'

I swallowed the toffee so I could speak (which was quite painful). 'Thanks.'

'I think you left your phone in the pocket. Well, the pocket keeps barking anyway.'

'Yeah, that would probably be my phone then.'

He laughed. 'Probably.' He sort of nodded at me and I couldn't think of anything else to say. It wasn't much of a conversation, definitely a backward step from the *Open Outcry* banter, but it made me happy. Given that the last time we'd been together I'd sobbed all over him, the fact that Archie was still talking to me at all was a result. Also I was eternally grateful that he still hadn't 'liked' the slap video, far less commented on it, and I was even more grateful (pathetically grateful?) that he hadn't said anything to me about it in class. I wasn't even going to go down the road of worrying if he was just sorry for me. I'd decided to be nice to myself for a bit.

'You were a great Harpy today,' he said.

'Thanks. Sort of,' I said. Good to know I'd impressed as a rapacious monster.

'You OK about the *Open Outcry* thing?'

'Sort of,' I said. I wanted to say, 'Sure!', but I didn't think I could pull that off, not after all the sobbing on his shoulder stuff.

'I wouldn't be cool about it either; it sucked.'

I really liked him for saying that.

'Do you want some?' He held out a seriously large bar of chocolate.

'Just one square.'

'Sure,' he said and broke me off four.

'God, I love chocolate.' I think I said it with real feeling because Archie looked at me like I was a bit strange. 'No, I really, really do.'

'Milk or dark?'

'Don't care; it's not really about the taste.'

'Then what's it about?'

How could he not know? 'It's always been there for me,' I said simply.

'Whatever gets you through?'

I nodded. I'd been eating a lot of chocolate recently. I'd probably got to the stage where on any analysis chocolate would register as one of the major elements of my body composition, right up there with carbon and calcium.

'So ... I guess I'll see you next week.'

I thought that he might hug me, I mean in a friends way (we both did drama and there was a lot of hugging), but he just kind of smiled and shrugged and crossed the street and stood at his bus stop. I stood at the bus stop too – but my bus was going the other way. It was kind of funny, the two of us standing on opposite sides of the street, trying not to look at each other. It was like a romcom moment.

Romcom moments were outside my usual experience (but nice).

I texted Mossy. **Archie . . . still hot. Just saying.**

My phone barked. Yay! She was picking up for once. **Did u _talk_ to him again?!!!!!! (PS I know he's hot, we've stalked him often enough**

Sort of . . .

OMG, it's love!!!!!!!

Hahaha!

There is very little excuse for text exchanges like this so I won't try to make any. Don't judge.

Mum was stressing when I got home. 'You're really late. Why didn't you call? I was worried. I almost called the police.'

That was typical her. She doesn't think like anyone else would: 'Elektra must be having a nice time at ACT; she's probably talking to all her friends after class.' Or: 'Oh, the traffic must be slow, which will be a little irritating for dear Elektra.' No, no, no, my mum thinks: 'Elektra is thirty-five minutes late; she must have been attacked by a child molester

221

or a headless phantom.' (Or something equally statistically unlikely in our part of London at 7 p.m. *when it's not even dark*.) Then she goes pacing around and wringing her hands. When she said she'd almost called the police, that wasn't just parental hyperbole, it was fact. She'd phoned them before. I probably had a file. She was outside normal.

'Sorry.' Maybe best not to point out her irrationality while she was still in the meltdown zone. 'Sorry.' I'd just keep repeating it.

'And you *didn't answer your phone*,' she said (as she so often did). 'I called a hundred times.'

This was, like, her number-one complaint; it bugs her even more than me saying 'like'. It probably wasn't a good idea to explain that I'd temporarily misplaced it. I had noticed the three missed calls when I was texting Moss, but I sort of forgot to ring Mum in the excitement of the whole Archie encounter.

Priorities.

She was going on and on and on – a sort of white noise of 'disappointed'.

'Sorry,' I said again, butting in before she started on some horrible statistic about how many hours it takes before missing children are chopped into small pieces by their abductors or something equally traumatizing. 'What's for supper? I'm starving. I haven't eaten all day.'

Ha, the siren call to my mother. Excellent distraction. No need to mention the chocolate.

I didn't hear from Daisy till after the weekend.

She sent me a text **Had a bug, back at class soon. xx**

I texted my reply under the desk. My lesson was a particularly trying one on ionic and covalent bonding, so I was grateful for the distraction. **Get better soon. We all want you back.** And then I added, **Big Brian wants you ... badly** because she would appreciate the irony.

I want him too. We are in a deep and meaningful relationship.

Hahaha

I heard about *Open Outcry*. That's grim. I'm sorry.

I didn't mind sympathy from Daisy because I knew that she'd get it. Like Archie. It's only when you've failed to land a heap of auditions yourself that you can really get acting stuff going wrong. I wasn't surprised that Daisy knew about *Open Outcry*. Everyone did. Even people who weren't on Facebook.

And I didn't hear about callbacks for *Fortuneswell* yet, did you?

No

☹

Big Brian got a part playing a delinquent in some BBC thing

Not a stretch for him

Archie got a voice-over for a new biscuit

Seriously? (trying not to mind that Daisy knew and I didn't and failing) **That voice**

☺

Why did it seem like this was easier for guys? With too few exceptions, the ones I know didn't grow up on a diet of *Fame*, *Glee* and *Ballet Shoes* or fantasize about what to wear to the Oscars. Most of them didn't nag to go to drama classes; they got sent to football and, if they weren't any good at it, either they didn't care and did it anyway (which is just not a girl attitude) or they just went inside and bitterly played *FIFA* on the computer. And there are way more (better) parts for boys than girls. You don't get a whole mob of boys turning up to castings – casting directors have to go out and look for them. They *stalk* them.

Casting directors are basically like teenage girls – they're all on the lookout for the next hot boy.

Whatever Daisy had must have been quite a bug because she wasn't in class the Thursday after that either. We had a stand-in teacher (or 'drama mentor' as he grandly styled himself) who was almost as ugly as Lens was hot. He spent thirty minutes lecturing us on Stanislavsky and his Method and the next thirty making us remember sad and/or distressing things that had happened to us. It wasn't a huge success as all the boys got embarrassed (so obviously the distressing things were all to do with sex) and all the girls started sobbing (so obviously the distressing things were all to do with love or maybe small animals).

Not me. I couldn't get into it. I just kept thinking about things that were sort of sad, but that I found bizarrely funny. I knew that wasn't what I was supposed to be doing. I knew that I was meant to be connecting with something that had really upset me and I knew that the teacher, sorry mentor, wanted me to use that. Despite the fact that he was so irritating and talked entirely in textbook pretentious phrases (*playing with risk in a safe environment* I found particularly ironic as I was standing next to Big Brian at the time), I could see what he was trying to do and on another day I would just have got over myself and done it. But the horrors of *Open Outcry* and now Flissygate were just too fresh in my mind.

From: Charlotte at the Haden Agency
Date: 27 April 18:02
To: Julia James
Cc: Stella at the Haden Agency
Subject: Elektra

Dear Julia,

I'm afraid that Mayday Productions have decided to go in a different direction on the *White Noise* project (mute, traumatized child role). They did ask us though to pass on their thanks to Elektra who was apparently *very* convincing in this role at the audition! I'm sure they'll bear her in mind for other projects.

Thank you for the messages asking for an update on the *Straker* (working title) project. As far as we know, no decisions on casting have yet been taken. It may be that they have decided to cast the net wider and see more girls or it may be that the delay has nothing to do with the casting process at all. Sorry not to have more exciting news for you and Elektra this time!

Kind regards,

Charlotte

WAITING

• Time (awake) spent at school: 63.1 per cent; time at school spent thinking about acting: 37.5 per cent (which has reduced, but I've been distracted by life drama).
• Number of auditions since Open Outcry: 4 (Stella's on a mission to get me over it); strike rate: 0 (but I am now an EXPERT on auditions).

Top Audition Rules
(as listed on google and annotated by me)

1.
Be yourself.
LOL don't be yourself; be the character. This is obviously a stupid rule.

2.
Wear all black so the clothes provide a neutral base for your characterization.
Unless you happen to have a stunningly vibrant purple school uniform at your disposal. If you do whip it out.

3.
Be off book.
This is true, learn your lines even if they say you don't have to then you can feel smug. Also your acting will be better.

4.
Be nice to the casting director.
Good plan. Playing hard to get really isn't going to work when there are seventeen girls who look EXACTLY the same as you sitting in the waiting room.

5.
Walk in with good vibes.
What does this even mean?

6.
Don't request feedback.
I think I must be looking at an American list. I don't know a single British actor who wouldn't be way too awkward to do this.

7.
Always celebrate/console yourself with cake.
I added this one in. You're welcome.

CHAPTER 22

'Each time my mum would ask me: "Are you sure you want to do this?" and I'd be, like, "Sure!"'
Dakota Fanning

'Elektra, do you want me to run these lines with you?' my mum called upstairs.

'It's for a dead child. I don't have any words,' I yelled back.

'No, not that one. The *Casualty* casting with seven lines before the operation,' she bellowed.

Obviously, I would learn my lines, but I was in the middle of a mildly satisfying Sunday evening gossip session with Maia so I ignored Mum. I *needed* to know if Jenny had beaten Bella in the battle to the death (well, *this* week's battle to the death) for Max's affections. I checked my phone. Excellent, she had (I liked Bella but I liked Jenny more).

What do you think of Torr? asked Maia, moving on.

He's nice

Bit up himself, right?

Bit

He was in my Tube carriage today. She attached a pic of him, enormous headphones squashing down his hair. You could tell he was nodding along to the beat.

Some indie band that he's 'early adopting', right? That was my guess.

He probs knows the drummer

Hahaha Did you talk to him?

No. He was pretending he didn't know me.

To be fair, as far as I knew, Torr did hardly know Maia.

My phone barked again. **Too cool?**

So cool

Bit weird?

LOL maybe

And Moss is so boring when she's with him

I know, right? And then I felt guilty so I texted, **But they're really sweet together.**

No reply.

'Elektra?' my mum called again (of course she did). 'Are you word perfect?' The words bounced off the walls.

'Yesssss.' No. Nooooo.

'I don't believe you.'

How did she always know?

'Come down and we'll just run them a couple of times.'

I knew she'd come up if I didn't go down and then she'd go on at me about the state of my room as well as how unprepared I was. Tidying it was on my list – but a long way down from learning my lines.

'I can practise them by myself,' I said, helping myself to a slice of sponge cake when I came into the kitchen. 'Hi, Dad.' He was practically hidden behind a perfectly constructed wall of files and just grunted a reply.

'Get a plate for that. You can't read the other parts on your own,' said Mum.

'Yes I can.' I scooped the cream out of the middle with my finger. The cake was good. She should make more cakes and leave me alone to learn my own lines.

'I want to help.'

My mother hadn't had this much to do with my life since primary school. I'd thought I was long done with needing to be picked up in the car and submitting to having my hair brushed and being reminded about my manners – but somehow I seemed to be right back there.

All that work I'd done, little by little, carving out

territory for *me* and Mum was barging back in. I wasn't talking about wild, open plains here, just enough space, any space.

And she *loved* helping me learn lines. She got so into it, reading every other part with *feeling* and a wide range of disturbing accents. It annoyed me more than it should have done.

'Seriously, Mum, it's fine. I've got ages and I'll run them with Moss at lunchtime.' That wasn't true.

'You've got two days and no you won't. You've got Spanish oral practice at lunchtime.'

How did she remember this stuff? *Why* did she remember this stuff? And that wasn't the real reason I wasn't going to run lines with Moss. The real reason I wasn't going to run lines with Moss was that Moss now spent every lunchtime 'catching up' with Torr over Snapchat (in case they'd missed some important development in each other's lives between 8.30 a.m. and 12.30 p.m.).

'I've emailed Stella saying no to the *Twisted* casting,' she said.

Well, that was predictable. Stella had asked (as a long shot) if I wanted to go up for the part of Holly in what she described as a 'harrowing coming-of-age' drama. I thought it sounded quite interesting. My parents thought it sounded *horrible* (I think they took the bit about how it would be a 'transformative experience' a bit too literally).

'Fine,' I snapped and Mum's shoulders went up and she looked hurt and made a big show of patting Digby and calling him a 'good boy'. I got the point she was making. Digby looked as smug as a Dalmatian can (which is actually quite smug).

'Walkies,' she offered and was gone before I could say sorry.

'I don't think you should talk to your mother like that,' said Dad, looking up from his work. His tone was quite mild, but that was deceptive; he was seriously pissed with me.

'Sorry,' I muttered. 'I was going to say sorry.'

'She's only trying to help.'

'But it doesn't help. It just stresses me out. She makes everything such a big deal.'

There was one of those horrible pauses when you have enough time to wish you hadn't said anything and your parent has enough time to think of something that will make you feel as bad about yourself as you should.

'She's stressed too, Elektra. Have a bit of empathy.'

'You mean because I'm stressing her?'

'Not just you ...' There was a pause and we both thought about all the myriad things that could stress out my mum. 'But yes, running you around to auditions and hanging about waiting for hours isn't something she chose to do.'

Fair.

'And she finds it stressful, waiting to hear if you've got parts or second auditions.'

'Why is that stressful for her? It's worse for me.'

'I'm not sure it is. But she worries for you because she loves you,' he said calmly, rearranging his papers so that they were precisely aligned with the edge of the desk.

'Well, you're not wasting your time worrying about whether I'm going to get some acting part that I'm probably not going to get.'

'No I'm not, but maybe I don't need to worry because I know your mum's worrying about it for both of us. And if she didn't drive you to these godforsaken locations I suppose I'd have to do it.'

I suppressed the thought that we'd probably get there and back a lot quicker. 'You took me to the *Fortuneswell* audition,' I said.

'Yes I did, but that was in Central London and it was so boring it gave me new respect for your mother.'

My phone barked. Text from Archie. I surreptitiously opened it. **Hey, Elektra, what are you up to?**

Yay. **Not much. What bout you?**

'Are you on your phone?' asked Dad.

'Sorry, yes I was.' I turned it face down.

Dad still had things to say. 'And if you do get

parts who do you think will have to sort out the paperwork? You're too young to do any of that.'

Also I'd probably forget everything and then lose it all.

'Your mum does a lot for you, Elektra, and she doesn't complain.'

Meaning that I did.

'But Dad, seriously, she's gone a bit mad. One minute she's telling me the acting world is a horrible, exploitative industry and I should just be worrying about getting into a good university and the next she's, like, searching for open auditions on weird momager websites and pressing refresh on my IMDb page.'

Why? Why did she do that? As if it mattered what my ranking was – there are over four million actors listed on that site, thirty-nine million credits, so it's kind of hard to stand out. At number one today in the STARmeter is Jennifer Lawrence, up 11,779 (little green arrow) one day, down 41,324 (big red arrow) the next – go figure that nobody's going be looking me up that isn't a blood relation. The STARmeter is a real thing – a sort of graph with little emoticons marking things like film releases and Oscar nominations or ... well, *death* (kind of sick to give death an emoticon – a cute little tombstone if you were wondering), little peaks and troughs of popularity.

'And she keeps going on about how well the girl in *Game of Thrones* is doing and I have no idea if she thinks that's a good thing or a bad thing.' Watching my parents watch *Game of Thrones* made me mildly uncomfortable.

'She's maybe a bit conflicted,' he said.

'And what about you, Dad? Do you want me to do this?'

He looked at me. 'I only want you to do this if you want to do it. It looks to me like it's not that easy for you right now.'

'Well, you're the one that always says you have to push through when things are a bit tough. Put the effort in and see rewards, all that stuff.'

'That's true about geometry. And physics. And pretty much all your subjects except maybe French – definitely not French. But it's not true about this. Acting is *optional*. Do it if it makes you happy. If it doesn't make you happy, then stop. Maybe you're a bit "conflicted" too?'

I didn't know if I were 'conflicted' or not. I didn't really want to think about that. Maybe people thought too much about stuff instead of just doing it. 'Can I check my phone now?'

He raised an eyebrow. 'Expecting an important message?'

'No,' I said and I blushed (of course I blushed).

'Go ahead,' he said, laughing at me.

Archie had texted back; this was now officially a conversation. **What you doing this weekend?**

Nothing. Just get the message out that I was 100 per cent available. But wait . . . now he'd think I had no friends and was tragic. **Hanging with friends, but nothing definite.** Pretty sure he would now think I had no friends and was tragic and was so self-conscious about it that I'd had to double text. **What bout you?** Be brave, keep the conversation going.

Got to go see fam in the country. Cows and stuff. Will be a mad one.

Disappointed expectations. Again.

'Interesting messages?' asked my dad mildly.

'Do you want tea?'

'You're changing the subject.'

'Yep.'

'OK, fair enough. Do you want to come and watch the footy with me and Digby?

'I'd be honoured. Shall I bring cake for you?'

'No thanks.'

'You need to eat more; you're too skinny.' And he was.

'You sound like your mother.'

That wasn't good.

From: Stella at the Haden Agency
Date: 11 May 15:41
To: Julia James
Cc: Charlotte at the Haden Agency
Subject: RE: Elektra and *Twisted*

Dear Julia,

Thank you for getting back to me so quickly on the *Twisted* casting. For what it's worth, I think you're making the right call: the script does deal with a troubling subject matter and there is some very strong language!

Kind regards,

Stella

★
CHAPTER 23

'Sometimes it's the stuff that makes you
uncomfortable that is actually the good drama.'
Natalie Dormer

'So, why did you say it if you didn't mean it?' Moss
was seriously annoyed with me.

'I didn't say *anything*.' And I hadn't, not technically.
I hadn't done anything that bad. Well, maybe I had.
I should have known Maia would show Moss our
conversation (I think I did know – I'd had a bad
feeling since I'd sent the texts).

'So Torr's "up himself" and "too cool"?'

'I didn't say that.'

'You pretty much did.'

'No, Maia said that. I just said "LOL".' I shouldn't
have said "LOL". Not just because nobody should
ever say "LOL", there is no excuse, but because I

should have defended Torr. Don't mention the other text. Please don't mention the other text.

'You said I was boring when I was with him.' Moss mentioned the other text. Of course she did. The other text was the biggest problem.

'I didn't say that. I just sort of agreed with Maia. And why aren't you angry with her?'

'Because she's not supposed to be my best friend.'

'No, just your informant.'

'She felt bad about it. That's why she told me.'

'You know that's not true.'

'Also she met up with some of Torr's friends in Starbucks and oddly enough they don't think he's up himself.'

Oh, right. So Maia fancied one of Torr's friends. And now she was going to majorly suck up to Moss in the hope of getting better access to him. This was making more sense every second.

'You obviously think my boyfriend's weird.' Moss wasn't going to drop it.

'I don't.' The temptation to mock the way she said 'my *boyfriend*' instead of just Torr was quite strong, but I didn't say anything.

'Did you just say it for *LOLs* then?'

'I was just being *lazy*. I wasn't being mean.'

'Sure, just lazy. That's why you replied. Several times.'

'I like Torr,' I said, but it sounded kind of weak and Moss did that shrug thing to let me know that she thought I was lying. But I wasn't really. I don't know very many sixteen-year-old guys who are *capable* of being boyfriends full stop. He deserves a lot of points for that. But Moss was so totally into him that I *missed her*. She was practically at the poetry stage (and I mean proper written-just-for-the-beloved, dedicated odes and sonnets) and we'd promised each other that we would never, ever be at the poetry stage. She never sat in a chair any more when she could sit on his knee and she whispered things in his ear which pretty much excluded everyone else (me) from the conversation and when she wasn't with him (which wasn't very often) she wanted to *talk* about him.

And it was always what Torr wanted. Moss's Moss-yness had sort of dissolved. She went to see things she didn't want to see, she went to cafes that didn't sell cake and she spent a lot of time (when they weren't making out) listening to Torr talking about things that she had no interest in. She went to *gigs*. And she was so loved up that there wasn't even any beef. Talking about Torr didn't mean complaining about him, it just meant going on about how sweet/cute/hot/clever/indie/into her/supportive, etc. he was. Honestly, it was boring and sometimes it was boring *and* awkward (I am not cool with public displays of affection).

'Maybe everyone's not as obsessed with Torr as you are.' Honest but not really an apology.

'I don't want you to be as obsessed with him as I am.' Moss wasn't even looking at me now.

'So you admit you're obsessed with him?'

'Why do I have to admit it? Why are you being so horrible?'

'I'm not being horrible.' I was and I knew it, but now I'd started I couldn't stop.

'You don't have to love him, Elektra, you don't even have to *like* him, but it would just be nice if you didn't go behind my back and talk about him.' I could see that she was nearly crying.

'That's not fair ... Look, I *miss* us hanging out.'

'Half the time you're busy with all your acting stuff and I don't moan about that, and anyway we do still hang out loads.'

'Er, no we don't.' My acting stuff took up way less time than her love life, but I wasn't going to get into that.

'We're hanging out now.'

'Having an argument outside the school loos doesn't really count as quality hanging-out time.'

'What about last Saturday?'

'I'm not sure awkwardly watching half a retro movie round at your house while you and Torr make out really counts either.' I would never know if Bridget Jones got with Mark Darcy or not (although I could guess). *Bridget Jones* wasn't Torr's kind of film. 'We don't even hang out virtually.' I missed our stupid Snapchats and texts.

'You sound jealous.'

I was but not for the reason she thought. 'Not everyone wants to spend their every moment in some exclusive Disney relationship.'

'I don't have a *Disney* relationship with Torr. If you'd ever actually had a relationship with any guy, you'd know that.'

Brutal.

'Anyway, how would you feel if I started bitching behind your back?' Moss was pulling at a loose thread on her tights. She'd been doing it the whole time we were talking and her tights were more shred than fabric.

Her voice was getting louder and louder and a gaggle of girls were gathering round us like Roman citizens at a small and exclusive gladiatorial bout.

'For Christ's sake, I Did Not Bitch about you behind your back. Why are you making such a big deal about this? Everyone gossips. You do it too. Don't be a hypocrite. Anyway, I hardly said anything and I didn't mean it.' I know that my argument wasn't entirely logical, but I was under pressure. Also I was getting defensive because the more upset she got, the guiltier I felt and the guiltier I felt, the angrier I got. 'Stop being so whiny and self-righteous. It's a miracle any guy – even a weird one – can put up with you.'

There was a gasp from the ever-growing audience. Moss looked shocked for a moment then set her jaw and drew herself up to her full and not very imposing height. She was almost shaking with anger. This wasn't good. Less gladiatorial private show than throwing Christians to the lions – I was the Christian.

'You know what, Elektra,' (amazing how much disdain she loaded into the word Elektra), 'it's fine. Totally fine.' She spat out each consonant. 'No, really, I get it. It's not your fault that your life is so boring that you have to moan behind my back and create drama out of my happiness because your own drama stuff's not working out and so you have something to talk about when you've exhausted everything you can say about your tragic little crush on Archie.' She drew breath. 'I'm sure if my life was as sad and dull I'd do the same. By the way, just a piece of friendly advice – it's obvious that Archie isn't into you so stop being desperate and save what's left of your dignity.'

There was more of course because there were lots of different and increasingly mean ways to say the same thing and make (multiple) snide comments about people changing and growing up and apart.

Somehow we both managed not to cry; it was colder than that. Bitter, like how two people who don't like each other would speak to each other.

I wish I hadn't sent those texts.

CHAPTER 24

'I like burgers, but do I want to see my face all over the burger cartons? Not really.'

Kristen Stewart

So Daisy's bug wasn't really a bug. No surprise there. She still hadn't turned up to ACT and she hadn't answered my last ten 'are you all right?' texts.

Hey, Elektra. Soz for not replying. Want to meet for coffee on Saturday?

We met in Pret. It was warm enough to sit outside.

'Daisy ... you look *amaaazing!*'

'You like it?' She did a sort of awkward little twirl; she obviously wasn't sure herself.

She'd cut her hair to within a few centimetres of her scalp. All the ringlets were gone and most of the blonde (I'd never even guessed she'd been dyeing her hair) and there was *nothing* bonnet and bodice about her any more. She looked seriously good.

'I love it!'

'You really like it? You're not just saying that to be nice to me.'

'Really. So ... either you just got cast in some sci-fi or prison drama thing and they cut your hair off or you're halfway through a hard-core production of *Les Mis* or ...'

'Or ... I've quit.'

'For real? What made you do it?'

'A little bit you saying "just stop" that day we were at the *Fortuneswell* casting, but mostly because my mum started to talk about LA and pilot season and Oakwood.'

'Not *Oakwood*,' I said in the tone of horror that most teenage girls would reserve for discovering that Robert Pattinson and Daniel Booth were married to each other.

Oakwood Toluca Hills is this apartment complex in LA where all the drama kids and their momagers go and stay for pilot season (or, in the case of some desperate souls, years). Look, some of my best friends are actors (weird defensive statement right there), *Archie is an actor*, but I couldn't think of anything worse than being holed up in some complex with a bunch of desperate kids and (worse) their mothers with everybody talking about auditions and callbacks and competition and making money and motivational mantras and disappointment. Hell.

'I couldn't do that.' Daisy obviously agreed with me. 'And I definitely couldn't let them spend any more money when I felt the way I did – it was *awful*; there was all this talk about cashing in pension schemes and remortgaging to "support my dreams".' (She did that air quotes gesture with her fingers, but I forgave her because I liked her.) 'So in the end I just told them no.'

'What did they say?' I said through a mouthful of lemon drizzle cake.

'They were weirdly OK. I mean, initially they were just a bit shell-shocked and kept going on about not understanding me and doing that unshed tears thing, but then the next day they were just like whatever and started to talk about going to Spain on holiday. I think maybe they were relieved.'

'Do you reckon they knew already?'

She hesitated. 'No, not really. I don't think they wanted to know or rather I don't think they knew that they wanted to know before they did know so they just didn't know.'

Okaaay, that was hard to follow, but I *think* I got what she meant.

'I mean, they knew I was stressy a lot of the time, but it's not like there weren't tons of other possible reasons for that.'

'Like?'

'Come on, Elektra, like normal stuff: panicking about GCSEs and not wanting to get fat and worrying that you'll never get boobs – or that you will get boobs, but that they'll be too big and end up under your armpits – and wanting to get off with guys who don't want to get off with you and not wanting to get with the guys who do want to get with you and not being invited to parties.'

Oh, yes, right, *that* stuff. Fair enough.

'Are they going to make you do something else?'

'Nope.' The whole time Daisy was talking she kept running her fingers through her new pixie hair, making it stand up in sharp little spikes like stiff meringue mixture. It was as if she were making friends with it. 'Well, probably they will at some point; chances are my mum will dream up some whole new escape route for me when I don't actually want to escape. Maybe it's her that does.' She paused as if that were the first time that rather obvious thought had occurred to her. 'Whatever.' She shrugged. 'Not much I can do about that.'

She was probably right. 'What did Stella say?' I asked.

'She was really, really cool. She said she'd known

for a bit that I wasn't that happy with it and that she'd been meaning to talk to me. She just said that she didn't want me to do it unless I was sure I wanted to. She meant it too, I could tell. Did you know she used to act?'

'No. What like in the sixties?'

'Harsh. She used to be a stage actress and she was in tons of plays, just small parts, but with really famous people and then she gave it up practically overnight because she got stage fright, real can't-go-on-any-more stage fright.'

I shuddered at the thought of getting that scared of doing something you'd loved. 'Are you still going to come to ACT?' I asked Daisy.

'No, I don't think so. I spoke to Lens and he's OK with me dropping out halfway through a term. I'll miss the people – I'll miss lusting after Lens.' She didn't mention lusting after Archie. That was good, right? 'Well, I'll miss some of the people, not Christian or Brian obviously, but I think it's better if I just have a clean break. I don't really want to hear about what everyone else is doing each week. I'm happy with my decision, but I just want to be done with it. Anyway, I've probably done enough improv games to last me a lifetime.'

'No more Superhero or Mirror Mirror? How are you going to *live*?'

'I know, right,' she laughed. 'It'll be tough. I'm

going to do some school drama, audition for the school play and stuff like that. That's enough for me. We'll still stay in touch though. I got Facebook.'

'Facebook? Seriously? I thought you disapproved of it. I thought you were too indie for it.'

'Ha, no, I'm not that pretentious. My mum was just scared that I would post some bikini photo or someone would post some dodgy comment and it would end up all over the papers.' She saw my face. 'I know, I know, it was mad, but this was in her phase of believing that only my possible bad rep could get in the way of me being the next Emma Watson.'

I struggled with the idea of Daisy having any sort of bad rep; she had 'good girl' stamped all the way through her like holiday rock. I thought about some of the things on my page (not posted by me) and cringed a bit. There are advantages to a life as one of the plankton.

'Now my mum doesn't care. It's like I have parental permission to be normal.'

'What, like normal have guy friends and things?'

'Yep.'

'Got anyone in your sights?'

She nodded and drew a little heart in the sugar crumbs on the tabletop. I think, well, I hope that it was an unconscious gesture.

'Anyone I know?' I asked, praying that it wasn't Archie. I would have to be cool about it and I really didn't think I was that good an actress.

'No. Someone in the year above at school. Nothing to do with acting.'

'A civilian?' I used the term in a properly ironic way.

'A clever, hot, *year above* civilian.' Whoop, status. She laughed a big, unapologetic, un-old-Daisy laugh. She was really happy. 'I'm still in lower-set maths though.'

'Maybe "Hot Year Above Guy" can tutor you?'

'Maybe he can or maybe we'll find more fun things to do.' She smirked.

Well, this was a bit disconcerting. It was as if aliens had abducted Daisy, shaved her head, brainwashed her and returned her to earth. (Quite like the plot of a student film actually; maybe I should mention it to Ed.)

'What's going on with you?' she asked me.

'Not much.'

'Really? You look a bit … well, you just look like something's wrong. Are you still upset about *Open Outcry?*'

'No. I'm a bit bruised mostly because it was so embarrassing, but I'm really OK about it now.'

'Is it other acting stuff? Were you really hoping to hear on *Fortuneswell?*'

'Well, yes.' Of course I was; it was a brilliant series with *good costumes*. What was weird to me was that Daisy had been serious: she really didn't care. 'But no, it's not the acting.'

'What then?'

'I just had a stupid fight with Moss this week and it's still not OK. We basically haven't spoken for days.'

'What happened?'

I told Daisy because she was easy to talk to. She'd only met Moss once when Moss had come to meet me after ACT, but she got it. I wasn't the first person to fall out with her best friend. It wasn't exactly top gossip, but maybe the pettiest argument since Year Six.

'Does it really matter whose fault it is? Maybe just say sorry anyway.' This was such Daisy-ish advice. 'Call her now.'

'I can't, I've lost my phone.' Well, it probably wasn't *lost*, but it was definitely misplaced again.

'Borrow mine,' she said, handing it over.

Thank God Moss never lost her phone; I knew her number off by heart. '*Hi, this is Mossy and I'm not ...*' Torr's muffled voice, then laughing, '*... here right ...*' laughter. I really, really hated that voicemail message.

'Try texting her,' said Daisy.

Hey, Moss, are you around?

Who is this? So she actually still had a phone.

Sorry, it's me, Elektra. I'm on Daisy's phone.

Have you lost yours again?

Not exactly. Well, maybe. Do you want to meet up?

Sorry, I can't. No crying face emoticons, nothing.

Actually can't or won't can't?

Actually can't. My mum's making me redo my English essay under her personal supervision. That was plausible.

Nightmare. I just wanted to say sorry.

Five minutes of looking at Daisy's phone, then, **Don't worry bout it**. No kisses.

Seriously?

No answer.

'I'll get emergency cake,' said Daisy.

WAITING

- Half-term: no good parties (no bad ones either).
- Three days' staying with Granny Gwen (too traumatic to talk about).
- One day shopping with Eulalie (too spoiling to talk about).
- Number of auditions: 2 (went so badly that I refuse to talk about them).
- Number of conversations with Moss: 0.

From: Charlotte at the Haden Agency
Date: 1 June 21:51
To: Julia James
Cc: Stella at the Haden Agency
Subject: Elektra updates

Dear Julia,

I'm afraid that Mid Hyphen Night Productions have decided to go in a different direction on the *Nobody Cares* project (Alice role).

Thank you for the telephone messages asking for an update on the other projects. As ever, we will be in touch the minute we have any news (good or bad!).

Kind regards,

Charlotte

P.S. Can't quite believe it's June already! Don't forget to let us have up-to-date holiday dates!

From: Jonathan Tibble, Deputy Head at Berkeley Academy
Date: 1 June 21:52
To: Year 10
Subject: Summer exams

Dear Girls,

You will be delighted to know that the exam timetable is now up on the school portal. I am confident that your revision preparation is already underway (if it is not, now is the time to panic).

Further to the *disappointing* incident that occurred during the chemistry test last year, snacks are henceforth strictly banned from the examinations.

Mr Tibble

Berkeley Academy: Believing and Achieving since 1964

★
CHAPTER 25

'I don't really have disappointments because I build myself up for rejection.'

Nicholas Hoult

'Moss?' I practically had to stand on her toes to get her attention. 'Don't want to sound paranoid here, but is there some reason you moved seats in history?' *And haven't spoken to me for the whole of this miserable Monday?* I didn't say that bit because there was a limit to how pathetic I was prepared to sound. I knew there was a reason and I knew it was the stupid argument about the texts – or maybe the argument about the stupid texts. I kept hoping it would magically sort itself out. Pretty clear that wasn't happening.

She shrugged.

OK, she could sit where she wanted. That wasn't

fatal. Or was that fatal? I tried again. 'Did you have a good half-term?'

She shrugged again.

This was brutal. 'Are you literally not going to speak to me?'

'There's not much going on. Or did you have *acting* news you wanted to share?'

'No. No news that would interest you.' Like we'd needed 'news' to talk about. Also there was no acting news except for a little tsunami of rejections.

'I suppose you've got Daisy if you want to talk about that.'

'Yep,' I said, a little bit because it was true, but mostly because I wanted to hurt her back. 'And I suppose one of Torr's many attractions is that he's a *really good listener.*'

'I think he's a bit surprised by how mean girls are, but yeah.'

'Well, he's hanging out with you at the moment, so he'll get used to it.'

Moss didn't answer that which was fair enough. She just elbowed her way past someone who was half cello, half girl and started to walk away.

This was horrible.

'Why are we fighting like this, Moss? It was just a stupid text.' I was practically shouting after her. It was pretty needy. Half Cello/Half Girl stopped to listen in. There was always someone listening in.

'We're not just fighting about the *texts*, Elektra.' Moss turned and stressed the plural. 'We're fighting because you can't cope with me having a boyfriend and I can't be bothered with you guilt-tripping me out about it.'

That was sort of true, but not the whole picture. 'Or maybe it's because you can't be bothered with your friends now you have a *boyfriend* and you're too self-absorbed to care.'

'That's not true, Elektra.' Maia had materialized out of nowhere and was standing 'supportively' next to Moss. 'You're so dramatic about everything.'

It wasn't a compliment.

'You're enjoying this, aren't you?' And Maia was. Probably mostly because it was good gossip and Maia lived for gossip – which I suppose is why she'd kicked it all off in the first place. Also because she could have long, whispering, sympathetic conversations with Moss and that was her idea of good drama.

'And apparently you're the one obsessed with getting a boyfriend. How's it going with Archie?'

I'd got to the point where I couldn't even remember why I'd ever liked Maia. Moss looked a bit awkward, but she didn't defend me, just played with her fringe, which she always did when she felt uncomfortable. (She'd obviously just had it cut way too short, but it wouldn't be funny if I pointed that out right now.)

'Are you getting the bus?' I asked Moss and I knew I sounded needy again.

'Or we could go get a coffee,' said Maia, very obviously just to Moss, and Moss nodded. I watched them walk off and Half Cello/Half Girl watched me watch them. Great.

I could have got the bus with Jenny. Jenny was still being nice to me. Well, she was making a massive effort not to take sides, but I was scared that she'd go Team Moss (and more scared that there was a Team Moss in the first place). But then Jenny *hated* conflict; she was going to have to toughen up if she was to survive Year Eleven. It probably wasn't fair of me to get the bus with Jenny: she wasn't some sort of human shield.

The walk would do me good.

There's a sentence I never thought I'd think.

For once, it was Dad who was at home when I got in and not Mum (she was out trying to find herself somewhere). He was in the kitchen, building little white models of kitchens.

'Do you want to help, Elektra?'

Any other day, I would totally have wanted to help him, i.e. play (I still secretly missed playing with Sylvanians and this was pretty close). But I wasn't feeling constructive. 'I can't. I've got too much homework.' That was a lie. I just wanted to be on my own. I checked my phone. No messages from Moss. No messages from Archie. The only person who'd communicated with me was Mrs Gryll and that was just to say that I was late with my essay on erosional landforms. I buried myself in the fridge. There was nothing appealing.

'Are you OK?'

How could he tell from my back that I wasn't? Was I giving off some sort of sweaty misery vibe? I leaned deeper into the fridge to cool my hot face. If I could have crawled inside and curled up next to the leftover rice pudding, I probably would have.

'I'm fine.'

'Fine, leave me alone? That sort of fine?'

'Yep. That sort of fine.'

'And if you stop wanting to be left alone you'll tell me?'

'I will.' I would have given him a hug just for not saying anything more, but if I'd done that I'd probably have started to cry and for someone who never cried I was doing it a lot lately. As long as no one was nice to me, I'd be *fine*. I loaded a plate with a large chunk of dried-out cheddar, two slightly squishy tomatoes and some leftover pesto pasta because I wasn't too upset to eat (or maybe I was eating because I was too upset: it didn't look very enticing). Even Digby didn't follow me when I took my snack upstairs.

*

It would have been a good night to have had homework. Even two hours doing an essay on how the Treaty of Versailles weakened Germany would have been better than sitting under the duvet, making a list of parts that I'd been up for and hadn't got, but that's what I did.

If I was going to feel sorry for myself, I might as well wallow in it.

1. *Part of 'Young Girl' in a 'challenging, contemporary' fairy tale.* Opening scene – the young girl is skipping through a forest surreally comprised of knives and forks. I got a callback for that one even though it was obviously a part for a six-year-old or maybe an older girl with an eating disorder. It didn't come to anything; it ran into funding problems. Can't imagine why.

2. *Part of 'Young Girl' in an episode of Casualty.* (Daughter standing beside mother at sink, drying dishes and cheerfully chatting as if without a care in the world as the knife her mum is holding slips ...). OK, this was maybe the tiniest role in the whole entire history of tiny roles, but I really wanted it, not just because it was the BBC and therefore classy, but because *Casualty* is a rite of passage for actors. EVERYBODY has been

in *Casualty*; I suppose it's down to the high death rate. If it was good enough for Kate Winslet and Orlando Bloom, it was good enough for me. More than good enough I suppose because I didn't get it and the part went to some random ten-year-old who lives in Cardiff and will probably turn out to be the next Kate Winslet. Hate her already.

3. *The 'Holly' part in the 'harrowing, coming-of-age drama', Twisted.* Of course I don't know how far I would have got with that one if my parents hadn't freaked out at the 'challenging' subject matter and banned me from auditioning.

4. *Part of 'Alice' (playing age sixteen, Caucasian, accent RP) in intense and occasionally foul-mouthed multicultural friendship drama.* I don't know why I didn't get that one. Frankly, I was perfect.

5. *Part of 'Dead Child' in:*
   student's short film about an vampire invasion;
   student's short film about a worldwide viral contagion.

If I were a grown-up actor, I would probably say that I was 'resting', but being a fifteen-year-old schoolgirl with parents like mine and a school like mine that would have been a seriously inaccurate statement.

Maybe they just weren't that into me.

It was time to have another mammoth session of googling 'actors who got rejected a lot before making it'. That was a surprisingly upbeat thread.

Anyway, there were worse things than acting rejection. Things like your best friend moving her seat in class so that she isn't sitting next to you any more. Yep, I think that's real rejection.

From: Stella at the Haden Agency
Date: 10 June 09:05
To: Julia James
Cc: Charlotte at the Haden Agency
Subject: *Straker* (working title) project
Attachments: Character scenes Straker and Jan.doc

Dear Julia,

Just a quick email to confirm our recent telephone conversation
and the good news that they loved the extra material we sent
over on tape and Elektra is now one of the final three girls being
considered for the role of Straker in the *STRAKER* project.

Would she be able to attend a meeting on Monday 22 June? At
the moment, we need to make sure that she is free for the whole
day so it will be necessary for her to have permission to miss
school. All three girls, as well as the three boys in the shortlist
for the role of Jan, will be taking part in a morning workshop
with the casting team and the director: this will mostly involve
improvisation exercises and there is no preparation required. I
am also attaching two new scenes (duologues, Straker/Jan) that
they will be working on in the afternoon and Elektra should be
off-book with her lines.

She should wear clothes that she can move easily in and bring
drama shoes or ballet flats with her. Again the casting team has
asked that the girls don't wear make-up.

The venue is the offices of Panda Productions at 100 Charing Cross Road, WC2. The nearest Tube station is Leicester Square.

<u>Once again, I must stress the confidential nature of this project.</u>

Well done to Elektra for getting this far! ☺

Kind regards,

Stella

CHAPTER 26

'*You improvise – especially with Shakespeare.*
People really appreciate it at the end of Hamlet.'
Nicholas Hoult

Lens was in a foul mood. In light of the whole Moss mess, I wasn't in a great mood myself, but his was *special*. He'd been standing silently in the middle of the stage, tapping his foot as though he wished there were a big red button labelled 'nuclear detonator' underneath it for a full ten minutes.

'Do you think he's had an argument with Aidan?' Archie asked me.

'God, I hope not.'

Aidan was Lens's newish boyfriend and we were all a bit obsessed with him because he was funny and he was hot and he always bothered to come in and gossip with us when he came to meet Lens.

'Maybe it's just that Lens's childhood pet has been run over or something,' I suggested hopefully. Lens and Aidan were ultimate couple goals.

Lizzie and Carrie straggled in, unsuspecting. This was not going to be pretty.

'You are two minutes and *thirty-six* seconds late. Do you know what that would mean if you were at an audition or, God forbid, a job?' The heavy implication being that the apocalypse and not mild embarrassment would follow. 'Your career would be over. Just like that.' Lens snapped his fingers dramatically. 'A *brutal*, *heartless* end to something that you've invested time and emotion in.'

I really hoped that wasn't a poorly veiled reference to his relationship with Aidan.

The girls looked very confused and extremely uncomfortable. Lizzie began to take off her jacket in slow motion as if a sudden movement might cause Lens to attack.

'Right, I'm not going to delay the lesson any longer. Get into groups of four and not just with your friends, please.' It was like Lens had done some sort of freaky body swap with Madame Verte. 'I'd like you all to devise a short piece starting with the line "mother, how could you". Make it dark.'

The rush to form groups began. I really missed Daisy.

'Do you want to group up?' asked Archie – to which

the only and obvious answer in every imaginable situation would be: 'Yes. Please.'

'Yes, please!' Ah. I hadn't planned on that coming out quite so loudly or quite so enthusiastically. I blushed (of course).

'No!' shouted Lens. For a painful moment, I thought he was just talking to me, but he went on, 'I'll put you into groups myself. I don't want any messing around.'

I was pretty sure he meant he didn't want any happiness full stop.

I ended up in a group with Brian, Carrie (who still looked like she had post-traumatic stress disorder) and a twelve-year-old who didn't speak. At least I wasn't going to find it difficult to emote the despair Lens wanted.

'I have a great idea,' said Brian once he realized that there was nothing he could say or do that would get him out of this group.

I gave Archie an I-may-not-survive-the-next-fifteen-minutes-tell-my-family-I-love-them look.

'So, it's about this family, yeah?' said Brian. 'And there's this main boy yeah ... ?'

Who could he possibly be referring to?

'... And he has special powers.' It really was a mystery. 'And the government, which is evil, yeah, want to abduct him to harness his powers against the Rebels. So, when all these government robot fighters turn up at the family hut, his mum sells him to them, yeah?'

. To be honest, I wouldn't have blamed the mother if she'd given him up for free.

'We could call this special boy Bry ... an ... o,' I suggested.

'Yes, perfect, I love it.'

The twelve-year-old sniggered. Carrie still looked like she was on the verge of tears.

'OK, so Carrie can play my mother and you,' Bry-an-o pointed at the twelve-year-old, 'can be the evil dictator.'

While I was all for playing characters outside your comfort zone, I wasn't sure that a small twelve-year-old in school uniform could really pull this off.

'And what about me?' I asked.

'You can be a robot soldier.'

'*Okaaay*, maybe we could do something slightly more naturalistic?' And slightly less Year Seven?

'No, we're doing this.' He looked stubborn (he quite often looked stubborn).

'I just feel like it isn't going to work. At all. Couldn't we do something about a mother telling her kids she's going to get remarried or something?'

'No, Electra, we're already going. And this is meant to be a collaboration so I don't think you're being very helpful, yeah? I'll start ...'

There was a long pause. It was uncharacteristically subtle for Brian.

'I can't think of anything,' he said finally.

While this may have been a radical Brechtian reinterpretation of the fourth wall, designed to strike right to the heart of the audience's assumptions about the meaning of theatre, I strongly suspected he just had no idea what to say.

'Two minutes left!' shouted Lens.

'Right,' said Bry-an-o, shocked into action and coming over all masterful. 'So, we start with the scene with the boy, then the dictator discusses the deal with the mother, then the robot soldier grabs the boy and drags him off and the dictator gives a speech, then the boy makes a daring escape, kills the dictator and rallies the crowds, yeah?'

It wasn't a question. This was going to be special.

'OK, everyone!' Lens called for order and (for once) got immediate and perfect silence. 'Archie, we'll start with your group first.'

The fact we had literally nothing to show the class nearly made me too distracted to ogle Archie. But not quite. His group had had the sense to stick with your classic devised family trauma: a difficult stepfather/stepdaughter relationship plotline (very probably 'borrowed' from a weeknight soap, but none the worse for that).

'Well done, that was very real.' Reluctant praise.

'OK, Elektra, why don't you show us what your group's got?'

There were so many reasons why what our group had 'devised' should never be shown to anyone.

'Bry ... Brian is very much in charge,' I said.

'This is a collaborative exercise,' said Lens. 'Group responsibility.' His phone buzzed in his pocket. He took it out, read a text and smiled – a beatific smile. I caught Archie's eye and grinned.

'So,' said Lens in a voice so mellow it was like pudding after a really rank main course. 'Elektra's group. Elektra? Or Brian? Whoever. Show us what you've got. I'm sure it'll be great.' And he *beamed*.

Oh, dear. I would very much have liked to have given him something lovely. At least the robot soldier had no dialogue.

'That was *incredible*,' said Lens when we'd finished. He gave a wide smile (like a crocodile).

Brian looked proud, but I knew what was coming.

'Unfortunately, I was looking for credible.'

'Aren't you excited about the *Straker* callback?' asked Mum when I got home.

'Yes.'

'You don't sound it.'

'I am.' And I was (and nervous too), but it was ages away and it was still just an audition and I was trying really hard not to get overexcited about

273

auditions. The lower I kept my expectations, the less disappointed I got. It was my new approach and I was going to stick to it. Also (for unrelated reasons) I was still not in a great mood.

Mum did that 'looking at me really closely and seeing into my soul' thing. 'You look miserable. Are you and Moss still fighting?' I'm not entirely sure when I'd told her about my 'issues' with Moss. I hadn't meant to tell her, but obviously I had. That happened a lot.

'It's fine.' Except it wasn't fine. I think I'd rather Flissy pulled Archie than have to put up with much more of the silent treatment.

'It's obviously not fine.'

I shrugged and went back to looking at everyone else having a life on my Facebook feed. There were photos of Moss and Jenny hamming it up outside the juice bar near our school. I 'liked' it to make a point, although I'm not quite sure what point it was.

'For goodness' sake, Elektra, just go round there and sort it out,' advised/ordered my mother. 'You're being very childish about this.'

'Thanks, that's helpful.' Not. 'I'm not just going to turn up on her doorstep and beg her to let me in and be friends again. I'm not six.'

'No, but you're behaving as if you are,' said Mum, violently chopping some innocent carrots. 'You and Moss have fallen out before and it's always been fine.' There followed a long list of historic fall-outs none of which had anything to do with me and Moss now.

'We haven't been fighting over a guy before.'

'You're both too young to be bothering about boys. You should be putting your friendships first.'

More mixed messages and was it *impossible* for her to see that that was what I was trying to do? My father raised his head from the sports section of the newspaper. 'Just let her sort it out herself, Julia.'

'There isn't much evidence of her trying to do that, is there? And anyway Elektra hasn't left me with much choice. Somebody has to get involved; she doesn't know a thing about how to behave like a responsible adult or even a responsible *teenager* it would seem.' She briefly broke off from the aggressive dicing and slicing and handed me a glass of water and a vitamin tablet so enormous it could have supported the immune system of a rhino.

I looked at Dad hopefully, but he was gratefully embracing the stereotype and had retreated back into an in-depth analysis of whether Chelsea should have played a 4–3–3. Normally, I quite liked that he didn't get involved in my friends stuff, but actually, when Mum was being so harsh, reinforcements would have been nice.

'Thanks for the help, Dad,' I said.

'Your mum's got a point. You're being a bit wet

about this, Elektra,' he said without raising his head. Another typical bit of parenting consistency right there. Plus, my father was calling me wet. Great. A new low point.

'What do you want me to do?' It was a rhetorical question. Stupid of me because I was going to get more advice whether I wanted it or not.

'Talk to Moss. Talk to Maia or whatever the other girl is called. Forget about it for a bit and enjoy all the other things going on in your life? I don't know.'

Sure, because it's that easy.

'I'm not the one who's refusing to speak,' I said, slipping the tablet to Digby who (predictably) spat it out immediately. I kicked it under the table and hoped for the best. 'Moss is the one avoiding me.'

'Then you're both being silly. I can't even see what you're fighting about.' That was my mum's contribution.

It should have made me feel better that she was criticizing Moss too, but it didn't; it just made me feel disloyal.

'Or if you're not going to sort it out with Moss then phone up some of your other friends. And not just your drama friends.' She said 'drama friends' like I'd have said 'performing seals'.

I knew that I should be making an effort with my other friends from school.

I knew that because my mum had already told

me so about one hundred times and I really, really wished that she'd stop.

The more I know she's right about something, the more it irritates me to hear her say it. Maybe it's because she never says it only once. I wish. I wasn't feeling social. *After* I was back being friends with Moss again, I would make an effort with everyone else at school that I'd managed to upset in the past three weeks.

Or maybe that wouldn't happen and I'd become best friends with Flissy. We could share make-up and she would advise me on guys. Right.

Or maybe I would just eat my body weight in chocolate.

'Well, if you're not going to take my advice, I can only suggest that you stop moping in my kitchen,' Mum said angrily, mashing some poor little potatoes. 'And if you're going to go out again later get changed first.'

'What's wrong with what I'm wearing?'

'The leggings are ... gynaecological.'

So I could add camel toe to my list of things to worry about. And I'd been wearing them to ACT. Brilliant.

Mum always got offended when I didn't take her 'advice', but the days when she could sort out my friends for me had passed. I thought about talking to Eulalie, but only because she would have ended

277

up offering to take me shopping to cheer me up. She wouldn't have had any magic answers either. But that wasn't even an option because she was away topping up her suntan in the Caribbean and all I was getting were Instagrams of her in sarongs (#stillknowhowtohavefuninthesun #poolparty) and I didn't want to rain on her (very sunny) parade.

Anyway, it was Moss I wanted to talk to. I wanted to tell her about the *Straker* audition, but mostly I just wanted to talk to her about all the things we always talked about – some real stuff like did Miranda in the year above have an eating disorder? And some stuff that was just gossip, like was it true that Maia/Claudia/Isobel got off with Ben/Josh/Anna/Ben (the same Ben)? And why did no one judge Ben? I wanted to talk to her about stuff that I was too embarrassed to ask anyone else (like was my left eyebrow higher than my right? Actually, I knew it was, so the real question was why did I care?). And other more embarrassing things that I'm definitely not going to list. I wanted to talk to her about stuff that I couldn't get out of my head (like did she think Archie still fancied Talia? Of course he did).

Forget it. None of that was what I really wanted to talk to her about.

I just wanted to say that I was sorry.

★
CHAPTER 27

'I just can't say no. I'm basically a circus bear.'
Tom Hiddleston

It was completely unacceptable for two people in their *late* forties to be dancing round a kitchen table in some sort of middle-aged version of twerking.

'What the—??'

They sort of trailed off and stumbled to a halt and looked sheepish, which was the least they could do.

'There has to be a reason for this behaviour.' I think I sounded quite stern. I certainly intended to. What if there wasn't a reason? What if this was just some horrible insight into how their marriage worked when I wasn't around?

'Sorry ...' said Mum.

'Sorry ...' mumbled Dad.

It's a good moment when you get a parental apology. And now two in a row. It almost made the 'dancing' thing worth it. Almost. Even without the half-empty champagne bottle, I should have realized by the goofy smiliness and sort of blurriness of the pair of them that they were both a bit drunk.

'And the reason for this singing and ... stuff would be?' There was a brief moment when I wondered if Granny Gwen had died and this was their idea of mourning. Not brief enough. I'm not proud of that.

'Your dad's been promoted!' I'm not going to lie, Mum *twirled*. 'He's off kitchens. He's going to be working on the Experimental House project.'

'Experimental?' I wasn't sure I liked the sound of experimental houses. I'd rather go for something a bit proven myself – at least structurally.

'It's *fine*. They've said they can be white. And minimalist.'

I was finding this quite hard to follow.

'I'm going to be busy,' said Dad as if being busy was the best thing anyone could ever wish for. 'No more kitchens.'

Experimental houses didn't have kitchens?

'Do you want a glass of champagne?' My mum was practically waving the bottle at me. I looked at the clock on the wall. It was 4.46 p.m. That was the sort of question Eulalie asked me after school, not my parents. I had two hours minimum of physics homework to do (the electromagnetic spectrum, fair to say not my favourite topic, but then it's not my favourite subject), but I took the champagne (are you kidding? Gift horse – well, gift foal: she only poured me like two centimetres). My phone woofed.

Hey, Elektra, what's up? x

It was Archie. On the upside, there were definitely more of these random texts and the 'x' was pretty standard now. Was Moss wrong? On the downside, they were all the sort of texts I would have sent to a friend. And I didn't want to be stuck in Friendzone with Archie Mortimer.

'Who's texting you?' asked my mum.

'No one,' I said.

'You don't normally smile like that when "no one" texts you. Do you want to talk about it?' She hiccuped.

Oh, great. My dad was singing quietly in the background with a silly smile on his face. Oblivious.

'Nope.' I ignored the whipped-puppy look Mum gave me. 'I'm just going to go upstairs and start on my homework.' Which meant: 'I'm just going to go upstairs for a bit of privacy.'

I sat on my bed and looked at my phone as if, in the absence of a best friend, it would start to tell me what to do next. Digby scratched at the door and I let him in because he only made a dog-sized dent in my privacy. He jumped up on the bed and pawed at my favourite jumper until he had got it into the best shape to curl up on. Should I make Archie wait for a reply? I probably should, right? Digby wagged his tail, but as advice went it was a bit equivocal.

I'm not great at waiting.

Nothing. Revision. x

Stupid, I'd replied too fast. And with a text that was both boring and depressing. Also stupid because I should have asked a question; I'd killed the conversation. Basic texting error. But moments later another text popped on to my screen.

Got my last paper next week. Seriously cannot wait. Life will begin again. x

Archie talking about GCSEs made me scared for next year. **Have they gone OK?**

Who knows?

😄😄😄😄😄😄😄😄😄😄😄

Thanks X

Capital letter kiss. Was that escalation or a typo? **You still coming to ACT this week? x** I admit that my failure to come up with witty text banter was beginning to look like a pattern, but this was a bit stressful.

Don't think so. x

Lower case x. Disappointing. Also very disappointing that I wouldn't see him at ACT. And then a second text a couple of minutes later.

Are you going to Steph's next Friday? Xx

Xx was escalation, wasn't it?

If you'd asked me ten minutes earlier if I'd wanted to go to Stephanie's house party, I would have said no. Chances were it wouldn't be any good because none of us (at least in my year) go to enough parties to behave anything like normal people at them. Everyone would be getting with everyone else and the girls wouldn't have eaten carbs for a week and wouldn't eat anything at all for the whole party day so they'd look skinny and then they'd hit the smuggled-in booze (unless Steph's parents just served it – it happens). Somebody/many people would throw up. There would be at least one fight, although chances were nobody would get hurt because everyone (even the guys who played rugby) fought like girls. Also I wouldn't be able to get ready with Moss or gossip about it after with Moss. In my very limited experience, those were the best bits.

It's not like I'd expected Steph to invite me because I didn't know her that well. Anyway, she'd invited Moss and she probably thought there'd be another fight if we were both there. (Maybe she *should* have invited me: we could have provided the entertainment.)

So, if you'd asked me ten minutes ago if I minded not having been invited, I'd have said no and I'd have meant it. Now I wasn't so sure.

There wasn't any point lying about it to Archie. Everyone knew everything.

Nope, not invited. x

You guys not friends?

We're not exactly not friends, but it's complicated.

I didn't put an x that time because he hadn't, but then an x would have looked a bit odd after a question mark. Oh, God, maybe his kisses were just punctuation?

Minutes passed, long minutes, and he wasn't replying. I'd killed the conversation by including an honest reference to the complexities of female friendship.

Stupid.

I might as well do my homework.

More long minutes passed. I was finding it hard to concentrate on the difference between ultraviolet and infrared radiation.

I doodled on my textbook (a little cartoon of Squirrelina dumping Colonel Kernel) and refreshed my phone again.

Nothing.

Did gamma radiation have the shortest wavelength or the longest? I was finding it very hard to care.

My phone barked. **Soz, parents around. Too complicated to come as my plus one? xx**

Back to double x'ing and a plus one invite to a party. No way was this Friendzone. Or maybe it was. Maybe we were so deep in the Friendzone that kisses escalation was irrelevant. Maybe Archie wasn't carefully considering the nuance of every single character in every single text? I was so *confused*. There should be a manual.

Obviously, I needed to ask Moss, but obviously I couldn't ask Moss.

I didn't know what to do.

I typed **Sorry, too complicated. xx**, stared at it for a full ten minutes, deleted it and typed **Why not? Sure. xx** and pressed Send before I could change my mind.

The phone woofed immediately: **xxx**

Even I was getting the message.

CHAPTER 28

'*Low expectations is what I'm after. Honestly.*'
Cara Delevingne

My phone barked. **Good luck for Straker callback.**
Long scroll of fingers-crossed smiley emoticons. Not
from Moss.

Thanks, Daisy, I'm soooo scared
Nah, you'll be great. Text me after.

I was seriously nervous. Excited, sure, but mostly
nervous. I still hadn't seen the whole script, just
some more casting scenes. The callback was at the
offices of the production company and they were
quite cool offices, modern, with lots of glass and
white walls peppered with posters from previous
productions. We were all shepherded into a big
room. I guess it was usually a conference room, but

they'd pushed back all the chairs to turn it into a rehearsal space. There were six of us in the room who were up for parts and I recognized three of them.

The two other girls were shorter and girlier than me (no surprise there). The girl I recognized was called Amy and the reason I recognized her was because she was beamed into my sitting room every Thursday night as a regular cast member on *Sunningtown*. *Sunningtown* is this sort of rustic drama/soap series, not my sort of thing, but obviously people watched it because it had been running for at least a decade and Amy had been in it all the time, growing up in front of us (despite at least two near-death plotlines – it may have been a small town, but it was one that attracted an extraordinary amount of incident). She was glued to her iPhone and wasn't making eye contact with anyone. Her mother was sitting beside her, reading a magazine with a picture of Amy on the front. Just weird. Everyone else had got rid of their parent at the door.

The other girl, the one I didn't recognize, came over straight away. She had a nice smile.

'Hey, I'm Lana. Were you at the *Hetty Feather* casting? I'm *sure* I recognize you. You had, like, a purple uniform on.'

This was the first time I'd ever been recognized

from my acting stuff, and it was from a casting for a part I hadn't got and because my school uniform was tragic. Score.

'Yeah, I didn't get the part.'

'Me neither. So we're up against Amy Underhill.'

We both looked over at Amy, who didn't look back at us. Now she was doing some rather ostentatious vocal warm-ups.

'She'll get it,' I said resignedly.

'Yep,' said Lana. 'I'm definitely looking at today as a free masterclass and nothing more.'

I already liked Lana. She seemed sane and normal. Also it was true: money couldn't have bought a masterclass with the director of this film. Looked at that way, today was going to be good. Oh, and we were missing school. I thought of Flissy in double physics and smiled. Win-win.

My phone barked. **Good luck for today. xx** Not Moss (bad). Archie (good) – two kisses (not as good as xxx but still good). I switched my phone to silent (it was a very demanding ringtone).

'She's wearing make-up,' said Lana, looking over at Amy.

She was right. Amy had on *at least* foundation and mascara and probably liner and lippy as well. We'd been told quite firmly not to wear any, but maybe different rules applied to actual actors with jobs. Lana and I were both wearing black leggings and white T-shirts. Amy was in skinny jeans and a teeny tie-dyed T-shirt.

'Maybe we'll get her autograph,' I suggested just a little sarcastically.

'Well, that'll make it all worthwhile,' replied Lana in the same tone, offering me half a Mars bar. A girl who ate Mars bars for breakfast was a girl to swap phone numbers with.

The three guys had clustered together on the other side of the room. Pack-animal instinct?

I sort of knew two of them. Alex was Jenny from school's older cousin and I'd met him a couple of times. I was a bit in awe of him because he was two years above and seriously hot in that English blond, blue-eyed way. He'd modelled for some T-shirt brand. I hadn't known he acted, but I wasn't surprised. He would have been perfect in war movies playing the heroic RAF fighter pilot who does eventually die, but not until the last scene and not until he has saved his best friend and not until he has seen his newborn son in the arms of his girl-next-door sweetheart wife (preferably played by me, but probably played by Amy).

The other guy that I recognized straight away was called Damian. I'd met him at castings before and he'd been on *Casualty* (he died in that one; there's a strange, positive correlation between the gruesomeness of your screen death and the success of your future career – his was a nasty incident with a lawn mower if I remember rightly so he'd probably do well). I'd never really spoken to him. He wasn't nearly as good-looking as Alex, but he was passable.

The third guy was the fittest. He was black so the three guys had – weirdly for a casting – completely different looks. It made me think that they probably hadn't cast 'Jan's' parents yet.

None of them were Archie, but none of them were ugly either, and although I was in the throes of a major crush I did still have eyes. Hypothetically, this attraction thing mattered because of Straker and Jan's young love subplot (which was a distraction from the whole flesh-eating-survival stuff apparently dominating the rest of the script).

I didn't think I was going to get this part, but I can't pretend I wasn't thinking about plotlines when I was checking out Alex, Damian and the mystery guy.

'OK, guys, gather round.' Janey, who we'd met at the first casting, did that sort of clapping thing that primary-school teachers do when they're trying to get their class to come to order.

'Right, you all know me and this is Sergei Havelski,' she gestured, 'and sitting either side of him are Selim and Rhona.'

So the short, middle-aged guy sitting quietly in

the corner was the director, Mr Havelski. In his photos on the web, he'd looked more vivid, more powerful. In real life, he appeared fairly ordinary, a bit older, shorter and a lot more tired. I hadn't recognized him. To be fair, he'd probably just flown in from LA or been up all night mentoring an Oscar winner or divorcing his fourth wife or something. He was clutching the most enormous mug of coffee so he'd probably perk up later. As far as I could work out, Selim and Rhona were his sidekicks – there to fill the coffee mug and take notes.

Janey went on. 'We all know who each of *you* are, but I know some of you haven't met before so can we just go round and each of you introduce yourselves? Just say a couple of sentences that really sum up who you are.'

I got really nervous and blotchy doing this sort of thing. It was meant to be casual, but we were already being tested and we all knew it. Who was going to be the wittiest/have the best voice/ projection/delivery/eye contact, etc. etc.

Amy went first as befitted her star status. 'Hi, everyone.' She broke off to give us all a saccharine smile. 'I'm Amy Underhill and I guess what's important about me is that I live for acting. *It's my life.* I've played Kelly in *Sunningtown* for years now and it has been an *awesome* experience. The cast are like *family* to me, but I really want to *stretch* myself as an *actress* and take on more *demanding* roles and I think that the role of Straker—'

'Thanks, Amy,' Janey cut in and motioned to Alex to take over (which was just as well as much more of Amy talking *emphatically* about what mattered to her and I would have thrown up).

'I'm Alex, I've got four brothers and ... I live in London and ... this is my first shot at trying to do some acting. Er, if it doesn't work out, I'm quite into football.'

He hadn't bigged up the modelling; Alex was OK. I wondered what the brothers were like.

'I'm Damian. I'm an only child. I've done a fair bit of acting at school and professionally and it's definitely what I want to do when I grow up.'

'When I grow up' – seriously, who says that? The jury is still out on Damian.

'Hi, I'm Lana and, um, I like acting too and singing and dancing and ... er ...' Long pause. 'I'm suddenly a bit nervous.'

'Don't be nervous, Lana, this isn't some sort of test. We just want you all to *relax* and have *fun* today. You've all done *really* well getting this far.' Now Janey was emphasizing every word, but how stupid did we look? By definition, this was some sort of test.

It was my turn and I had a bit of a brain freeze

too. There was an even longer awkward pause. 'Hey.' I did a strange sort of little wave. 'Sorry, I'm Elektra and I'm nervous too ... obviously ...' My voice was a bit squeaky. I forced it low, maybe a bit too low. 'I haven't really done much acting, but I do enjoy it. Erm, there are quite a lot of things I enjoy.' I really had not intended that to sound suggestive, but Alex was definitely smirking; focus, Elektra, focus. 'I haven't got any brothers or sisters.' Not cool.

'Thank you, Elektra,' said Janey, nodding intensely as if I'd said something really clever and deeply insightful.

And finally, 'I'm Carlo, I'm seventeen, I used to live in New York and I've done a bit of acting out there. Music's my thing.'

Risky to say that something that wasn't acting was his thing. Carlo was cool, maybe too cool. Time would tell.

'*Okaaay*,' said Janey, 'that was GREAT.' Every word she said now came with its very own exclamation mark she was trying so hard to make us all feel good. 'Let's do one more round and this time I want each of you to tell us one, just one,' I swear she looked at Amy when she said that, 'secret thing about yourself that nobody would guess. It's important as actors that you can lay yourselves open to others. Alex, you go first.'

I think Janey fancied Alex, which was fair enough.

'I like One Direction.'

That was brave. Carlo raised an eyebrow, but the rest of us just looked at him adoringly.

'I can speak Polish. *Powodzenia*, everyone!'

That was Lana and that was impressive. I have no idea what it meant, but there was lots of what we actors call positive energy.

'I won a beautiful baby competition.'

That was Damian and I *was* beginning to judge him.

'My mum dropped me on my head when I was baby.'

Well, it didn't damage your good looks, Carlo.

'My left arm is one inch longer than my right,' said Amy, giggling winningly as if that were her only flaw. Physically, it probably was. I can't say that I was warming to Amy.

'My left boob is *at least* one inch smaller than my right,' I said because I had temporarily gone out of my mind.

I had certainly laid myself open to others. The guys laughed, Amy looked faux shocked and Lana cringed and whispered in my ear, 'Me too.'

Havelski just stared into his coffee morosely.

'*Okaaaay*,' said Janey, 'I think we all know each other a bit better now. Time to get you guys warmed up. Form a circle, everyone. Now who here does yoga?'

Amy and Damian's hands went up like rockets. I'd say Amy pipped him to the post. Carlo raised his arm at a much slower pace (the movement equivalent of a drawl – sexy) and – almost apologetically – so did Lana.

'*Greaaat*,' said Janey, 'so who wants to lead us all in some stretches?'

No prizes for guessing that Amy was up for that.

So we did Downward Dog, we did the Warrior, we did Boat, we did the Cobra, we did Child's Pose. When I say 'we did', I mean that some of us did (rather beautifully – how the hell Amy managed it in skinny jeans, even stretchy ones, was beyond me, but she did) while others of us (basically, me and Alex) failed miserably and got the giggles. Weirdly, the more I humiliated myself, the less nervous I felt. Janey only stepped in when Amy tried to make us all follow her into the Crow; the Crow would have finished me off.

★
CHAPTER 29

'I expect I'll have to talk a lot about The Kiss. We did it two weeks ago. Four takes one way, and two takes with the camera in the other direction. Six takes altogether.'

Emma Watson

We'd got all the yoga stuff out of the way and we'd played some pretty standard improv games and we'd run around a bit so that even Amy was hot and sweaty and had started to forget that her hair was meant to be perfect. Basically, they gave us three hours to muck around and chill out a bit.

The afternoon was for script work. We all had the same sides, two scenes, both short, between Straker and Jan. For once, we were all doing the scenes in front of each other, swapping partners around. That wasn't as daunting as it sounds

because once you've done Downward Dog in front
of someone anything goes. There was a quarrel
scene and a love scene.

The quarrel scene was short.

EXTERIOR. FOREST: DAY THREE

A clearing in the forest. Tall, black,
dark trees, menacing shadows. Two figures
facing each other. Stiff, exhausted and
obviously angry: Straker and Jan. Straker
is holding a spear.

STRAKER
(*aggressively*) Why the hell did you have
to interfere? I had it under control.

JAN
(*matching her aggression, moving closer to
her*) You. Had. Nothing. Under. Control.

STRAKER
(*Backs away from him as if from a
dangerous animal. Trying not to cry with
frustration and anger.*)
I don't want your 'help'. You're not some
action hero — well, except maybe in your
pathetic imagination — and I'm not some

297

helpless little girl. You know what? You
make everything worse.

JAN
(*shouts*) No. *You* make everything worse.

STRAKER
(*Drops the spear. Quietly, to herself as
much as to Jan.*)
I thought it was as bad as it could get.
I thought nothing and nobody could make
anything — this thing, this place, this
world — worse, but you do.

JAN
(*Doesn't answer. Looks at her as if he
will never understand her.*)

(*Hearing roaring off camera, they both
turn, fear uniting them immediately.*)

JAN
Run!

It was good starting with the fight scene because we
were so pumped with adrenalin that it was kind of a
relief to swear and shout. The pace was fast, no time
to get uptight. The love scene was the one we were

more worried about. It wasn't a full-on love scene, nothing really happened, but we knew that it was a big point in the script because it was the first scene where the romantic connection between Straker and Jan was really brought out and you realized that it was going to be a love story (possibly a tragic love story given the whole world-ending, flesh-eating scenario).

INTERIOR. SHELTER

A rough wooden shack, earth floor. In the dim light from the moon outside, we can see two figures, Straker and Jan. Straker is washing the blood off Jan's hands with a rag. Her voice is harsh, she is angry and afraid, but her actions are gentle.

STRAKER
I don't know how you managed to fight him off, Jan; he was twice your size.

JAN
(Jan *winces; he is quite badly cut.*) Ouch. You're hurting me more than he did.

STRAKER
Don't be such a baby, stay still. I need to get this properly clean. If it gets

infected, we're in even more trouble.
You're such an idiot.

JAN
(*He tries to laugh it off.*) Come on, admit
it, Straker, you're impressed.

STRAKER
(*serious*) I'm not impressed, Jan. I think
you're a fool. I think you're a fool who
nearly died. And what if he'd attacked me
too? Did you think about that?

JAN
(*Jan looks away; his voice is almost
inaudible.*) Yes, I thought about that. I'd
have kept you safe.

STRAKER
And if you couldn't? What then, Jan? What
are you going to do when he comes back
with others and he looks for you and
he looks for me? Do you think he'll not
try again? Being Warri isn't going to be
enough to keep you alive every time. Not
any more. You think you're so bloody brave
and you're just so bloody stupid.

JAN

(*Jan looks up at Straker and this time his voice is firmer, more the voice of a man than a boy.*) I promise you, Straker, I *will* keep you safe.

STRAKER

(*Straker is crying now.*) Nobody can keep anyone safe here, not any more. You shouldn't make promises like that.

JAN

(*Jan puts his hand up to her face and brushes away a tear. They are standing very close.*) I won't let you down, Straker.

STRAKER

(*Straker takes his hand and says very gently*) Better now?

I was first up with Damian so we hadn't seen how anyone else was tackling it. We started off OK, although I probably enjoyed calling him a fool more than I should have done; I had to keep reminding myself that this wasn't the fight scene. Then we got to the line 'I won't let you down' and Damian, well, I don't know how else to put it, he lunged.

It was a pretty effective guerrilla attack; I had

301

zero chance of escape. His mum had obviously advised him to 'really go for it' before the audition so he had *really* gone for it. His technique was pretty pragmatic, well suited to a not particularly hot teenage boy. He'd obviously calculated that he had about three seconds before a girl would work out what was happening so, instead of going for a slow, romantic, lean-in and an exchange of romantic, sensuous looks of longing, he just sort of *fell* straight in the direction of my face, hoping my lips would be where he expected and he might just make contact. He did. Unfortunately, my teeth were also there.

He 'kept calm and carried on' (probably another of his mother's mantras) and started on stage two, the face sucking followed immediately by stage three, the tongue. A *lot* of tongue. Was that *normal*? How were you meant to breathe doing this? What if I suffocated? Would the production's insurance cover lunge-related deaths?

How did I get him to stop?

'STOP!' bellowed Havelski. 'What the hell do you think you are doing?'

Damian leapt away from me as if he had been electrocuted, I gasped for breath and we both stood there, looking like primary-school kids who had been hauled before the headmaster.

'One, you … you …' He looked over at Rhona who muttered, 'Damian,' nervously. 'You, *Damian*, do NOT kiss ...' He looked over at Rhona who mouthed my name. '... Elektra unless and until the script tells you to kiss her. Where does the script say Jan kisses Straker? Nowhere. The reason it does not say Jan kisses Straker is because at this point in the script *Jan does not kiss Straker*. Are you the scriptwriter? Are you a better scriptwriter than the scriptwriter who is working on this project and has worked on a dozen high-grossing Hollywood movies? I can answer those questions for you – no and no.'

Wow, Havelski was intimidating. My legs were actually shaking and I'm pretty sure that hadn't been caused by anything Damian had done.

'Two,' he went on, '*I did not tell you to kiss her.* Three, if you had to kiss her, you should have kissed her properly. That wasn't a kiss, that was an ASSAULT.' (He'd obviously had the same insurance freak-out.)

There was complete silence in the room for several very long minutes. Poor Damian, he might never lunge again, ever. Which was probably not a bad thing.

'But I thought you were testing for chemistry,' he said in a tiny little voice.

'Well, Damian, you have a lot to learn about women if you thought that kiss demonstrated chemistry.'

This time there was some laughter, nervous laughter. I wasn't laughing.

'I presume you have kissed a girl before?'

Damian nodded sulkily.

Please don't let him ask me if I'd kissed a guy before. Please.

He didn't. 'Sorry about all this, Elektra.'

'It's OK,' I mumbled, resisting a very strong inclination to add 'Sir' to the end of my sentence.

'In a way, you're right, Damian. Part of the reason all six of you are here together in this meeting is so that we can watch how you relate to each other and what sort of "chemistry" there is between you. You've all had a script synopsis; you know that Jan and Straker fall in love. They do kiss and down the line, whatever actors are cast, we will talk about that and we'll talk to your parents about it. But that is not for today. What is important in Jan and Straker's story is *love*. They fall in love when everything around them is in pieces and that love is the only thing that makes the audience believe that things might get a little better.'

Heavy. Made heavier by the slight accent. Russian? Hungarian? Meerkat? I needed to google Havelski some more.

He went on. 'The actors that play Jan and Straker need to make the audience believe that they have fallen in love, otherwise this narrative doesn't go anywhere. Don't you think we were all watching for chemistry when you were reading the fight scene? Don't you think that people who are in love fight with each other differently, talk to each other differently, look at each other differently? It's not about body parts.'

Nobody was looking at anybody else. We all talked about body parts endlessly, but when sixty-year-old men started talking about them it was undeniably awkward.

'Well, it's not *just* about body parts. It is about an emotional connection, an intellectual connection, a shared sense of humour; it is not just about a physical connection. Each of you is a strong actor. I don't doubt that and you mustn't doubt it, whatever happens or doesn't happen next. If you weren't strong actors, if you hadn't already impressed, you wouldn't be in this room right now. I certainly wouldn't have flown five and a half thousand miles to meet with you. *But* any guy can grab a girl and stick his tongue down her throat. And by the way, Damian, it is poor etiquette for an actor to use tongues, at least without permission—'

'I didn't know that.'

Havelski gave him a 'don't interrupt me' look and went on. 'OK, let's do this scene once more and this time I want you all to think about chemistry; I want you to think about it from the beginning

of the scene until the end and if anyone locks lips
I will personally come and separate them and it
won't be pretty.'

We didn't doubt that.

'Elektra, take a break. Lana, come back out here
and read with Damian.'

OK, so the bad news was total humiliation
(again), the good news was that I was technically
no longer a snogging virgin. That was possibly the
least romantic first kiss in history. It might also
have been the most public. Not totally sure about
that because even I had seen some pretty public
making out (not very many guys under eighteen
who have the slightest chance to get with a girl
will hold off until they're someplace private – and
now I come to think of it most of the girls I know
aren't that bothered either). But not very many
people have their first kiss in front of a Hollywood
director and his entourage – most people are
spared that.

My break was all of ten minutes and I was up
again, this time to read the scene with Carlo. Carlo
obviously thought that because it was a love scene
it was important that we read it practically standing
on each other's toes we were so close. That was fine
by me and to be fair that *was* in the script. Damian
had tasted of cheese Quavers; Carlo's breath
smelled of mint and aniseed. By the 'I promise

you, Straker, I will keep you safe' line, we were maintaining serious eye contact and when he put up his hand to brush away my tears (yep, I can cry to order, real tears and everything; it's my drama USP) I was totally into it. I think it went quite well because the room was very quiet when we finished. It took a couple of minutes before I realized that I was still holding Carlo's hand. Embarrassing. This was a guy whose ego was big enough already.

Watching the others play out the scene made me feel insecure again. They were all really good. I was an amateur.

I was sad when we got to the end of the session: it felt like the end of something. Well, it probably was; it probably was the end of the *Straker* project for me. We all hugged. Even though we were in competition, we'd been in it together. Don't want to sound trite here, but we'd *bonded*. I was just going over to my mum's car when someone called out my name. It was Carlo. He motioned me over and of course I went (like Digby to a treat). He leaned in close to me. 'You know that scene?'

I nodded.

'Unfinished business. See you at rehearsals, E,' and, without waiting for an answer, he turned away and walked off. So he obviously didn't feel that it was the end of the road.

Carlo was arrogant, no question, but he was hot with it.

I quite liked him.

I was still laughing when I got into the car.

'How did it go?' asked my mum (inevitably). 'You look happy.'

I'd survived and I was quite proud of that. And it had been fun – well, it had been fun in parts.

'It was ... interesting,' I said, which was the truth.

The Damian lunge had been pretty disgusting, but if I added in the whole Carlo flirtation thing it hadn't been a bad day. The great gods of drama (Dionysus and Bacchus, the bad boys of booze and drama, and Saint Genesius who converted to Christianity in the middle of a performance which must have been a moment) had handed me a script with some sort of a 'love' scene and I'd got it over and done with.

Better late than never.

Sure, it hadn't been with Archie, but then I hadn't wanted my first kiss to be with him. I *really* liked Archie.

There was way too much at stake to have risked a first kiss with Archie.

From: Stella at the Haden Agency
Date: 24 June 15:44
To: Julia James
Cc: Charlotte at the Haden Agency
Subject: *Straker* (working title) project – dates

Dear Julia,

Further to our phone call today, can I just say that I've had another email from Janey at Suited Casting. She just wanted to emphasize that although they really do need to get an idea of everyone's potential availability for this project as soon as possible <u>no decisions have yet been taken about casting</u>.

Elektra's done extremely well to get this far, but Janey has made it very clear that they thought all three girls performed very well at the audition and it's a strong field (the other two girls do have more experience). I don't want you all to read more into this request for information than you should.

Don't hesitate to call me if you want to talk about this.

Kind regards,

Stella

⭐ CHAPTER 30

'Acting has done a strange thing to me though. I often sit there, thinking, "I love this, but I wouldn't put my daughter on the stage."'

Eddie Redmayne

'I just don't know, Elektra; they're asking if you would be free for *two whole months*. Two whole months and you've got GCSEs round the corner.'

'*Hypothetically*. They're asking hypothetically, Mum. It doesn't matter; it's not worth getting all het up about. It's not going to happen.'

'They might be asking hypothetically, but I'm expected to give them a real answer. Two whole months,' she wailed.

'Two whole months *in the summer holidays*. Two whole months that aren't going to happen.'

'But *exams*. The work you do over the next few

years is going to determine your future,' she said (as she so often did).

'Oh, come on, Mum, do you seriously think I'm going to be revising for my exams this summer? Do you know what people do in the summer holidays at my age? They drink beer in parks or, if they can afford it, they go to Reading or Bestival. Or if they're loaded maybe they go and drink beer somewhere foreign and sunny . . .'

She shuddered ostentatiously. 'You're fifteen, Elektra. I don't believe that fifteen-year-olds do that sort of thing. What makes you think we'd let you go to any festivals? I've heard the stories. Do you know how many drugs there are at events like that?'

Well, yes, I had a vague idea, I'd listened to the stories of the girls in sixth form, but now wasn't the time for that. 'I'm not saying I would go to festivals.' And I wasn't, not yet; I'd fight that battle after GCSEs like everyone else (or maybe I'd find something better to do than spend three nights in a tent in the rain in a field with scary loos).

I was just winding her up. It was *so easy*.

'Don't worry, Mum, I'm just saying that it's not like I'd be starting on my exam reading list. Actually, now I come to think of it, I'd probably get more time to do reading on set than I would anywhere else over a summer. And if you're worried about teenage summer behaviour then surely I'd be safer on some set with a chaperone or with you.'

She sighed dramatically. 'I don't know. I just think the whole thing could derail you.'

That's the problem with parents: they not only think that they have you on rails, they think that's a good thing.

'I'm not even going to get the offer. They'll cast Amy; they're bound to.' I liked Lana (a lot) more and I thought she'd read the fight scene the best of everyone, but my opinion didn't matter and Amy was way the most experienced of the three of us (and the prettiest). 'Stella said they were only checking everyone's availability upfront in case there were any problems. And she's not just managing our expectations.'

'I know, I know, but what if they don't? What if they ask you, Elektra? What then?'

What then? I hadn't really got that far ... 'Dad's OK with it,' I said.

'Dad's not OK with it. Dad just hasn't had time to think about it and anyway he'd agree to anything right now.'

That was true. Dad was happy (even though the client wanted to incorporate a curved wall – experimental since the Stone Age), he was busy and he was completely distracted. Which was quite frankly probably the best mixture in a parent.

'Eulalie thinks I should definitely do it if I get the chance.'

'Eulalie would think you should strip naked and swing from the chandelier if you got the chance.'

I was having difficulty visualizing that, but Mum was probably right. I should probably just drop the Eulalie line of persuasion.

'Molly said that when Miranda let her son take a part in some film he went *completely* off the rails and ended up in rehab.'

'Oh, for goodness' sake, Mum, Miranda's son was *destined* for rehab: it's their family tradition. Why do you care so much what your friends think?'

'And you don't care what your friends think?'

That was a low blow. She knew that I hadn't spoken to Moss about the *Straker* callback because I still wasn't speaking to Moss about anything. Mum knew that I really, really cared what Moss would think. I thought I knew what she would say, but maybe not; maybe I'd got that wrong too. Mum was pacing round the kitchen now, completely confusing poor Digby, who kept trying to get out of the way and ending up under her feet.

'You're making Digby dizzy – you're making *me* dizzy – please sit down.'

She ignored me. Even more worryingly, she ignored Digby. She never ignored Digby.

'Mum, please, look at me!' I grabbed her hand as she went past.

'I spend hours looking at you.'

'Sort of, like you notice every time I have shadows under my eyes or my forehead is threatening to break out or I'm not wearing the right sort of sports kit, but you don't seem to have noticed much else. And I don't just mean I've, like, got taller.'

'Don't say "like",' she said (as she so often did). I ignored her (as I so often did) and she went on. 'Of course I notice that you're growing up.' She said 'growing up' in that heavy way that made me squirm and looked a bit upset like I was suggesting that she was doing something wrong. I wasn't. It wasn't her fault that she wanted me to stay her little girl.

And it wasn't my fault that I didn't.

'Really? Do you *really* notice? Or does it take you about a year to catch up all the time? I think it does because you treat me exactly the same as the day Stella signed me up.'

She sat down next to me then and waited.

I went on. 'We've had this exact same conversation a hundred times and that's not fair. You shouldn't keep saying the same things to me all the time because I'm not the same.' I thought I was making a pretty obvious point (actually, I *was* making an obvious point), but Mum just looked baffled. 'I don't do all the same things.'

'What things? You mean boyfriends and stuff?'

'No, I'm not talking about that.' God, this was hard work. 'I'm talking about learning lines and getting to auditions on time and not minding about them not wanting me and still doing my homework.' Mostly. 'Just, like, dealing with all that.'

'I know and I'm proud of you. But it hasn't even been a year.'

'It's been a long time. You've got to start to trust me.'

'We do trust you.'

'Not really. You sort of trust me not to get drunk or smoke or get pregnant, but you don't trust me to know my mind about my future.'

'I just don't know.'

'I think I will know,' I said.

She looked at me. 'Will know?'

I nodded.

'So you don't know? You don't know for sure?'

Months and months of *stuff* scrolled through my mind: waiting rooms packed with the competition, church halls, the other Elektra smiling up at Daniel Craig, crying on Archie, Daisy crying on me, lovely Ed directing me, mucking about at ACT, *being* Squirrelina, the phone not ringing, the phone ringing.

I hesitated. 'Not for *sure*. Now it's just something

that might but probably won't happen. I'm not stupid, Mum, I know it would be a big decision.' It would be a much bigger decision than whether to take a bit part or do a voice-over for a minor squirrel. It would change things. I'd thought about this. 'I know it would be hard work, not some cushy ride. I just really, really want to be the one who decides. I don't mean I won't listen to you and Dad, of course I will. It's just ... it's just that it's my life and I *want you to listen to me too.*'

She looked at me for a long minute. 'You know what we need? We need a List.' (And yes, she did say 'list' like it had a capital letter.) 'We need paper and we need pens. Well, you do – you need to be the list-maker.'

She was right. There's nothing like being the list-maker to make you feel as if you're in control.

'What shall I put first?'

'What do you want to put first?'

That was quite an annoying answer. I looked at the blank sheet of paper and wrote:

1. Stella and Charlotte to email/phone me, not Mum.

'Agreed?' I asked her.

'I think maybe they have to contact me because you're under sixteen,' Mum said. 'How about you put that they should always email you *and* me. And you have to check your emails. I don't care which of us they phone, but you're usually at school.'

I crossed out my first attempt and started again:

1. Stella and Charlotte to email/phone me, ~~not Mum~~ as well as Mum. Mum to promise to tell me exactly what they said on any phone call the minute she next sees me.

'Agreed?'

'Agreed,' she said. 'What's next?'

2. Mum will not discuss my 'career' with Stella and Charlotte without me there.

'Agreed?'

'Agreed,' she confirmed.

3. Mum and Dad will not discuss my 'career' without me there.

'Agreed?' I asked.

'Not agreed.'

'Room for negotiation?'

'No room.'

I crossed that one out too. I needed a clean sheet of paper.

3. I will go to auditions and meetings without a
   chaperone.

'We've talked about this, Elektra. Stella says it's usual to be chaperoned under sixteen.'

'Tons of kids turn up on their own. Honestly.'

'How about we agree that if Stella says it's OK and it's in London and it's near a Tube station then you can go on your own?'

'Is that your final offer?'

'Yes.'

'Then all right.' I wrote it out.

'If this is turning into a contractual negotiation about your independence, is there any chance we could add in some additional stuff like you agreeing always to sort out your own laundry and cook the occasional meal?'

I gave that the thought it deserved. 'You know what I was thinking?' I said.

'No, what were you thinking?'

'We don't really need an actual list. We can just wing it.'

She laughed. 'Sounds like a plan. So, I guess I'm making supper?'

'I'll help,' I offered.

'And I promise I'll call Stella and ask her to email you first if she hears anything about Straker.'

I wasn't holding my breath. I was all but resigned

to the fact that I'd be going to the movies in about a year to watch a gigantic Amy make out with a gigantic Carlo on a gigantic screen. Hopefully, not in 3D.

The sane thing to do was try to forget about *Straker* and concentrate on what I was going to wear to Stephanie's party.

★
CHAPTER 31

'I'd rather be the designated driver and be in
control of where I'm going and what I'm doing.'
Lindsay Lohan

'So, who is this Stephanie?'

'I've told you a hundred times, Mum. She's in my
year at school.' Calm down. I didn't say 'calm down'
out loud. Obviously.

'But who is she? Why have you never mentioned
her? Who are her friends? What do her parents do?'

'Why the interrogation? This is *ridiculous*.'
Mistake, but we'd been through all this about five
times and Mum still couldn't get her head round
the fact that I didn't ask all my new friends for a list
of personal details about them and their extended
family. I really didn't get why she was so stressy;
she'd probably read way too many articles about

teenagers' house parties. It so wasn't going to be that sort of party (well, probably not).

'This is not ridiculous. If you expect me to allow you to go off to some girl's party in the middle of the night *one week before exams*, you can expect me to ask some questions.'

'This isn't "some questions", it's *every* question. I'm totally on top of my revision.' I wasn't. 'And it's not the middle of the night, it's *half past nine*. Stephanie's one of Jenny's best friends. She only came to our school last year which is why I haven't mentioned her.' No need to add that the other reason I hadn't mentioned Stephanie before was because I didn't really know her. 'I think her mum's a lawyer or something that people wear dark, sharp suits for, but I'm not sure because we don't really talk about what our parents do, oddly enough.'

'There's no call for sarcasm, Elektra Ophelia,' said my mum, handing me a brownie fresh out of the oven. 'How are you planning on getting there?' She was weakening.

'I'll get the Tube.'

'You *cannot* be serious. Dressed like that?'

There was absolutely nothing wrong with how I was dressed. My skirt was on the shortish side, I admit (new, very expensive and perfectly balanced on the verge of classy and slutty – thank you,

Eulalie), but I had decided to own my stork legs instead of apologizing for them. (Stork legs is not a self-deprecating way of saying I have very long, slim legs – they actually do look like stork's legs.) I gave Digby a corner of brownie because he looked so tragic.

My phone rang and Stella's number came up on the screen. This was quite scary.

'Hi, Stella,' I said (unfortunately, it came out squeaky). Inside my head, I was shouting HAVE YOU HEARD ANYTHING ABOUT STRAKER? but I didn't say that because I was a cool and rational working actor – an actor whose agent now phoned *her* to discuss her career *and not her mother*.

'You must be wondering if I've heard anything about *Straker*,' she said.

'Not really,' I lied and Stella laughed because I wasn't that good an actor. My mum was making 'What? What?' faces at me – role reversal. 'I haven't heard a thing,' said Stella after a painful pause. 'That wasn't why I was phoning.'

Then why? *Fortuneswell*? Please let it be *Fortuneswell*. A crisps advert?

'It was just to say that unfortunately the role I was putting you up for in *Doctors* has been cut.'

'Oh.'

'It's not going to someone else. They just need the screen time to resolve a bit of infidelity among the medical staff.'

'Oh.'

'I just wanted to let you know so you didn't keep that date free.'

'Thank you,' I said and resisted the temptation to grill her on every other project we'd ever talked about.

'My pleasure,' she said without a trace of sarcasm and hung up.

My expectations management still needed a bit of work.

'Mum? Did you find it a bit scary talking to Stella on the phone?'

She laughed. 'Sometimes.'

'Thank you,' I said. And then (because it was worth a try and she looked pleased with me), 'Any chance of a lift to Stephanie's house?'

'Can't this boy you're going with pick you up? That's what used to happen on a date; it's basic good manners.'

'It's not a date.'

'I thought you told me he asked you to go with him.'

'That doesn't mean it's a date.'

'Of course it does.'

She just didn't get it. I thought about all the steps between being plus one'd by Archie to Steph's party to getting with Archie (would he even try?) to going out with Archie. We had some way to go. I thought about explaining all that to my mum. No, just no.

But she did agree to give me a lift.

Stephanie had a big house and it looked even bigger because all the lights were on and the door was open. Two older guys (I think they were her brothers) were checking that nobody got in that wasn't meant to. Her parents were nowhere to be seen, but I guessed her father was probably drowning his fears at the local pub while her mother was secretly watching from a neighbour's upstairs window.

'Hi ... er, I'm Elektra James.' (Like there would be two Elektras; that couldn't happen again in one lifetime, could it?)

One of the guys skimmed down a list with his pencil (he was taking this very seriously). 'Nah, sorry, I can't see your name.'

'No, I'm Archie Mortimer's plus one.' Complicated mixture of pride and embarrassment right there.

There was another *long* pause as he checked out the names. Either he was enjoying making me cringe or he was a bit stupid. It was a long list. I wished he would hurry up; there were three people lined up behind me.

'Can't see him either ... Oh, yeah. OK, he's already here. Go on in.' He turned his attention to the two girls next in the line. I didn't recognize them – they must have gone to Stephanie's old school – but I half wished my mum could have seen what they were wearing, only because it made my outfit look nun-like.

It was packed. Stephanie was sitting halfway up the stairs and I would have said hello, but she had her arm round some girl who was crying.

I saw Archie before he saw me. He was chatting to Jenny. Maybe he was chatting *up* Jenny; they were standing really close to each other and she was looking amazing in a little red bandage dress with her hair all big and messy and her eyes kohled and her big lips glossed. She looked at least eighteen.

'Hey, Jenny,' I said awkwardly because I didn't want to say 'hey, Archie'.

They turned as one and I could tell straight away by how pleased they both were to see me that he hadn't been chatting her up. Jenny gave me a big squashy hug; she'd obviously had something to drink and was at that sentimental stage where everyone was her best friend in the world. Frankly, Archie looked relieved that I was rescuing him.

'Elektra, you're here. Sweet. I've been texting you all afternoon. I was going to pick you up.'

My mum would have been proud of him.

'Sorry, my phone went AWOL for a couple of hours.' Strangely, I'd found it in the fridge, but I didn't really need to tell him that.

He pulled me towards him for a hug and I let him because it was a party and I was technically only invited because I was his plus one, but mostly because I really wanted him to.

'How did it go?' His arm was draped round my shoulders like it was meant to be there.

'What?' I was a bit befuddled, but in a good way. He smelled nice, a little bit of beer and a little bit of clean T-shirt (a way nicer combination than it sounds).

'The *Straker* callback!'

Oh yeah, the callback, that had been the biggest thing going on in my life until about twenty-five seconds ago when Archie had started to run his fingers up and down my arm. He was one of the very few people who would understand about *Straker* (and yes, I'd told him about it too – apparently, secret-keeping wouldn't go on my list of 'skills'). 'It was OK, a bit weird,' which was one way to describe it. 'We did yoga.'

He didn't look that surprised, but then Archie was used to drama workshops. 'Did they like you?'

'You know that I have no idea what the answer to that question is.'

'Sorry,' he said and pulled me even closer. Nice. 'What were the rest of the shortlist like?'

Carlo entered my conscience and crossed right out of it again. Carlo, Carlo who?

'Amy Underhill was there. So I definitely won't get it. She was up for the same part.'

Archie looked blank.

'You know the girl who plays Kelly in *Sunningtown*?'

He still looked blank – obviously, not his sort of show.

'It's a soap and Amy's famous-ish and I reckon she's got it in the bag.'

'You'll be better than her and you're way hotter,' he said.

That would have been an even better compliment if he'd had a clue who Amy Underhill was, but I'd take it (not too seriously but still).

The room was heaving now, the music really loud. Jenny and Hugo (this guy she'd fancied forever) were draped all over each other. I wasn't sure if that was because they were both drunk and needed the support, but whatever: they looked happy. No matter how closely Archie and I stood together, we kept getting jostled and there wasn't anywhere for us to sit (there was already a queue for the snogging sofa). We went outside and perched on a low wall in the garden. It was nice out there. Someone, Stephanie I suppose, had lit heaps of little tea lights and dotted them all around the flower beds. Don't want to be cringey here, but it was romantic, if a bit of a drunk-teen fire hazard.

I was just imagining Flissy (who I could see

making out athletically with James in the bushes) catching her hair on fire when I felt Archie's hand on my cheek turning my face towards him. I looked at him for a minute. Was he waiting for me to say something? I stared desperately at the bushes, willing them to lend me a line. Nope, nothing.

'Don't you just, like, love what she's done with the candles and lights and stuff?' I babbled. Where were the Hollywood scriptwriter and director when you needed them?

I could feel Archie looking at me; it was intense.

Or maybe he was just worried about my lack of social skills.

I dared another proper look at him and stopped. God, he was hot. I could feel his hands moving up my arms, down over my shoulders and my back and round my waist again, holding me tight, and then he started to kiss me. I didn't realize until it had started, not because it was a stealth attack like in the audition, but because it happened naturally. When Damian had lunged, my brain had gone into horrified overdrive, but this time I didn't *think* anything at all. Anyway, my optimism about kissing had been well founded.

I sort of sensed another couple coming and sitting next to us. I would have preferred us to have been on our own, but I wasn't going to stop unless it was my mum who'd just sat down.

Even if someone knows what they're doing (and Archie did), you need to break off eventually. I didn't really know what to say so I just sort of smiled at him goofily, but to be honest he just sort of smiled goofily back.

'Hey, Archie.' It was a familiar voice.

I peered out from under Archie's arm; I was a bit blurry-eyed with the kissing, but yep, I was definitely sitting next to Moss. And Moss was sitting next to (well, on) Torr. This was awkward.

'Hey, it's Archie, right?' Torr was introducing himself and within minutes Archie was getting up, leaving a cold, Archie-shaped space, and he was talking to Torr, not me, and Torr was nodding and getting up, no doubt leaving a cold, Torr-shaped space.

'Shall we leave them to it for a bit?' suggested Torr and Archie was nodding and – and there is no other word for it – they *abandoned* us.

Moss and I sat next to each other in a loud sort of silence for some long minutes.

'So you finally got with Archie.' She broke it first.

'Obviously.'

'About time.'

'Uh-huh.'

'Good decision.'

'Uh-huh . . . So, things going well with Torr still?'

'Obviously.'

'That's a long time now.'

'Uh-huh.'

'Good decision.' It was *her* decision so I meant it.

There was another long pause during which we kept giving each other sideways looks. 'Nice ... distressed thingy,' I said, gesturing at what she was wearing (a skinny, black, distressed thingy which on her, of course, looked amazing).

'Your legs have got longer,' she said, gesturing at my very short skirt, which had ridden up even higher. We both started to laugh a bit nervously, but it was still laughter.

I stopped. 'I'm so, so sorry,' I said and I was so, so serious.

'Don't. I'm sorry too.'

'I've missed you so, so much,' I said and she was saying it back at the same time and we couldn't talk because it was a party and really, really loud so we just did the whole girly, huggy love thing until Archie and Torr judged it safe to come back.

Then we did more hugging but less girly.

It was kind of predictable that I got home late. Not that late but late enough. It was predictable that Mum waited up. It was also predictable that she'd been having a nervous breakdown.

'Why do you never pick up your phone?' she said (as she so often did).

'I didn't hear it ring,' I protested (as I quite often did).

'If you can't behave responsibly when you're out, then you can't go out,' she said (she didn't say that very often because I didn't really go out very often).

'You've no idea how responsibly I behaved.' And comparatively speaking that was true.

She paced and tutted for a bit, but couldn't help herself. 'Are you hungry? Do you want pasta?'

'Yes, please.' I was starving.

'Fine. I'll make you pasta and you sit down and tell me everything.'

Oh. OK, this pasta had strings attached.

'Moss was there,' I said.

She looked worried. 'Oh, dear, did you have another argument?'

'No, it was really nice to talk to her. It was all good.'

'I'm pleased,' said Mum simply and for once had the sense not to ask me any questions about something that mattered. It didn't mean she wasn't going to ask *any* questions. 'So, did you have fun?'

'Uh-huh.' I went as non-committal as possible; I didn't want her to think I hadn't had fun, but I definitely didn't want her to know how much fun I'd had.

'So you didn't have fun.'

'No, no, I did.' I just really didn't want to tell her about it.

'Was it awful? You hated it? They were mean to you?' Every teenage parenting book she'd ever read had been preparing her for this moment. 'Darling, if anything happened, anyone peer-pressured you, you did anything you regret, you can tell me.'

'NOTHING HAPPENED! I LOVED THE PARTY!'

'Why do you sound angry then? Something's obviously upset you. Just tell me – stop being so defensive.'

I spoke very slowly, like you'd speak to a small, rather stupid child who was threatening to throw themselves under a train. 'No, I had a very, very nice time. The party was amazing. I didn't drink anything. I did no drugs. I did not engage in sexual contact.'

'Oh, all right.' She almost looked disappointed. 'Who did then?'

She was a lost cause. I ended up telling her about Flissy's 'moment' in the bushes because my judgement was a bit impaired, it was seriously funny, I owed no loyalty to Flissy and Mum deserved payment for the pasta.

She took this as proof that the party was a rampant orgy, then she let me go to bed, her fears about not having anything to worry about allayed.

✦
CHAPTER 32

*'I'm just going to do some mad stuff. It's about
living and being my age. That's what success is.'*
Suki Waterhouse

My phone was ringing, but by the time I found it –
under the bed, under a tangle of tights – whoever
was phoning had given up. A minute later, there
was a single woof and a text glowed on the screen.

Are you awake?

I am now. I love Moss, but she has an abnormal
body clock and is stupidly conversational in the
mornings.

I had a seriously weird dream last night

Unlikely to have been as weird as mine. I'd
dreamt I was at the callback, stark – completely
no knickers – naked. Also I couldn't find my script.
That was the bad bit. **Was I in it?**

Yes. Good. I would have been offended if I hadn't been.

Was it good?

Er, not exactly

Then don't tell me

It wasn't pervy. But Archie was in it ☺

Did it end well?

Not really

THEN DON'T TELL ME. I really didn't need any more dream-related stress.

I'll save it. Happy bout Archie?

Yes. Come over later and we can have a deep convo.

Yaaaaay. Will you give me ALL the goss?

I'll give you the highlights

Can't come till evening — is that OK for you?

I was pretty sure that meant she was seeing Torr.

Perfect. I've got to revise. And it's just possible that Archie might drop by . . .

😶 **You're not going to go all . . . unavailable on me, are you?** 😶

LOL. I was taking a risk there.

Hahaha

Mum yelled up the stairs. Apparently, if I wasn't down for breakfast within five minutes, I wouldn't be getting any. Also, apparently, I didn't really deserve breakfast on account of being late home.

'You look tired.'

I didn't say, 'You always look tired,' because that would have been harsh. Also I didn't say, 'You shouldn't have waited up,' because that would have just started her off again.

'I suppose you're hungry.'

'Starving.'

'I thought you might be. Bacon sandwiches?'

'Thanks, Mum. Love you.' It was the best smell in the world again; Digby was beside himself. 'Did Stella call?' I asked through a mouthful. I'd propped my mobile up against the milk jug so I could keep an eye on it at all times.

Mum shook her head, 'No. Anyway, under our new regime she'll call *you* first.'

I'd forgotten. 'Do you think we'll hear on Monday?'

'I don't know. I think you should try to put it out of your head. You've got school; how about just concentrating on finishing your homework?' I could see her fighting the temptation to add 'for once' to the end of that sentence.

How could I be expected to concentrate on $E=VxQ$ with everything that was going on?

'And you've got exams. They're not going to revise themselves, you know. Parties or no parties. Boy or no boy. Film or no film.'

She said the strangest things. I escaped into the garden where I could sit under a tree and *no one*

335

would talk to me. If the price for solitude was a stab at revision, it was a price I was prepared to pay.

Also I really didn't want to fail my exams.

At least it was revision for English and not physics. Newton might have managed insights under a tree, but it wouldn't work for me. Our set drama text was *Waiting for Godot*: an odd play, the point of which is that there isn't a point. Most of the time there's just two old guys with only a tree for company, waiting – just waiting – for Godot; and who or what he is nobody knows. You couldn't call it *gripping*, but I secretly liked it. How could you not like a play with lines like: 'Nothing happens, nobody comes, nobody goes, it's awful!'? Actually, they should have made it with teenagers – just substituted the tree for a phone and that's about 90 per cent of my life. They could have called it *Waiting for Something to Happen/Anything to Happen*.

I couldn't concentrate. It wasn't just the heat – although there was a trickle of sweat running down my arm and threatening to drown a tiny ant running the other way – it was the waiting for the phone to ring. This was drama waiting. Waiting so active that I would have lost weight doing it if it wasn't for all the comfort eating. Drama waiting was worse than waiting for a guy to call. Really.

'Hey, Elektra.' Archie was coming across the

garden, carrying two enormous ice creams. 'Sorry. I'm a bit early.'

Like I minded. He'd shown.

'Your mum let me in.'

'Oh, God, did she interrogate you on your parents/hobbies/predicted exam results/preferred university/career choice?'

'Nah, she was cool.'

She was? That was a first.

He handed me one of the ice creams. 'It's melted a bit.'

''S OK, it's good,' I said, licking the melted ice cream off the cone, feeling seriously self-conscious because he was looking so hard at me. 'Come sit down.' I patted the grass next to me and we sat side by side under the tree and ate the ice creams, acutely, almost painfully, aware of each other. Last night we'd had the music and the beer and the whole heat of the party and it had been easy. This was daytime and I wasn't wearing a tiny skirt and mascara; I had on an old pair of denim shorts and a Snoopy T-shirt that used to be a nightshirt before my latest growth spurt. Archie hadn't given me time to change ... or brush my teeth for the third time. He crunched the end of his cone and slung his arm round my shoulders. That was way better. I leaned into him and it was sort of familiar. Clean T-shirt and some lemony soap or shampoo this time. Oh, yes, this I could do.

'You're not going to finish that, are you?' He eyed up the end of my cone greedily and I handed it over. It was good to share. He finished it in two bites, which meant that both of us had free hands.

'Elektra!' It was my mum.

I thought the look of shock on her face was because she'd seen us kissing, but then I saw that she had the house phone in her hand and was looking at it as if it were radioactive. I don't think she'd even noticed what we were doing.

'Elektra. It's *Mr Havelski* ... for *you*.' She was all weirded out.

I looked at her, and I looked back up at Archie who was, frankly, looking very good indeed.

'We keep getting interrupted,' he whispered in my ear. His breath tickled.

I smiled at him. 'Thanks, Mum. Tell Mr Havelski I'll call him back.'

~~THE END~~

(Because that's how cool and collected I was; an actor one hundred per cent in control. Seriously? Seriously? Well … no. Let's try that again. PTO for Take Two)

Strangely enough, I wasn't cocky enough to leave Mr Havelski waiting for *me* to call *him* back. That is a game I wouldn't play with a sixth former, far less a *Hollywood director*.

And Archie was in the business. He was the one that put the phone in my hand.

'Hello?' I squeaked in a teeny-tiny voice.

'So ...' (Havelski still sounded like a meerkat – a *really important* meerkat.) There was a terrifying pause. 'So ...' Another scary pause.

I was going to pass out. I clung on to Archie (mostly for support).

'So ... Is that my Straker I'm speaking to?'

And I could *hear* Havelski smiling all the way from LA.

(Take 2)

THE END

Acknowledgements
[In the style of an embarrassing Oscar speech...]

Both:[Falling up the stairs to stage]
We'd just like to thank everyone who has supported our dream along the way. We'd like to thank The Academy ... [Realize that's not strictly relevant and pull themselves together.]

Jonathan, if it hadn't been for Scraps playing his trump card and dying you'd have earned the dedication. We love you. Thank you to our awesome, kind and very lovely agent Hannah Sheppard, for well *everything*, you deserve ALL the pugs (and thank you to The Literary Consultancy for their excellent match making). Thank you to the whole team at Simon & Schuster who have helped make this book the very best it could be inside and out and all the way on to bookshelves. Especially our brilliant editor Jane Griffiths, Rachel Mann, Jade Westwood, Elisa Offord, Jenny Richards and Laura Hough (and to Jane Tait who would be horrified by the repetition of 'thank you'). It's been a team effort and we are very glad that we called you back (to be honest you had us at cake). Thanks to James Barriscale for reading the novel with his actor's eye and giving us lots of help (but agreeing that reality shouldn't always get in the way of a good line). Thank you to all at The Golden Egg Academy especially Nicki Marshall (we hope Daisy likes Daisy). To all the lovely children's book people that have made us feel so welcome and shared so much of their expertise and friendship with us on and off line (Abi and Jim you get a special mention).

Perdita: [grabs the microphone] And thank you to my mother, Sheila, for force-feeding me books and not vegetables (except for Enid Blyton about whose work she was irrationally snobby) and my lovely sister Linnet and all my family and incredibly supportive friends (especially for all the recent hand holding Hannah, Juliet, Natasha, Lia, Krystina and Grace), I'm so lucky to have you ... wow ... This is just ... so ... overwhelming [breaks down in tears and is escorted from the stage].

Honor: Moving swiftly on ... Thanks to everyone I met through acting for being so supportive/fun/weird enough to inspire this novel. Special thanks to Andrew and Dyana at YAT. Thanks to my school for ignoring the rising number of 'orthodontist' appointments I had during sports lessons as publication approached. Thanks to the very cool 'real' Elektra for letting us steal her name. Thanks to my incredibly supportive and staggeringly handsome boyfriend. LOL jokes he doesn't exist. But massive thanks to all my friends especially my gals Chiara Richardson, Katerina Lelikova, Reeny Eyi and Tash Jeans. I love you to bits weirdos. So yeah, in conclusion, thanks. [Falls down stairs from the stage.]

ABOUT THE AUTHORS

PERDITA

I used to be the least numerate tax barrister ever to practise in the English Courts. Frankly it was a relief all round when I hung up my gown & wig and turned (after a bit) to writing. I'm pretty geeky and a bit of a wimp. On the upside I do like teenagers. Actually I like quite a lot of people.

HONOR

I'm doing A Levels at St Paul's School for Girls. I've done lots of acting mostly just school plays but a tiny bit of professional too and, although I'm nothing like Elektra, I feel her pain because her most humiliating moments are strangely similar to mine. Actually she has it easy, not only was my first kiss on stage but it was in front of my parents and my headteacher!! So naturally I decided to write about it so you can all mercilessly enjoy a little laugh (or two, or three, or more) at my expense!

Find us online!
website: waitingforcallback.com

 honorcargill   Waiting for Callback   @perditact

Permissions

Quotation Nicholas Hoult, pg. 39 from *The Telegraph* 14th January 2007 (Catherine Shoard); quotations Tom Hiddleston pp. 128 and 281 from *The Telegraph* 14th January2014 (Chloe Fox); quotation Jessica Chastain from *The Telegraph* 11th January 2015 (Celia Walden); quotation Natalie Dormer *The Telegraph* 9th August 2015 (Olly Grant); quotation Eddie Redmayne pg. 312 from *The Telegraph* 23d November 2009 (Georgia Dehn). **All reprinted by kind permission of the Telegraph Media Group and pursuant to Licences dated 16th June 2015 and 1st September 2015.**

Quotation Daniel Radcliffe, pg. 95 from *The Sunday Times* 10th July 2011; quotations Emma Watson pp. 106 and 298 from *The Times* 27th June 2009 (Kate Muir); quotation Elle Fanning pg, 142 from *The Times* 19th October 2012 (Kevin Maher); quotations from Asa Butterfield pg. 152, *The Times* 30th August 2008(Kevin Maher) and 5th December 2011 (Alex O'Connell); quotation Max Irons from *The Times* 10th September 2014 (Helen Rumbelow); quotations Kristen Stewart pg. 210 and pg. 248 from *The Sunday Times* 6th September 2009 (Will Lawrence); quotation Cara Delavigne pg. 288 *The Times Magazine* 16th August 2015 (Shane Watson); quotation Lindsay Lohan pg. 322 from *The Times* 19th June 2004 (Lesley O'Toole); quotation Suki Waterhouse pg. 335 from *The Sunday Times* 9th August 2015 (Giles Hattersley). **All reprinted by kind permission of News UK and Ireland Ltd.**